DEATH
AND
RESTORATION

A Jonathan Argyll Mystery

IAIN PEARS

S C R I B N E R

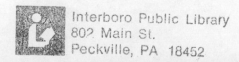

SCRIBNER
1230 Avenue of the Americas
New York, NY 10020

First published in Great Britain by Collins Crime
SCRIBNER and design are trademarks
of Simon & Schuster Inc.

Manufactured in the United States of America

1 3 5 7 9 10 8 6 4 2

Library of Congress
Cataloging-in-Publication Data
Pears, Iain.
Death and restoration : a Jonathan Argyll
mystery / Iain Pears.
1. Argyll, Jonathan (Fictitious character)—
Fiction. I. Title.
PR6066.E167D42   1998
823'.914—dc21   97-39932
CIP

ISBN 0-684-81461-7

To Ruth

1

Business meetings are more or less the same all over the world, and have been since the beginning of time. There is the man in charge; the man supposedly in charge; the man wanting to be in charge; their minions, their enemies and those waverers who float gently downstream, hoping things won't get too choppy. And there is always a dispute, which serves the purpose of making half-felt antagonisms real. Sometimes these are of importance and justify the energy expended on them. But not often.

So it was one afternoon in September in a large but utilitarian room in a shambling, run-down set of buildings in that section of Rome loosely known as the Aventino. There were twenty people, all men of between thirty-five and seventy-five years old; fourteen items on the agenda, and two factions, each determined to sweep all before them and rout the forces of (on the one hand) dangerous and puerile innovation and (on the other) hidebound traditionalism irrelevant to the needs of the modern world. It was, the chairman thought as he took a deep breath, going to be a long afternoon. He only hoped that the two hours they had just spent praying together for God's wisdom to infuse their collective decision would stop the imminent debate from getting too acrimonious.

But he doubted it, somehow. Much as he felt himself teetering on the brink of heresy in even considering the idea, he did sometimes wish the Lord could make his wishes just a bit plainer: then his fear might not be realized that he, Father Xavier Münster, thirty-ninth head of the Order of St John the Pietist, might also be the last. His heart sank as he saw the glitter of battle in the eyes of those souls nominally

7

submissive to his total authority. Above all Father Jean, organizing his papers in front of him like so many divisions of tanks, waiting for the moment to advance. Determined to oppose, mindless of the problems he had to face. Although, in the circumstances, that was just as well. 'Perhaps,' Father Xavier said with determination to the assembled collection of his order presently in Rome. 'Perhaps we might begin?'

Five hours later, it was at an end, and the shattered brothers staggered out. Ordinarily, there were apéritifs on the terrace after such a meeting; this time only a few people, those who had not become too involved in the unseemly brawling, turned up. The rest went to their cells (such they were called, although they were little different to the sort of rooms students occupy) to meditate, pray, or fume with rage.

'I'm very glad that's over,' murmured one of the most youthful of the brothers, a tall, handsome man from Cameroon called Paul. It was selfless of him to say it so mildly; he had hoped that his own concern might have been dealt with. But, yet again, his little problem was too far down the list to be discussed.

The words were addressed to nobody in particular, and were heard only by Father Jean, an old man who had stationed himself next to the Pernod bottle at the table. He peered upwards in the general direction of Father Paul's face – which was a good eighteen inches above his own – and nodded. He was exhausted; that sort of combat does use energy and sometimes even he was surprised and alarmed at the deep sources of hatred that Father Xavier's efforts at reform had stirred up in his usually placid soul. He had not come on to the terrace to be social; unusually for him, he was there because he needed a drink.

In the past he had always refused to be sucked into such disputes and still could not quite believe his new role as leader of the opposition. It was not what he had wanted; not his ideal way of spending his declining years. He still thought of himself as a natural loyalist. So he had always been ever since he was plucked out of village school at the age of twelve by a priest who had spotted his qualities.

But not this time, although the vehemence unleashed by the contest between himself and Xavier appalled him. Even at the height of the doubts and anguish thrown up by the great Vatican Council, he remembered nothing which could compare with the sheer unpleasantness the meeting room had witnessed that afternoon. But there was nothing to be done about it: the soul of the body was at stake; of that he was absolutely sure. Xavier was a good man, no doubt; a courageous one, even. And many saints had been as ruthless and determined to follow their vision, despite all opposition, as he was. Look at St Bernard; look at St Ignatius. Neither were exactly known for their ability to see all sides of an argument. But this was not the Middle Ages, nor the seventeenth century. Other techniques were required. Patience, tact, persuasion. And none of them were Xavier's speciality.

So Father Jean nodded sadly to himself. 'Over? Only for the time being,' he said. 'I fear we have not seen the last of this dispute.'

Father Paul arched his eyebrow. 'What more is there to say? It's settled, isn't it? You got your way. Surely you should be happy.'

Paul could speak with little heat because he, almost alone of the brothers, had not taken sides. Indeed, he wasn't entirely certain what the dispute was about. He understood the *occasion*, of course, but the underlying *cause* meant nothing to him. All he understood was that it wasted a lot of energy that, surely, could be better spent.

'It was only defeated by one vote,' Jean replied. 'Only by one vote. Last year – what did he try to do then? I don't remember – he was turned down by five votes. Which means this will be taken as an encouragement, rather than as a defeat. You just wait.'

Father Paul poured himself an orange juice and sipped thoughtfully. 'Oh dear. I do wish I could go home. I hardly seem to be doing the Lord's work here.'

'I know,' Father Jean said sympathetically, wondering whether a second Pernod would be permissible. 'You must find us shocking, and you're probably right. And I'm sorry we've put off discussing the business of your going home yet again. Next time, perhaps; when tempers have cooled, we might bring the subject up. I will do my best, if that's any help.'

A few kilometres away, in the very centre of the city, a quite different, more worldly, organization was ploughing its quietly effective way through life. The main door (newly electrified at hideously unnecessary expense) swished to and fro as eager policemen walked purposefully in and out. In small, windowless rooms technicians and filing clerks pursued their careers with keen concentration and devotion to duty. Further up the building greater harmony reigned, as detectives in their offices read, telephoned and wrote in their determined pursuit of Italy's stolen artistic heritage. And from the top floor, from the room which was frequently described in the more respectful press as the brain centre of Italy's Art Theft Squad, came a low rumble which was disturbed only by the persistent buzzing of a large, fat bluebottle.

The efficient machine was on autopilot; the brain was off duty. It was a hot afternoon and General Taddeo Bottando was fast asleep.

Not that this mattered, normally. Bottando was handsomely into his sixties and even he was now ready to agree that youthful sprightliness was no longer one of his dominant characteristics. Experience more than made up for this loss, however. So what if he husbanded his resources now and then? His overall strategic grasp was as good as ever, and his organizational powers unfaded by the years. Everybody knew what they were meant to do, and they got on with the business of doing it, without any need for him to supervise them day and night. And if something happened when he was not around (so to speak) then one of his team, such as Flavia di Stefano, was fully able to deal with the situation.

Such had been the way in which he had described his role that very lunchtime, to a pair of senior civil servants who had taken him out to a fine, excessively fine, restaurant to make up. For reasons which he couldn't quite understand, Bottando had suddenly become popular, after years of battling for money and continued existence. Now, perhaps due to a major success a few months back, everybody loved him, everybody had always loved him, and everyone had always been his secret supporter against the machinations of others. All those years, and Bottando had never noticed. He had all but purred with pleasure, and had permitted himself to wallow in complacency as he played a significant role in the destruction of a second, then a third bottle of good Chianti.

Perhaps he should have seen it coming, an old hand like himself. The bonhomie, the admiration, the friendliness. But the wine and the warmth lulled him into assurance. Deep down, he was a trusting man, despite years in the police force contending with crooks and – what was worse – superiors. For once, he permitted himself to think that everyone was on the same side; we are all colleagues. Perhaps I really am admired and appreciated for my efforts.

His mood was one of confident, generous urbanity by the time the most senior of his colleagues – a man he had transferred away from his command years ago in a different life in Milan – leant forward with an ingratiating smile and said: 'Tell me, Taddeo, how do you see the department developing? In years to come. I want you to take the *long* view here, you see.'

And so he gave a peroration, about international co-operation and regional squads and all that sort of thing. About new computers and new techniques and new laws which would all make the business of retrieving stolen works of art that little bit easier.

'And *yourself*? How do you see yourself?'

If he hadn't been wary before, the alarms should have gone off now. All the signs were there; but he never for a moment even suspected the existence of the huge and omnivorous trap doors creaking open to swallow him up. He talked about teams and leadership and overseeing functions, talking the foreign language in which he had become fluent, if not entirely comfortable.

'Good, good. I'm so glad we are in agreement. That does make our task so very much easier.'

Finally, at long last, despite the heat and the drugging

11

effects of the wine and food, a warning tickle activated itself at the base of his thick and powerful neck.

'You see,' the man said as Bottando mentally assumed a crouching posture but kept silent, 'there are all these reorganizations. This new promotion structure.'

'Which ones? Have I missed something again?'

A nervous chuckle. 'Oh, dear me, no. It hasn't been published yet. In fact, you're the *very first* person to be told of it. We thought it best, as you may well be the first person to be affected.'

More silence, more caution and a raised eyebrow.

'It's all structural, you see, and I'd like it known that I am not happy with it.'

Which means, of course, that he is. Probably his idea, in fact, Bottando thought.

'So many people, all crammed up with no promotion prospects. The demographic age bulge. What's to be done with them? All over the government, the very best people are leaving. Why is this? Because they've come to a dead end, that's why. And then there is Europe. We are entering a new age, Taddeo. We must be prepared. The time to start planning is now. Not when it is all too late. So it has been decided – by people other than myself – to introduce some, ah, changes.'

'What, ah, changes?'

'Two things. Specifically, there is to be an intra-governmental liaison group to coordinate all aspects of policing. It will start with a particular area as a way of testing procedures and operations.'

Bottando nodded. He had heard all of this sort of thing before. Every six months some bright spark in a ministry decided to nail his promotion prospects to yet another piece of liaising. Never came to anything much.

'And the second, which will ultimately be linked with the first, is to sort out the relationship between your department with the new international art safety directive.'

'The what?'

'A European affair, funded entirely from Brussels, but the minister has managed to establish that it will be headed by an Italian. You, in fact.'

12

'And sit around writing memoranda which no one will ever read.'

'That depends on yourself. Obviously you will encounter resistance. You would have resisted it fervently yourself. It will be your job to turn this initiative into something.'

'Does this mean lots of foreigners?' he asked dubiously.

They both shrugged. 'It will be up to you to decide what it is you want to do. Then to get the budget to pay for the staff to do it. Naturally, the staffing structure will have to be balanced.'

'It does mean foreigners.'

'Yes.'

'And where will this fine example of Euro-nonsense be located?'

'Ah, there now. Obviously, the most *sensible* place would be in Brussels. However . . .'

'In that case I'm not going,' Bottando began. 'The rain, you know . . .'

'However,' the civil servant continued, 'other factors come into operation here.'

'Such as?'

'Such as the fact that money spent in Brussels benefits Belgium; money spent in Italy benefits us. And, of course, we are the greatest centre for art. And, come to think of it, for art theft. So we are lobbying hard for it to be located here.'

'And what about my department?'

'You continue in charge, of course, but you will obviously have to delegate day-to-day operations, which will run in parallel, with some interchange of personnel.'

Bottando sat back in his chair, his good mood dissolving as the full implications dawned on him.

'What choice do I have about this?'

'None. It is too important for personal preference. It is a matter of national honour. You accept, or someone else gets your job. And you will have to go to Brussels in a week to explain how you will run this organization. So you have a lot of work to do.'

Not knowing whether to be pleased or irritated, Bottando

went back to his office to try and figure out all the subtleties and, as was his habit, ended up sleeping on it.

It was not the best time for an anonymous tip-off to come in, warning about an imminent raid to steal one of the city's works of art.

Jonathan Argyll walked home across Rome at half past six in the evening, taking some, but not a great deal, of pleasure in the bustle of a city anxious to get home for its dinner. He was tired. It had been a long day, what with one thing and another. A lecture in the morning, which was becoming routine now that his stage fright had left him and he had gauged the low expectations of the audience, followed by two hours of sitting in the little broom cupboard officially called his office, fending off students in various levels of distress who came to waste his time. Could they be late on this? Could he photocopy that to spare them the trouble of actually sitting in a library themselves?

No, and no. Much to his great surprise, his random career change nine months previously from art dealer to temporary lecturer in baroque studies had brought out a hitherto unsuspected authoritarian side to his character. Combined with a tendency to grumble about what students were like in his day, he had managed to institute a reign of terror for all who were lured into the great mistake of signing up for his course on Roman art and architecture, 1600 to 1750.

The Baroque. The Counter-Reformation. Bernini and Borromini and Maderno and Pozzo. Good lads, all of them. No need for slides or illustrated lectures in this of all cities; just send the idle good-for-nothings on walking tours. On their own on a Monday, escorted by him on a Wednesday. *Mens sana in corpore sano*. Health and knowledge, all in one package. Cheap at the not inconsiderable price the besotted parents of the little urchins coughed up to add a patina of cultivation to their offspring.

Even more surprisingly, he was quite good at it. His boundless enthusiasm for the more obscure and impenetrable aspects of baroque iconography slowly transferred itself to some of his students. Not many, admittedly; half a dozen out

14

of thirty of so, but this was held by his colleagues to be pretty good going considering the motley collection of raw material they had to work on.

And the great virtue of it all was that he didn't really have to prepare anything: his only problem was deciding what to leave out. And marking. That was depressing, of course.

'Medieval monks scourged themselves with birch rods; we do the same thing with essays,' the head of his department, a Renaissance man himself, explained in a philosophic vein. 'It comes to the same thing in the end. Painful and humiliating, but part of the job. And purifying, in its way: it makes you see the futility of your existence.'

There was, however, a snag. Lurking ambition, somnolent or at least beaten into submission, had been awoken once more by the transition. Old habits and pleasures came back to haunt him. Having taken the job as a temporary measure because of the flaccid state of the art market, Argyll found himself rather liking the business, despite the students. He had even taken out his doctorate, long since forgotten and mouldering on the shelves while he tried to make a living as a dealer, and dusted it off. The itch was upon him once more: the desire to see his name in print. Nothing grand. A little article, with a decent array of footnotes on some minor topic, to get him back into the mood. An excuse for ambling around in the archives. Everybody else was at it; and it was a bit awkward to have lunch with a colleague. What are you working on? It was an inevitable question. It would be pleasant to be able to answer.

What indeed, though? He had been flailing around, trying to come up with something for a couple of months. Nothing, so far, had struck his fancy. Too big, too small or done already. The universal chorus of modern academia. It occupied his mind mightily these days.

Except when there was marking. That was the little nagging detail in the back of his mind which stopped him enjoying the view of Isola Tiburtina as he trudged through the thick fumes of evening carbon monoxide and across the Ponte Garibaldi on his way home. Fifteen essays on Jesuit building programmes. Could have been worse; they might all have managed to pull themselves together and produce something. And judging by the look of it, some of the offerings were going to be a touch thin. In abstract, he loved the conscientious students who worked hard and tried. When he had to mark the result, he loathed the little swots for the reams of paper they produced. But there was nothing to be done about it; a couple of hours of his evening were going to be devoted to reading their efforts, and trying to stay calm when, as was inevitable, one of them informed him that Raphael had been a pope, or that Bernini taught Michelangelo everything he knew about sculpture.

When what he really needed was a nice quiet evening with Flavia, who had promised faithfully to be home early and cook dinner for the first time in weeks. Now that they had, tentatively, decided to recognize reality and get as married in law as they seemed to be in practice, and Argyll had settled into his new job and was no longer fretting continually about his career, life had become as blissful as it could possibly be when you were proposing to link your life's fortunes to a woman who never knew when her job would allow her to come home.

Not her fault; police work was like that, and she did her best. But it was galling, occasionally, to be so obviously pushed into second place by a purloined chalice, however much a marvel of sixteenth-century Tuscan workmanship it undoubtedly was. All very well, once in a while. But these things kept on vanishing. The thieves never rested. Did they not feel the need for a quiet evening with their feet up now and then like everyone else?

This time, Flavia would be home; she had left a message to that effect not half an hour ago, and Argyll was looking forward to it; he had even done his duty and got all the shopping on the way home so they could have a properly civilized meal together. He was so much looking forward to it that he felt a little anticipatory skip as he turned into the vicolo di Cedro, and began the last stage of the journey home.

And met Flavia coming down the street. She gave him a quick kiss, and looked apologetic.

'You're going back to the office, aren't you?' he said accusingly. 'I know that look.'

''Fraid so. Just for a while. I won't be long.'

'Oh, Flavia. You promised . . .'

'Don't worry. I won't be long.'

'Yes, you will be.'

'Jonathan. There's nothing I can do. Something's come up. It really won't take a long time. There's a little problem.'

He scowled, his good mood evaporating.

'I'll go and do my marking, then.'

'Good idea. And I'll be back by the time you're finished. Then we can have a quiet evening together.'

Grumbling to himself about essays, Argyll mounted the stairs to the third floor, said good evening to the old signora on the first floor and nodded coolly but politely to Bruno, the young lad with a taste for filling the night air with very loud and extremely bad music on the second, before fumbling in his pocket for his keys. Odd, he thought. There was a very strong inverse relationship between the volume of music and its quality. He'd never noticed it when he was young.

Two hours later, he'd finished his marking; Flavia had not yet returned. Three hours later, he'd eaten his dinner and she was still not there. Four hours later he went to bed.

2

'*When* did this come in?' Flavia asked incredulously when she got back to the office and saw the slip of paper containing a brief summary of the anonymous phone call.

The office trainee, a young, fresh-faced girl called Giulia who looked as though she should still be doing her homework before washing up for her mother, blushed with distress. It was hardly her fault; the call had come in, and there was no one to tell. She said as much.

'About five. But you weren't here, and I did go up to the General's office.'

'And what did he say?'

'Well, nothing,' she said reluctantly. 'He was asleep.'

'And you didn't want to wake him because you're new here and don't know that it is quite acceptable to give him a prod. I know. Don't get upset. It's not your fault.'

She sighed. Being just and fair is hard sometimes. It would have been much more satisfactory if she could have shouted at the girl.

'OK. Let's forget about that now. Did you take the call?'

The infant nodded, realizing that the worst was over. 'It was very imprecise.'

'No code-words? Not one of our regulars?'

'No. Just that there was going to be an important raid in the next few days. On this monastery, or whatever it is. San Giovanni.'

'What do they have? Are they on our list? Have you checked the computer?'

She nodded again, grateful that she had done the basics. 'They were burgled a couple of years ago, and were put on the register then.' She pulled out a piece of paper the computer had disgorged an hour ago.

'In fact, they have very little. Quite a lot of gold and silver ornaments, but that is mainly kept in a bank safe deposit; General Bottando recommended that after the last time. The only thing on the list which would seem to be worth anything is a painting by Caravaggio. Which is an important painting, although according to the book, not one of his best. And according to another book, isn't by Caravaggio at all.'

'Insured?'

'No note of it here.'

Flavia looked at her watch. Damn. Jonathan would not be pleased. She could see his point. It was some time . . .

'Have you rung them?'

'No answer.'

'Where is this place?'

'On the Aventino.'

'I suppose I'd better go there on my way home,' Flavia said reluctantly. 'Just to tell them to lock up carefully. Do we have anyone who can watch the place?'

Giulia shook her head. 'No one except me.'

'You're minding the desk. Oh, I'll see what I can do. If you'd get some patrol cars to drive past the place periodically during the night. And while you're sitting here drinking coffee all night, go through all the lists of coming and goings and sightings and arrivals. Anything at all. OK?'

Father Xavier, still at his desk and attending to the business generated by meetings, received Flavia in his office without ceremony and listened to what she had to say quietly.

'You must get reports like this all the time, don't you?'

She shrugged. 'A reasonable number, but rarely this specific. It would be foolish to disregard it. I thought it would be best to let you know so you could be on alert. Probably nothing will happen, but if you could put that painting into safe storage for a while . . .'

Father Xavier smiled indulgently. 'I don't think so. And I'm also sure that if any thief saw it at the moment, he would change his mind quite quickly.'

'Why's that?'

'It's being restored. By an American gentleman, called Daniel Menzies. Who is doing a very thorough job of it, I must say. He tells me that people who know nothing about the restoration process are always frightened at this stage of proceedings, and no doubt he knows what he is doing, but it is in a very poor state indeed at the moment. He has removed the old canvas, large portions of what he says is nineteenth-century paintwork and a good deal of grime. As far as I can see, there is nothing left at all for any thief to steal.'

'And is there anything else?'

There was a slight hesitation as the priest thought, then shook his head. 'We have many things of value to us; nothing of any great value to anyone else. You are aware that we were burgled?'

Flavia nodded.

'A bitter lesson,' he continued. 'We had always maintained a policy of leaving the church open on to the street. There is a street entrance, as well as one from the cloister. Some local inhabitants always preferred it to the parish church. It was a mistake, as we discovered. Since then, the door has been firmly locked. It was one of the first things I had to contend with when I took over as superior. The only other way in is through the courtyard, and the door on to that is locked as well.'

'Alarms?'

'No. There are limits. It was considered unseemly that we should defend ourselves in such a fashion. I didn't agree, but that was the decision of the council who have the last word in such matters.'

She stood up. 'It may have been a hoax. But I thought it was wise . . .'

He nodded, stood up to show her out and shook her hand. 'It was very kind of you, signorina. Very kind indeed, especially at such a late hour. And I will make sure that all precautions are taken.'

And Flavia, finally, felt her day was coming to an end. On her way back, she called in to Giulia, to see if anything else had happened. She shouldn't, she knew. There is nothing worse than an interfering superior, constantly meddling and looking over your shoulder. It does no good at all, and merely makes you uncertain of yourself. She remembered that from her own youth. But she felt uncomfortable.

'Anything?'

'No. I've been going through the lists. Airports, hotels, sightings at railway stations, reports from dealers. Nothing of importance.'

'What about the unimportant?'

'Not much there, either. The only thing I did note was that someone vaguely involved in one of your cases last year arrived yesterday evening. Just a witness, though: no involvement in anything illegal. Quite the opposite, in fact.'

'Who?'

'A woman called Verney. Mary Verney.'

Flavia got that little turning sensation in her stomach that always happened when she realized that, if disaster was going to be averted, it would be by sheer good fortune rather than skill or observation or intelligence.

'Some report you wrote seems to have been absorbed into the immigration computer. I don't know why. It just came up as routine.'

'Any idea where she is?'

'No. But I can try and find out, if you think it's important.'

'I do. I really do. Think of it as your night-time's entertainment. Ring round every hotel in Rome if need be. The sooner you find her, the better.'

'Who is she?'

'An old friend. And a very clever woman. You'll like her.'

'Ah, yes. Mary Verney,' Bottando said the next morning. 'The English country lady. Why are you so interested in her? All she did was provide evidence against that man Forster last year. So you told me. Or was there more to it?'

'We got back eighteen pictures, thanks to her,' Flavia said. She didn't like this bit. 'And because of that I was happy to end the enquiry. Getting things back is our main job, after all. But once all the reports were written and the whole affair

21

finished I became convinced she was responsible for most of the thefts in the first place.'

'And you never mentioned this?' Bottando said with a suggestion of slight surprise around the left eyebrow. She avoided looking too embarrassed.

'I couldn't pin anything on her, and if I'd tried earlier we would never have recovered the pictures. It was a trade-off and, in the circumstances, a reasonable one.'

Bottando nodded. It was, after all, exactly what he would have done himself. He couldn't complain too much.

'But she's on the loose? A bit unwise, that, don't you think?'

'Unexpected. She's not so young any more, and I was pretty sure she'd retired. She's no spring chicken, you know. And hardly needs the money.'

Bottando nodded. For some reason Flavia got the idea he was only half listening.

'But here she is,' he observed. 'You want to bring her in?'

Flavia shook her head. 'No. It may be a completely innocent visit, and it would be a waste of time. I don't want to start anything official unless we have to explain our interest. But I don't like her being in Rome. I thought it would be a good idea to let her know that we are aware she's here. I'll have her for a drink. It would accomplish the same thing. She's staying in the Borgognoni hotel. With your permission, I'll ring her up this morning. And put someone on to watch her.'

Bottando came out of his reverie long enough to frown with disapproval. 'We can't afford that. Don't have the people. Besides, this monastery business seems a higher priority. If either of them is.'

'Well . . .'

'No. You can have Giulia. Time she got out of the office, and we can put the cost down to the ministry's training budget. A bit of practice for her. But that's all. Get her to stand outside San Giovanni all day . . .'

'She's already there.'

Bottando peered at her. 'Oh,' he said. 'Good. You can have her follow this Verney woman afterwards, for a bit of variety, if you like. Couple of days of that and she'll begin to realize what policing is really all about. But don't use anyone else.'

He was right, she knew that; they couldn't spare two people. Even sending Giulia out would mean masses of extra paperwork for everyone else. But the very presence of Mary Verney in Rome rattled her. She nodded, nonetheless.

Bottando grunted. 'Good. Now, is there anything else? Thank you,' he said to his secretary as she slid into the room and deposited a vast file on his desk. He transferred it immediately to a drawer, which he closed with a satisfying slam. 'Because if not, I'm going for a coffee.'

She stopped and looked carefully at him. 'You all right?' she asked. 'You don't seem your normal self at all this morning. Did they give you food poisoning or something yesterday?'

He grimaced, and hesitated, and then gave into the temptation. 'Come back in and sit down. I need to tell you something,' he said with a sigh.

'Sounds bad,' she said as she settled back on the armchair.

'Maybe, maybe not. I haven't figured it out yet. I'm being promoted. I think.'

Flavia blinked and looked at him as she tried to think of the right thing to say. 'You sound uncertain. These things are normally clear. Am I meant to congratulate or commiserate?'

'I don't know. But basically I was given the option of being promoted and taking over some useless new department which seems to have been set up solely to soak up more money from the European taxpayer, or being booted out. With all the consequences for pay and pension that entails. I've been making some phone calls and I don't as yet see any way out.'

She leant back in her chair and bit her thumbnail as she thought this one through.

'But you stay here?'

He nodded. 'Nominally. That brings me to you.'

'Oh, yes?' she said cautiously.

'Essentially, you have two choices. Stay here and take over the day-to-day running of the department, where you will have to spend much more time in administration. Or help me set up this new Euro-nonsense. Where you would have to be junior to some Englishman or Dutchman or something and still have to spend much more time in administration. The second option will be exceptionally well paid, of course. Riches beyond the dreams of avarice. Tax free, as well. And more regular hours.'

'Which do you recommend?'

He shrugged. 'I hope I have your services either way. Apart from that, you'll have to make up your own mind on the matter.'

'When do I have to make up my mind?'

He made an expansive, all-the-time-in-the-world gesture. 'End of the week? I hate to rush you, but I have to lay my plans. You can get some practice in this week. I'm going to be busy writing memos. Consider yourself on your own. And the eyes of the ministry are on us at the moment. If you could fend off all raids on the national gallery and the Presidential art collection until this is sorted out, I'd be grateful. And it would be best if raids we've been told about in advance didn't happen.'

'Looks bad, you think?'

'Not ideal. Not ideal.'

3

Dan Menzies was a painstaking, methodical worker, labouring in a fashion which was totally at odds with both his bulk and his reputation. Despite the flamboyant gestures and the frequent use in his speech of dramatic metaphors – always talking about expunging this or that part in his campaigns of restoration – when engaged on a job he went slowly and extraordinarily carefully. Normally, of course, he commanded small armies of people, and it was typical of him that he talked in military terms while his more subtle colleagues headed teams. But that was for large projects, with lots of money. Then he would behave like an artistic General Patton, rushing from one place to another, shouting encouragement and advice and orders. But in this church he was on his own. He found it all strangely restful; he was restoring, he felt, more than the pictures. It was many a year now since he had worked alone, just him and the paint, trying to feel his way with his scalpel and his chemicals back to an instinctive idea of what the artist had in mind. And as he crouched there, oblivious of the hours passing by, and not even feeling the strain as his back muscles began to protest about the unfair treatment they were receiving, he realized that he was entirely happy. He must, he decided when the light had become so bad that he could work no longer, do this more often. Once a year, he thought as he stretched and washed the grime off his hands, he should do a painting on his own, with no one around. Well, maybe once every two.

Any of his colleagues in the restoring business, had they known about this tranquil, introspective mood would probably have been stunned into silence, so little did it fit his reputation or normal means of behaving. Menzies was known as something of a showman, never missing an opportunity to thrust himself into the limelight, and had earned plaudits and criticism in equal measure through the dramatic, and some said vainglorious, way in which he went about bringing pictures back to life. This he knew and accepted; it was an inevitable part of a competitive business, as far as he could see. For his own part, he thought he did his best, however much he might dress it up dramatically to please the audience. He also wanted very much to be liked, for he considered himself a likeable fellow, and never understood why his colleagues and rivals were so unfair. Dissimulation was simply an unknown skill, that was all. He had opinions, lots of opinions, and when someone asked him, he could never resist the opportunity of giving full chapter and verse. Was it his fault some of his rivals were fools?

And that was why he was here. He did not believe the best man won without working for it. There was a big project dangling there, waiting to be plucked, and he was determined to get it. If it meant spending six months in Rome in advance, that was part of the price. Restoring this dubious Caravaggio was a way of keeping himself occupied. A work of charity, just the sort of thing to arouse favourable comment. And a perfect excuse to be in the right place, talking to the right people as they made up their minds. It would be the highpoint of his career, if he could get it. No one was going to stand in his way.

Suddenly, he was aware of a presence standing behind him, watching what he was doing. Bloody tourists, he thought. He tried to ignore the unpleasant sensation that tickled at his concentration, and succeeded for a while. But he ended up trying so hard not to be bothered that eventually he made a small mistake. His patience snapped.

'Piss off,' he said furiously, turning round to face the man. His eyes narrowed when he saw the figure, standing meekly there, foolish look on his face. That look of bovine stupidity on his face. Jesus.

'I'm sorry . . .'

26

'I don't care if you're sorry or not. Just go away. How the hell did you get in here, anyway?'

'Well, I . . .'

'You have no right to be in here. It's not a public monument. Aren't there enough of those in this city without you having to come barging in here?'

'I'm not . . .'

'Go on. Go away.'

The little man stood his ground, so Menzies, who weighed maybe twice as much as he did, lost his temper. He rose from his knees, walked over and grabbed him by the arm, then frogmarched him to the main door that led on to the street, taking the vast old key from the hook as he went. Unlocked it, pulled it open a foot or so, then ushered the man out.

'So nice to have met you,' he said sarcastically as the pathetic fellow walked blinking into the sunlight. 'Do drop in again sometime. Like next century. Goodbye.'

And as he waved, Giulia, sitting on the steps of the church as she had been all that day, furtively took a photograph of Menzies waving in what seemed to be a friendly fashion. No reason to do so, but she was bored beyond endurance. Apart from spending her hours wondering whether the police was the right career for her, this was the first moment of excitement for hours. Then she scribbled down some notes, very precisely and carefully, leaving nothing out.

For the second night in a row, Argyll got back in the evening in the fond hope that this time he was going to get his quiet evening with Flavia. They didn't seem to have had time to speak about anything at all for weeks and he was concerned that unless they got in a bit of practice, they might lose the knack entirely. He was a bit late himself this time, and walked in expecting her to be there already. She wasn't. The apartment was occupied nonetheless.

'Oh, my God,' he said despairingly. 'What the hell are you doing here?'

A small, elegant woman in her mid-to-late fifties sat serenely on the sofa by the window. She had a lovely face, which seemed kind, and looked as though she was fond of laughing. The sort who knew how to grow old graciously, a rare talent. A bit reserved, perhaps, but good company. An honest face. The sort you instantly felt you could trust.

Which just went to show what a lot of nonsense it was to place any sort of reliance on the interpretation of physiognomy. He must remember to point that out to the students. A very important aspect of seventeenth-century artistic theory and one which, in his experience, was completely wrong. Mary Verney, sweet-faced criminal that he knew her to be, proved this pretty conclusively.

'Jonathan!' this woman said, rising from her chair and coming to meet him with a warm smile and outstretched hand. 'How lovely to see you again.'

Argyll growled with annoyance. 'I'm afraid I cannot say the same for you, Mrs Verney,' he replied stiffly. 'How you have the nerve . . .'

'Oh, dear,' she said, brushing his protests aside. 'I suppose I couldn't really expect a great welcome. But that's all water under the bridge.'

'No, it isn't.'

'Oh, Jonathan. What a fuss you make.'

'Mrs Verney, you are a liar, a thief and a murderer. You organized it so that there was nothing I could do about it. Fine. But you really don't expect me to be pleased to see you, do you?'

'Well,' she said doubtfully. 'If you put it like that . . .'

'I do. Of course I do. Don't be ridiculous.'

'I take it you never mentioned that little matter to Flavia?'

'Not exactly.'

'I wondered why she was so keen to see me,' Mrs Verney said with a slight frown. 'A harmless little old lady like myself.'

Argyll snorted.

'No, really. I am. I confine myself to good works and repairs to the house.'

'Paid for by your ill-gotten gains.'

'Ill-gotten gains? Really, Jonathan, you do sound like a Victorian melodrama at times. But if you want to put it like that, indeed. By my ill-gotten gains. And it uses up all my time.'

Argyll snorted again. 'So why are you here?'

'Gin, please. And tonic, if you have it.'

'What?'

'I thought you were asking me if I wanted a drink.'

'No.'

She smiled sweetly at him. I know this isn't easy, dear, she seemed to be saying. Argyll, who in fact rather liked the woman, however much a monster of turpitude she really was, crumbled into abject politeness.

'With ice?'

'Please.'

He assembled it and handed it over.

'Now,' she went on. 'Let me make it clear that I am not here of my own volition. The last thing in my mind when I came to Rome was seeing either of you. I hardly expected a warm welcome from you, at least.' She held up her hand as he was about to interrupt. 'I'm not blaming you in the slightest. But Flavia rang and invited me for a drink. In the circumstances, I could hardly refuse.'

'In what circumstances?'

'She had taken the trouble to find out that I was here. Which means that I am a marked woman. And I don't want to waste police time, so I thought it best to reassure her that I am here merely for a holiday. Then she can devote herself to catching real thieves.'

'You are a real thief.'

'Was, dear. Was. There is a big difference. I told you. I'm retired.'

'Somehow I find that difficult to believe . . .'

'Look,' she said patiently. 'I am on holiday. Nothing sinister at all. I just hope that I can convince you eventually. If I can, I am sure your sanctimoniousness will evaporate and you'll become a normal human being again.'

'Sanctimonious? Me? You turn up here out of the blue . . .'

'I know. You're in shock . . .'

'Really?' asked Flavia brightly as she came in through the door with pasta and a couple of bottles of wine. 'What about?'

'With sheer pleasure at seeing me,' Mrs Verney said smoothly.

'Yes,' Flavia said. 'Isn't it nice? When I noticed she was here, I thought, how nice it would be . . .'

Mrs Verney smiled. 'And here I am. I'm delighted to see you both again. I'm most anxious to hear all your news. How are you both? Married yet?'

'In the autumn,' Flavia said. 'That is the plan.'

'Oh, congratulations, my dears. Congratulations. I must send you a wedding present. I hope you will both be very happy.'

'Thank you. I was wondering whether you would like to have dinner with us. Unless you're busy, that is . . .'

'I'd be delighted. But I was going to invite the both of you. If there's a decent restaurant nearby . . . ?'

'That is kind. Why not?'

They smiled at each other with total lack of sincerity. Argyll scowled at both of them.

'Not me, I'm afraid,' he said with entirely fake regret as he saw his opportunity and patted the pile of essays by his side. 'Confined to barracks.'

Five minutes of a routine attempt at persuasion followed, but he stood firm, and although it cost him disapproving comments about being an old misery, he eventually saw the pair of them off to the restaurant round the corner which was their usual eating place when cooking seemed too much to bear. He had a miserable meal of pasta instead, followed by two hours of essays. Not an ideal evening; not what he'd planned at all. But in comparison to the alternative it seemed positively heavenly.

It was an agreeable meal; no doubt about it. Pleasant little trattoria, simple but delicious food and that combination of amiable informality that only Italian restaurants ever seem to manage properly. The two women chatted happily throughout, working their way through a fund of gossip like long-lost friends. Flavia even enjoyed herself. The same could not be said for Mary Verney.

She was seriously, deeply alarmed. It was too much to expect that the Italian police wouldn't notice her arrival, but she had assumed that demarcation disputes, bureaucracy and lack of manpower would delay things. She had done her best to be invisible, arriving by train rather than aircraft because checks at airports were better, not using her credit card, that sort of thing. It must have been the hotel registration that did it. Odd that; she'd believed no one bothered with those sort of checks any more. Evidently wrong. Maybe it was the computers. It just showed how old she was getting.

And instead of coming to police attention in a week or so, or not at all, they had noted her on her first day, and gone out of their way to make that clear. It was obvious that Flavia didn't know why she was here, but it was likely she would be watched; and that would cramp her insufferably.

She poured herself a whisky when she got back to her hotel room to think it over. She had stayed in the Borgognoni once before, in 1973. It was an ideal hotel, even nicer now it was under new management and had been redecorated. Then it had been comfortably luxurious and had the inestimable advantage of being within a few minutes' walk from the Barberini Gallery. As she had been in Rome to steal a picture from the Barberini – a small but delightful Martini, which she had been seriously tempted to keep for herself – it could not have been better. But the feature which tipped her finally in the hotel's favour, now as then, was the number of exits it possessed. Front ones, back ones, side ones. For guests and employees and delivery men. She had always insisted on this when working; you never knew when a discreet disappearance might come in handy. Like now.

So she made her phone call, set up an appointment, and slipped out the back when she'd changed and finished her drink. As she walked across Rome to the Hassler hotel, she cursed her ill-luck once again. She had been quite genuine about retiring. She had spent more than twenty-five years stealing paintings and had never been caught; only came close once. And that was enough. It had been the rule she had made in her youth, and she intended to stick to it firmly. Never, ever, take risks. She had totted up her winnings, disposed of her last embarrassing possessions, and settled back to grow old in comfort.

Until three weeks ago when her daughter-in-law, even

31

more hysterical than usual, telephoned. She never had much to do with the silly woman. Why her son – normally a sensible person – had decided to marry such a fusspot was quite beyond her. She was completely brainless but – and here Mary Verney had to give grudging approval – a doting mother to her grandchild. Louise, eight years old, was in fact the only member of her family Mary had a great deal of time for; the only one who had much in the way of spirit. You could see it in her eyes. An adorable child; Mary Verney's normally well-disciplined heart melted each time she thought of the little beast.

How Kostas Charanis divined this she could never figure out. She had worked for him once, more than thirty years previously, and it was the one time a working relationship had become more than merely professional. He paid, she acquired the painting he wanted. And then she had, over the next year, spent a great deal of time in his company, in Greece and elsewhere. A lovely man. With an edge of steel when he wanted something. As, at the time, he had wanted her, she found it exciting rather than frightening.

Nonetheless, when Mikis, his son, turned up out of the blue four or five months previously with another commission, she had been friendly but firm: no thanks. Never revive old flames, never take commissions out of sentiment, never come out of retirement. She had worked because she needed to, not for the hell of it. Now she didn't need the money, and saw no reason to take any risks at all.

And, quite apart from such practical reasons, she didn't like Mikis Charanis. Didn't like him at all, in fact. None of the father's intelligence, or subtlety or strength. A spoilt brat, with delusions of unearned grandeur. She remembered him as a six-year-old, the last time she had met Kostas and they had said their final farewells; the child was standing in the street with a friend. There'd been a fight, and the boy had deliberately and cold-bloodedly taken his friend's hand and broken every finger on it. To teach him a lesson, he said afterwards. Even if she'd been short of cash, the fact that he was involved would have made her turn it down, no matter what fond memories she had of his father.

32

She thought he'd taken it well, even though he'd made another approach, more pressing this time, a few weeks later. Again, she had no trouble in turning him down. Tell your father I'm too old, she said. Find someone more sprightly.

Then he took her granddaughter. One morning, she had been taken to school by her mother, dropped off at the gates. Two hours later a teacher had rung, wondering where she was. Even before the police could be told, Mikis had rung, warning against contacting anyone in authority. She remembered those broken fingers then, and the look on his face.

The child was well and being indulgently looked after, he'd said. Nothing to worry about. She'd been told it was a surprise holiday, and she would have a wonderful time for the next month or so. If all went well. Mary Verney was told that all depended on her. It was a simple job.

She was paralysed with anger and terror in equal measure, but had swiftly understood that there were no alternatives. She had tried ringing the old man in Athens to plead with him, but had not got through. She left messages, but he didn't reply. Eventually, she realized he was not going to. He wanted something, and the steel was showing.

This time, she didn't find it exciting.

For herself she could take risks, but this was the one area where she would never risk a thing. It was all agreed with Mikis that same day: she would go to Rome and would acquire the painting Charanis was so excited about. The sooner it was handed over, the sooner Louise would be restored to her family.

She had not yet figured out why it was so important to him; she'd done a little background work the first time he came, but couldn't even find the thing listed in any of the guidebooks, directories or inventories she'd consulted. Mikis hadn't been so keen to tell her, either. She'd found a little on the monastery, of course, but that was no substitute for a close examination.

The problem was the rush; she wanted her granddaughter back, and Charanis was in a hurry as well. A project she would usually plan for six months at least, to make sure everything went well, had to be done in a couple of weeks. Even worse was his insistence that she, and she alone, should be involved. She'd protested about this.

'Look: give me half a year and there would be no problem. But if you want it this quickly then slightly more direct methods might be better. Drive a truck through the door, grab it and run. It's not a method I approve of, but it shouldn't worry you. I know some people . . .'

Mikis shook his head. 'Absolutely not. I want only the smallest number possible involved. That's why I chose you. If I'd wanted a gang of bruisers I could have found them myself.'

That she believed. She seethed but accepted, then laid the best and safest plans she could come up with in time. In five days' time, a party of pilgrims from Minnesota would arrive in Rome and, because of local connections, would be offered bed and board in the monastery of San Giovanni. Mary Verney, aka Juliet Simpson, was already booked into the party through an old contact in America. All she needed was a few days in advance to double-check the plans and check for possible problems. In principle, it should be easy, as long as her luck held.

Less than twenty-four hours after she arrived, it broke; Flavia noticed her and, although the meal was entirely polite and unthreatening, made it clear that she would be watched. Looking out of her hotel window as she finished off her drink, she saw the Italian had meant it. Sitting at a table in a café opposite the entrance was the same youthful girl she had noticed behind her on the way back. Not doing a very good job of being discreet, but that was perhaps the idea.

So she changed, and slipped out of the back; she doubted they would have enough people to waste more than one on her at the moment. Then walked, by a slightly circuitous route, to the Hassler – very much grander than her own hotel, but she was in an economical frame of mind these days – marched straight in, up the stairs and made for room 327. Always be on time when possible. She was not in a good mood, but was damned if she was going to let it show.

'Good evening, Mikis,' she said evenly when the door

opened. The man who let her in and offered her his hand was in his thirties, but already overweight. He had been drinking, and she was pleased to see that he was nervous. She felt a wave of contempt flow over her.

'Bad news, I'm afraid,' she said unceremoniously.

He frowned.

'Very bad,' she went on. 'I've been to see the police. They rang this afternoon. They knew I was here, and they are buzzing like a nest of wasps. For which I hold you responsible.'

He frowned with displeasure. 'And why do you think that?'

'Because you're a clumsy amateur, that's why. Have you been talking to anyone else about this? Getting someone lined up in reserve? Boasting to your friends? If you have any, that is.'

He stared at her. 'No,' he said shortly.

'Are you sure? Absolutely sure? Because someone has been indiscreet. They must have been. It's the only possible explanation. And it wasn't me.'

He shook his head firmly. 'Absolutely not.'

'The whole thing is blown to bits,' she said. 'You'll have to abandon the idea.'

Again he shook his head. 'Sorry. I'm afraid not.'

'It's all very well for you to say that. Courage in adversity. I'm the one who goes to jail. And if I do, you don't get your picture.'

He didn't even reply, so she carried on, hoping to make him see reason. 'Listen, I told you how I work. This is exactly the sort of situation I have always managed to avoid. I don't want you talking to anyone else and above all I don't want you here.'

'That's unfortunate,' he said evenly. 'But there is nothing you can do about it.'

'And I want this whole thing cancelled, or at least postponed. Now.'

He shook his head, opened his wallet and handed over a small photograph, of a child. 'Came this morning. What do you reckon? Quite a good likeness, I thought.'

She took it and stared grimly at a picture of her smiling granddaughter for a few seconds. As is traditional in this most

35

ghoulish of modern art forms, there was a copy of yesterday's newspaper, clearly showing the date, in the foreground. Just so there would be no misunderstanding. Her attempt to push him off-balance hadn't worked. Back to the drawing board.

'So what do you expect me to say?'

'Nothing. But I want it understood I must have that picture quickly.'

'Why doesn't your father just buy it? He's got enough money. It can't be worth that much.'

He smiled indulgently. 'It's worth a king's ransom, in the right hands. And it is not for sale. So this is the only way.'

'Why's it so important? It's not a great picture. I could buy you one twice as good in a gallery for less trouble than this.'

'That is not your concern. Your job is to get it. For that you don't need to know why I want it. And you will get it. I have every confidence in you. So let us not waste time talking. You have a job, and you'd better get on with it.'

She was angry when she left five minutes later, with the suppressed fury of total impotence. It was something she was not used to and, yet again, she had that slow growing feeling of age creeping up on her. She felt lonely, in fact, having to rely on her own resources and discovering that, for once, they weren't enough.

It also made her vengeful in a way which was of no use but was no less demanding for all that. Had she been a man, she might have gone out and got drunk and ended up in a brawl. Instead she fixed on the one person nearby with whom she had some sort of acquaintance. When she got back to her hotel by the back entrance, Mary walked straight through the lobby, out the front and crossed the road to the bar.

'Excuse me,' she said to the young woman still sitting patiently and reading her book. Mary noticed with satisfaction the look of perplexed alarm on her face as the poor girl realized what was going on.

'Yes?'

'You must be a colleague of Flavia's, I assume.'

'What?'

'Well, you've been following me around all evening, and

36

look terribly bored sitting there with that book. I was wondering if you wanted to come up to my room for a drink? Then you could watch me in comfort.'

'Ah . . .'

'Please yourself. But as we seem to be stuck with each other for a bit, I thought I might as well introduce myself formally. So that tomorrow we could say good morning properly, rather than pretending we don't know each other.'

'I don't think . . .'

'Or I could just give you my itinerary for tomorrow, so you'd know where to go if you lost me. It's so ridiculous, your trying to be discreet.'

'Listen . . .'

'What, my dear? What's your name, by the way?'

'Giulia Contestanti.'

'What a nice name.'

'Thank you. But this won't do.'

'Why not?'

'Because it won't.'

'Oh, I'm not meant to know you're following me, is that right? Don't worry' – Mary leaned forward in a conspiratorial whisper – 'I won't tell. Promise. Do I take it that you don't want to come for a drink?'

'No, I don't.'

'Pity. Oh, well. I'm off to bed. I'll be up at about seven and I'll leave when the shops open. You'll find me pottering up and down the via Condotti most of the morning. I need a new pair of shoes. I promise not to wave when I see you. It can be our little secret, eh? Good night, my dear.'

And, leaving the poor girl red-faced with embarrassment, Mary Verney went to bed.

4

Argyll was in a sulky mood the next morning, and sat sullenly over his toast when Flavia came into the little kitchen after her shower. She peered at him to assess his mood, made herself a coffee and sat down.

A long silence followed.

'What's up with you?' she asked eventually.

'Nothing.'

'Yes, there is.'

He chewed his toast for a moment, then nodded. 'You're right. There is. Why did you invite that woman for a drink?'

'Mary Verney? I thought you liked her.'

'No.'

'Business.'

'What sort of business?'

'A warning shot. Just so that she knows we are aware of her presence. I've been meaning to ask you about her.'

Argyll sniffed cautiously.

'Do I conclude that she wasn't quite as innocent as my report said over the Giotto thefts?'

Argyll gave a hesitant nod. 'Since you ask,' he began reluctantly, 'I suppose I should tell you . . .'

But she held up her hand. 'No doubt. But it might be better if you didn't. We got the pictures back and closed the case to everybody's satisfaction. If she was more involved and knew more than she let on then it might be better to pass over it in silence. If you tell me anything else, I'd be obliged to report it. That is the way it stands, isn't it?'

He nodded.

'But if I suggested that she was as crooked as a corkscrew,

you wouldn't feel obliged to leap to defend her good name?'

He shook his head.

'Thought so. I was never entirely convinced by her story.'

'You weren't?'

'No. But we did get the pictures back, and that was all I was interested in. Keep the rest to yourself. But she may not be here simply on a holiday.'

Argyll shrugged. 'I really don't know,' he said cautiously. 'As far as I can see she has more than enough money. And her complaints about being too old had an air of truth to them. What are you going to do about her?'

'Nothing. Except watch her every step, bug her phone, read her mail and never let her out of our sight.'

'Which she will spot.'

'That's the idea . . . She assures me she is here on holiday. Maybe she is. I just want to be certain.'

'Is that why you were late the other night as well?'

She sighed. So that was why he was grumpy. In abstract she sympathized. In practice, she wished he had a bit more sympathy for her. What was she meant to do about it? Stay at home while things got stolen all around her?

'No,' she said patiently. 'That was something else. We had a tip-off about a possible raid. On a monastery. I had to go down and warn them. I don't like it, either, you know. But we're short of people ever since . . .'

'I know. Budget cuts.'

'Well, it's true. I don't hang around street corners at night for my own pleasure, you know.'

'I'm glad to hear it. Oh, well. I'm used to it, I suppose.'

'Don't be so long-suffering.'

'I am long-suffering.'

'And don't be crabby, either. That's my job. I'm a bit fed up too, you know.'

'Oh? Why's that?'

'Bottando's going.'

'Where?'

'Going. Just going. He's been promoted. Against his will. It's that or being demoted, it seems.'

Argyll put down his toast suddenly. 'Good God. That's sudden, isn't it? What happened?'

'A coup d'état, I think. But he's going in two months. To head some useless Euro-initiative, which will probably result in art theft doubling over the next few years.'

'You sound very certain. Isn't he going to do anything about it?'

'Apparently not. He says there's nothing he can do.'

'Goodness. So who takes over?'

'He remains nominally in charge. But he's offered the day-to-day running to me. If, that is, I don't want to go with him.'

'Do you want to run the place?'

'I don't know. Do I want everything to depend on me and be responsible for operations? I don't think I do. Do I want to work for Paolo, or someone brought in from outside? No. Not that either.'

'You want things to stay as they are.'

She nodded.

'And they're not going to. What will you do?'

She shrugged. 'I haven't thought about it.'

'What would going with him involve?'

'Sitting in an office from nine to five, organizing. Home every evening at six. No rushing around late at night. Vast amounts of money, tax free.'

He nodded. 'Every sensible person's dream, right?'

'Yes.'

He nodded again as he turned this over in his mind. 'Hmm. Do you want to do it?'

'I'd get to spend more time with you.'

'Not what I asked.'

'Oh, Jonathan, I don't know. I suppose you think I should go for the quiet life.'

'I didn't say that. Obviously I wouldn't mind seeing you every now and then.'

'I thought so.'

'But if you go with Bottando you could end up in a dead-end, boring job which drives you crazy, money or no. When do you have to decide?'

'He's given me a week.'

'In that case you should think about it for a week. And so will I. So let's change the subject. This monastery. Did you fend off the criminal classes? Which monastery was it, anyway?'

'San Giovanni. On the Aventino.'

He nodded. 'I know it.'

'Really?' The things he knew about this city never ceased to amaze her. She had never heard of the place before.

'It's got a dodgy Caravaggio in it.'

'Under restoration.'

'Ah. Who's doing it?'

'A man called Dan Menzies. Ever heard of him?'

Argyll nodded fervently. 'The Rottweiler of Restoration.'

'So it's worth a lot of money?'

'*If* it's a Caravaggio, and *if* Menzies hasn't repainted it as a Monet, yes. And the subject matter is a bit gloomy for your average buyer of stolen works of art, as I recall.'

'What is it?'

'The breaking of St Catherine on the Wheel. A bit morbid. And good evidence for it not being by Caravaggio. He didn't take to women much. These private collectors usually go for the more cheerful stuff, don't they? Sunflowers and Impressionists, and all that sort of thing. Baroque religion doesn't look so well in the dining room. Puts people off their food, in fact. Besides, it's probably quite big. Getting it out would need a removal truck, I'd imagine.'

'So what's the story on Menzies?'

'None that I know of. Very loud, bellows away so you can hear him from miles off, but it may be that his bark is worse than his bite. I've never met him. More than that I can't say. You think he's in cahoots with someone, do you? Tipped them off the picture is out of its frame so they can sweep in and roll it up.'

She shrugged. 'No. But if someone is going to pinch that picture, and would want to hit it before it goes back on its stretcher, they'd have to know when the best moment would be to go in.'

'Better put a tail on Menzies, then. Tap his phone, that sort of thing.'

'We don't have the people.'

The first thing Flavia had to deal with when she arrived was Giulia, who brought her crisis of confidence with her into the office. This did at least make her forget about major career decisions. 'Oh, stop making such a fuss,' she said crossly, when Giulia recounted her meeting in the café with Mrs Verney and then burst into tears. 'It happens, and it's partly my fault for not telling you that she's a bit more complicated than she looks. Now stop making that noise.'

Flavia paused for a moment when she realized how very much like Bottando she must sound to the poor girl. Except that Bottando would have managed to be a bit more avuncular, which was quite beyond her range. Naturally Giulia was upset; it was more or less the first time she'd been allowed out of the office since she'd arrived after her initial training; she wasn't very good yet and to have her nose rubbed in the fact like that must have been distressing.

'You go and recover yourself by writing the reports for a day, and then maybe you can have another go. It's just a knack. Don't worry about it. Who's following her at the moment?'

'No one.'

'Oh, for God's sake.' She stood up and reached for her bag.

'Where is she? In her hotel?'

Giulia looked at her watch. 'She said she was going shopping, and we could find her in the via Condotti most of the morning.'

Grumbling to herself that this was a ludicrous way of running a police force, Flavia walked out of the office to fill the gap. Tell Bottando, she said, to find someone to take over at lunch. If he's around. She'd ring in later to say where she was.

She tracked Mary Verney down in a shoe shop, as she was trying on a pair of fairly expensive shoes. The wince on her face suggested they were not perfect.

'You've taken over watching me for the morning?' Mary

said when she attracted Flavia's attention with a wave.

'*Faute de mieux*. I have.'

'Splendid. I hope you are not going to pretend you don't know me.'

'It was very unkind of you to do that last night,' Flavia observed gravely. 'Poor girl was in tears this morning. She's only young, you know.'

'I am sorry,' Mary Verney said, with every sign of meaning it. 'I was in a bad mood and felt like kicking someone. She was the only person available. I shall apologize later. But I could say that it was unkind of you to put a tail on me like that. Personally, I felt I deserved better.'

'No. Arresting you would have been unkind. Keeping an eye on you is merely sensible.'

'At least we don't have to play hide and seek all morning. If you're with me, you can help. You dress so much better than I do. I need a nice coat. Nothing fancy, you know. Or too expensive. Something fitting my age and the Norfolk countryside. One doesn't want to stand out too much. What do you suggest?'

Flavia recommended a place which her mother visited on the rare occasions she came to Rome. She was a touch stouter than Mrs Verney, and a little older, but very much more vain as well. It would be a place to start. She led the way, once Mrs Verney had tried on a few more pairs of shoes and given up the attempt to find something which matched comfort and elegance. Such things are hard to find.

'Such an expensive city,' she said as they walked up the street. 'I don't know how you do it, dear. After all, you aren't paid very much, I imagine.'

'We manage.'

'I was so glad to see that you and Jonathan are still together. When did you say you were getting married?'

'The autumn. That's the idea.'

'I am so pleased. I suppose it's too much to expect an invitation?'

'Probably.'

She sighed sadly. 'I thought as much. Are you *terribly* cross with me?'

'No. But only because I've taken care not to find out officially what it is I should be cross about. Otherwise I would be.'

'But you don't trust me any more.'

Flavia grinned. Mary Verney was quite impossible to dislike for long. 'Not an inch, no. I don't know what you are doing here. It may be that the story you have told me is the gospel truth. Even thieves have to have holidays, after all. But I have my doubts.'

'It's my own fault. However, this time I am being totally reliable. That I can guarantee.'

So they spent the rest of the morning shopping, Mary Verney buying a coat, with which she pronounced herself delighted, a pair of shoes which she didn't need but couldn't resist because they were so comfortable, and a leather hand-bag which was absurdly expensive but so awfully pretty. Then she led the way to a restaurant where they had a slow but (Flavia had to admit) very enjoyable lunch and she had a small brandy while Flavia went out to phone for a replacement. This wasn't quite the discreet surveillance she'd had in mind, but it was too late to do anything about that now. So she thought she might as well avoid making her manning problems worse, and removed Giulia from report writing.

'Oh, don't bother about that,' she said wearily when Giulia asked where she should pick up the trail. 'We're in Al Moro. Just come straight in.'

Then she went back to the table to find Mary Verney looking impish. She'd paid the bill for both of them.

'Look, do you want me to be had up for corruption or something? We've had the spooks all over us recently. I told you . . .'

'It's just a bill. But rather a big one. Don't worry. Your name isn't on anything. My treat.'

'I don't want treats.'

'But you deserve one. You have just spent three hours taking me shopping, after all . . .'

'It was a pleasure.'

'Shall we go?'

'No. We have to wait for Giulia. She will be your escort for the afternoon.'

'How lovely! This is the way to travel. I should have thought of this years ago.'

'We don't make a habit of it. Ah, here's Giulia,' she went on as the trainee arrived and crept cautiously up to their table, a worried frown of uncertainty on her face.

'I fear I owe you an apology, Giulia. Flavia was very cross with me for the inconsiderate way I behaved last night.'

'Oh, that's all right,' said the surprised, but well-brought-up, trainee.

'Splendid. Now, you go back to work, Flavia. And Giulia and I will have a lovely afternoon together. I thought I might visit some old art-dealing friends of mine. Some of them are a bit . . . perhaps, Giulia, you wouldn't mind being my *niece* for the afternoon? We don't want to frighten anybody, do we?'

Flavia just about managed to suppress a smile at the disconcerted and uncomfortable look on Giulia's face. 'Enjoy yourselves.'

'We will,' Mary Verney said. Giulia looked more doubtful.

Having nothing better to do that morning, Argyll walked across town to the monastery of San Giovanni to visit Dan Menzies and the Caravaggio. It wasn't in the slightest bit necessary, although it was in the back of his mind that perhaps, just perhaps, he might sniff around and see if he could find out something about this picture. Then he could write it up – and it didn't matter whether it was by Caravaggio or not – and get a little publication out of it. It also provided an opportunity to mess around with Flavia's case. Not that he should, of course, but the prospect offered a bit of variety. Teaching and marking things was all very well, but no one could say that it made the adrenaline run through the veins at high speed. Unless, of course, you found yourself in a lecture room with seventy students and then discovered you'd forgotten to bring your notes. Even then, it wasn't certain anyone would notice.

And it was a lovely day. The sun was shining and the bus routes were sufficiently complicated to make it not worthwhile waiting in the polluted street for one to come along. It was a decent stroll and put him into a sunny frame of mind. He crossed the river at the island, then did a slight detour through the prettier parts of the Aventino before climbing the hill and getting into the ever more out-of-the-way streets and alleys, one of which contained the surprisingly modest entrance to the monastery of San Giovanni. The baroque style is not normally associated with spiritual humility, but somehow the architect had pulled the trick off. The gateway, all peeling terracotta, had the regulation curls and swirls and twists, but it was all done on a small and almost domestic scale, as though it was the entrance to a private, and not very grand, house. The door itself, however, was well defended to keep the corruptions of the material world outside. Solid, sun-bleached oak was covered in a regular pattern of large metal studs for extra strength, and the little porter's hole was protected by a thick grid of iron bars. The only modern touch was a little doorbell drilled into the stucco, into which some-one had stuck a postcard. The Order of St John the Pietist, it said in several languages, so Argyll pressed it.

He had half hoped for a shuffling of feet and a creak as the porthole opened to reveal a bent-over old monk, tonsured and muttering. But no such picturesque details were forth-coming: what he got instead was a buzz and a click from the gate as the electric lock opened up. The modern world, he thought as he pushed and went inside. No romance.

It is one of the great delights of Rome that not even a long-term, assiduous resident is safe from surprise. Any street in the city, no matter where and no matter how seedy or shabby it looks at first glance, is capable of containing some little gem tucked away in an obscure corner, passed by nearly all the time and waiting to astonish. Sometimes it is a toy-box-sized Renaissance chapel, around which a twentieth-century developer has squeezed a vast, lumbering block of flats, or which has been accidentally turned into a traffic roundabout. Or the remains of a Roman palace nestling between a truck stop and a railway line. Or it is a Renaissance pile, converted into flats and hammered incessantly by fumes and the noise of traffic, but which still has its delicate, colonnaded court-yard, with moss on the cobbles and a sculpted fountain of nymphs and goddesses tinkling away to welcome home the weary commuters in the evening.

The headquarters of the Giovannisti (as such they were known, Argyll had learnt from a guidebook) was one such building. The street which contained it was not noisy, but it was unremarkable. A block or two of flats and empty, weed-covered waste ground awaiting the bulldozers and archaeologists on one side. The sort of street which contains nothing of interest to anyone.

Except for what was perhaps one of the prettiest collection of buildings that Argyll had ever seen. It was almost a perfect little miniature version of a monastery, with the chapel – much earlier in date, it seemed – on one side topped by a short tower that wanted to point to the heavens but was a bit too timid to presume; a range for the living quarters flanking it, but two storeys only, giving the effect of a row of country cottages, complete down to the green and orange of the old, rippling tiles on the roof, and then, slightly set aside, what was presumably the public building, with the library and the meeting rooms and the offices. Being on an uneven piece of ground helped, as the architect had so arranged his work that he fitted it into the terrain rather than the other way around; the result was an informality helped by the bits of classical statuary, evidently found when the garden was dug, stacked in one corner, and a bed of carefully tended summer flowers in another. Argyll breathed deeply and smiled in contentment.

'Good morning. Can I help you?'

Argyll was startled. Far from the shuffling old monk with matchstick legs and leather slippers he'd expected, he was confronted with the looming figure of possibly the most handsome man he had ever set eyes on. Nearly seven feet tall, powerfully built and nothing but muscle and bone, the sort of finely chiselled face a good draughtsman would long to have in his studio for a month or so, and a deep black skin which positively radiated health. He was dressed all in white – linen shirt, linen trousers and even linen shoes which made him all the more striking, and wore a small gold cross around his neck. That was the only indication at all that he was an inmate. Argyll felt pale and scruffy in comparison, which was largely because he was.

'Ah. Yes. Good morning. My name is Argyll.'

The man nodded politely in acknowledgement, but seemed to think that more was necessary. He didn't bother to ask anything.

'I've come to see Mr Menzies.'

It was only for the briefest fraction of a second, but Argyll thought he saw a tiny little twitch in the man's face, and believed that it indicated less than wholehearted warmth for Mr Menzies. But maybe not; he spoke perfectly graciously in a rich and elegant voice.

'I'm afraid Mr Menzies has not yet arrived. If you would like some coffee while you wait . . . ?'

'That's kind. But I'm awash with the stuff this morning. Could I go into the chapel and see what he's up to?'

'With pleasure, but I doubt you'll see much. Mr Menzies has cordoned off most of the transept as his work space and barred the entry. But you're welcome to see the rest of the church. It is, I'm told, very lovely.'

'You don't think so?'

'You may have noticed that I come from a very different tradition, sir. It means less to me.'

'Ah.'

'I think that the door will be open now. We have to lock it up these days, you see.'

'Oh? For any reason?' Such as the sudden arrival of a vastly valuable, but small treasure waiting to be stolen? he thought hopefully.

'There was a burglary a year or so ago, and the police recommended that if we didn't want to lose everything, we might think of locking the doors. There is, in truth, little that is stealable, I gather. But they say that if it can be moved, it will be. So they told us to lock it.'

'They do that.'

'We still don't like it, I must say. There is a group amongst us who believe there is something strange in an order which takes vows of poverty protecting its possessions from the poor and needy. Especially as they are not valuable.'

Argyll nodded. 'A lot of church history is against you, there.'

Father Paul nodded. 'I am learning this.'

'Where do you have your services at the moment? If Menzies has commandeered your chapel?'

'Oh, we make do. In the refectory, and sometimes in the library. Which, it must be said, is very much more comfortable. The chapel itself tends to be a little damp, especially in the winter months. And as many of our brothers are not in the prime of youth . . .'

'I see. Agonies at evensong, eh?'

'I beg your pardon?' He seemed puzzled by the remark.

'Nothing.'

'Please wait in the chapel if you wish. And do tell me what he's doing in there, will you? He discourages us from viewing his work.'

Then Argyll was left alone in the little courtyard and, to pass the time, went into the church to examine those bits which had not been boarded off by Dan Menzies. It was, in truth, very charming, or would have been. At a rough guess, Argyll reckoned it was probably fifteenth century in origin, and there was just enough clear space to see the elegant simplicity of the old church, which was fairly small but still had the dignity and harmony of its century. But it had been modernized, got at in the seventeenth century. Again, the architect had restrained himself. There was lots of gold leaf, angels and cherubs on the ceiling, and curls and quiffs stuck on all over the place, but somehow the effect was in keeping with the original structure. It was something of a relief. Argyll was a great defender of the baroque, normally, but sometimes they did go over the top and give even the loveliest buildings a distinct air of the Roman *nouveaux riches*.

So he turned his attention to the paintings, principally the Caravaggio. Not that there was much to see, as only the frame was left hanging on the wall, but it was clear even from that that it didn't fit. Much too big. Just the ticket for a huge place like San Andrea delle Valle, or San Agnese, but here it would seem so vast it would look as though it was wedged in, turning the airy church merely into supporting walls for the painter's gloomy notions of religion. The wrong mood, and as out of place as a mourner at a wedding party. And clearly vast. Twelve foot by eight, more or less. Stealing it would be a bit of a task. Although, for his part, he reckoned the church would be greatly improved if someone did remove it. In fact, he decided as he walked round, his feet echoing quietly on the stone flagging, the only painting which *should* be there was that little Madonna. He stopped and peered at the tiny painting in a minuscule chapel halfway down the aisle. It was very dirty, and he could scarcely make it out, but it was, he thought, a virgin and child. Very old, and an icon. Surrounded by a gold frame that came all the way down to the head, then curved simply round the outline of the shoulders and down to the infant resting airily in her arms. In front of it was a range of candle holders for the devout. There were no candles lit; no prayers or supplications that day. Argyll, who hated anyone to feel neglected and lonely, fished out a coin and dropped it in the box, then took a candle and lit it with his lighter, pressing it into the holder right in the painting's line of sight. There you are, love, he thought.

'Thank you, sir,' said a soft woman's voice, so gentle and so unexpected that Argyll, prone as he was to momentary bursts of superstition, almost jumped into the air.

'I'm sorry; I surprised you,' it continued, and Argyll turned round to see a middle-aged woman with a broom in one hand and an old plastic bucket in the other.

'No, no. That's all right,' he said. 'I didn't hear you. Who are you?'

'I clean the church,' she said. 'They allow me to. We always have.'

'We?'

'My family.'

'Oh.'

There was a brief pause, as Argyll examined this woman, and she, with great but benign curiosity, studied him. He saw a short, stocky figure, very Roman in appearance, with that broad, both-feet-on-the-ground air which is characteristic of the city's inhabitants. A kind face, with hands rough from years of being dipped into buckets of cold water, and scrub-

50

bing floors on hands and knees. An old floral house dress, and a cheap coat to keep off the dirt. She also wore a bizarre pair of pink velvet slippers with pom-poms on the end, which no doubt accounted for her being able to walk up behind him so silently.

'It's My Lady,' she said, nodding a greeting at the icon and making a half curtsey as she spoke. Odd, Argyll thought. Not Our Lady. Was that common among Romans? He'd never noticed before. 'She has great powers.'

'Oh, yes?'

'She protects those who are kind to her, and chastises the wicked. In the war, the people who lived round here gathered in the church when the troops were approaching and prayed for her help. Not a single bomb fell on this part of town.'

'That was fortunate.'

'It had nothing to do with fortune.'

'Of course not,' Argyll said hurriedly. 'She seems a little, um, neglected, now.'

The woman clicked her tongue against the roof of her mouth in disapproval and sadness. 'We live in a wicked age. Even priests turn from her, so how can anyone else know better?'

Argyll was beginning to feel uncomfortable. These sorts of conversations always had this effect on him, a slight feeling of claustrophobia and a desperate desire to be somewhere else. He didn't want to encourage her to talk on, but didn't want to be rude either, so he hopped up and down and said, 'Ah, indeed,' in a noncommittal way.

'They won't let people in any more; it's so sad and so foolish. The church used to be open for supplicants, who needed to come and ask her a favour. Or who wanted to thank her.'

'Ah.'

'And now only I am let in. I tend to her . . .'

'Morning!' A voice boomed and echoed across the church like an old cannon being fired, and simultaneously a bright shaft of sunlight cut across the loom of the church like a knife. Dan Menzies had walked through the door. 'Ciao, signora,' he said cheerfully to the cleaner. 'How are you this morning?'

'Good morning, sir,' she said politely, then picked up her

51

bucket and walked off to restart her work. Menzies made a face at Argyll and shrugged. No dealing with some people, he seemed to say.

'Who are you?'

Argyll began his explanation as Menzies pulled out a key ring from his pocket and gestured at the temporary wall put across the transept. 'I've seen you around. At the university, right? Come in, come in. Come and see the mess I'm making, if you must. Trying to prove it's by Caravaggio, are you?'

'Or not.'

'Not, in my opinion.'

'Why do you say that?'

He shook his head. 'The style's OK. But it's not good enough. Although there was so much nineteenth-century overpainting there's not a lot of the original left. Why don't you write about that? The nineteenth-century destruction of Italy's art? They did much more damage than modern restorers have ever done, you know. Despite our reputation, we're very careful in comparison to what went on before.'

'I'll think about it. I rather want a more modest topic at the moment.'

'Publish or perish, eh?'

'Not exactly.'

'Here it is, anyway. It still looks a bit shocking, but I'm nearly finished, despite the efforts of Father Xavier to stop me.'

He fumbled at the door then pushed it open.

'Who's he?'

'Head man. Got a bee in his bonnet about someone stealing it. Apparently the police were here and put the fear of God into him. Stupid man even had the idea that I should roll it up and lock it in a cupboard every night for security's sake. I tried to tell him that's impossible, but you know what a bunch of idiots these people are. Frankly, I couldn't imagine anyone wanting to steal it even if it was in perfect condition. Not my taste at all. Certainly not at the moment. Have a look. I'll put the lights on.'

Argyll stood in the cool and dusky light facing the altar,

until the whole transept was suddenly drenched in a harsh and brilliant glare. He gasped in astonishment.

'Oh, my God,' he said.

'Don't be ridiculous. That's quite normal,' Menzies called from over by the light switches. 'Don't you know anything about restoration?'

'Not really.'

'Well, you should. It's absurd for someone who calls himself an expert in art not to know the basics about the most important part of the entire business.'

'All I know,' Argyll said defensively, deciding not to mention that he'd always thought painting the things in the first place was more important, 'is that it looks as though it's been in a bar-room brawl. All that sticking plaster.'

'Dear God, how I hate the ignorant amateur,' Menzies said fervently. 'You'll be going on about respecting the wishes of the artist next.'

'Isn't that what you're meant to do?'

'Of course. If you know what his intentions were. But you don't, most of the time. What you normally have is a couple of square metres of peeling paint. Often heavily gone over by someone else. You don't really think that Caravaggio wanted that man watching in the corner to have side whiskers and the air of a nineteenth-century property developer, do you?'

'I don't know.'

'I do. He didn't. But a hundred years ago someone removed whatever he painted and stuck an entirely new face on. It must have been shortly after it came here.'

'Wasn't it painted for the place?'

'Oh, no. Of course not. Look at it. Doesn't fit at all.'

'Where did it come from?' No harm getting it started.

'Who cares? Not my business.'

'Does anyone know?'

'Probably. If you want to find out, go and look in the archives. Tons of stuff in there, I gather. Anyway, this face. I've taken it off, and there's nothing underneath. I have to put something back, and go by intuition. Guesswork, if you like. Someone's got to do it. It's all very well going on about minimal restoration, but that's the sort of nonsense normally

53

spouted by people who don't know what they are talking about.'

'My line is more historical.'

Menzies shrugged. 'In that case, the archives are the place for you. You should ask Father Jean. He controls them at the moment, although I don't think he knows much. Some old buffer before him was the expert.'

So Argyll left to find Father Jean and beg access to the archives. The itch was upon him, the yearning for the feel of old paper and the smell of dust in his hair.

Although Flavia was having a quiet and companionable mid-afternoon drink after leaving Giulia to the tender mercies of Mary Verney, she could, legitimately, claim to be working. Oiling up the contacts is a necessary part of the business and, on the whole, not too unpleasant: however loathsome and dishonest many art dealers are, they tend to regard the generous provision of food, wine and conversation as part of a public image necessary for the successful acquisition of clients. Sociability had been one of Argyll's least favourite activities and, in no small measure, contributed to the slow progress of his career before he did an abrupt turnabout and took refuge in teaching. All to the good, in Flavia's view; his mood had improved with his salary and, much to his surprise, he had sold more of his stock of paintings since he gave up being a dealer than he ever had when he was working on it full time.

Flavia, on the other hand, quite liked this aspect of the job – another mark against following Bottando into internationalism – as long as she was careful about who she associated with. It is, after all, always awkward to end up prosecuting someone who a few months previously had bought you a good lunch, but there was little to be done about it; if you want the best out of your contacts, you have to associate with the doubtful ones. Flavia was expected to be discreet, overlook any minor peccadilloes like taxes she might come across and give the occasional careful warning should that be necessary. Like, I'd be careful about having dealings with so-and-so for a few months. Or, if you were planning to buy that Domenichino in the auction next week, it might be advisable to think again. Things like that.

And in return, she expected a steady flow of information on the grounds that if it wasn't forthcoming, she might accidentally let slip about the taxes to the financial police, or time a raid for the very moment when a particularly important client was in the gallery and about to buy a major work.

Not that such tasteless matters were ever mentioned as the wine was poured or the coffee drunk; it was understood, and there was no need to be crude about it.

And Giuseppe Bartolo, whose gallery she reached at about four after fruitless visits to half a dozen others before him, was a wise, not to say wily, old-timer who knew the rules better than she did, being twice her age and many times as cunning. Indeed, he had virtually taught them to her, having taken her under his wing when she was little older, and even less experienced, than Giulia. In a similar manner to Bottando but from a slightly different perspective, he had given her useful advice about the seamier sides of the art business, and continued to do so. He regarded it as an insurance policy; he knew as well as Flavia did that the file on him in the bureau was bursting out of its second folder. Smuggling, handling stolen goods, failure to report income, operating rings at auctions, excess zeal in authentication, fakery, the works. A lovely man he was, and a wholly delightful companion, full of entertaining anecdotes and worldly wisdom.

Apart from the occasional fine, he had been left in peace; most of his victims were foreigners in any case and removing the money of strangers too stupid to know better was a centuries-old tradition which no mere police crackdown could ever prevent. Even getting the average Roman dealer to grasp that it was wrong was an uphill task. More importantly, he was a treasure trove of useful information and had never lied to Flavia once, as far as she knew.

Which is why she had chosen today to go and check up on old clients, asking the same question of half a dozen dealers. Had they heard of any raids being planned?

'Such as where?'

'A monastery called San Giovanni,' she said for the sixth

time as they sat in the back room of Bartolo's little gallery in the via dei Coronari, 'We had a call, but it doesn't add up. What we don't know is whether it was a hoax or not. The one painting worth stealing is unstealable. A man called Menzies is restoring it.'

Bartolo stiffened slightly, then nodded. 'I understand. But I am afraid I can be of no help. I've heard of nothing being planned at all. Tell me what you know.'

'That's about all there is. Have you ever heard of a woman called Mary Verney?'

Bartolo frowned as he tried to figure out in advance the purpose of the question. Then he gave up and shook his head. 'Who is she?'

'She's a professional thief. A very good one.'

'I see,' he said cautiously. Odd how dealers lost their *joie de vivre* when you asked them about thieves. 'What's she done?'

Flavia reeled off a list of thefts; Bartolo raised his eyebrow in unaffected astonishment. 'Bless me,' he said. 'Are you sure? I often wondered what happened to that Vermeer.'

'Now you know. You've not heard of her?'

'Not by name. Obviously, I hear every now and then about professionals for hire, but as I have no inclinations in that direction myself, I never pursue the matter. Besides, these people are rarely as good as the legends claim.'

'This one is. And she's in Rome.'

'I see. You think she might have Caravaggist inclinations?'

'Who knows?'

'Hmm. I will keep my ear to the ground, if you like. But I can't help you much. I don't remember ever hearing of this monastery before last week.'

Flavia finished her meal and leant back for the waiter to take her plate away. 'Last week? What happened last week?'

'This man Menzies.'

'Ah, yes. I noticed that you turned a little pale when I mentioned him.'

'Indeed. It's fortunate you are here. You can help. He has to be stopped, you know.'

'What are you talking about?'

'The Farnesina.'

'What about it?'

Bartolo sighed. 'You really don't pay much attention to things, do you? The Farnesina project. Cleaning and restoring the Raphael frescoes. Galatea.'

'Oh, yes. Now I'm with you.'

'Good. A great masterpiece and one of the most important restoration projects for years. The ministry will be assigning the project in due course. There are two candidates – Dan Menzies and my friend Gianni d'Onofrio. Menzies has been lobbying hard to get it, saying that it should go to someone with an international profile, as he terms it. And he's already lined up subsidies from rich Americans, which is the sort of thing poor Gianni can't do. And Menzies is prepared to use methods which Gianni would never descend to.'

'Who is this man of yours?'

'He works for the Borghese, and has a freelance business. He comes from a different tradition to Menzies. No university courses in restoration theory or any nonsense like that.'

'I see. Artisan versus Professional, is that it?'

Bartolo nodded. 'He followed in the family business, you see. D'Onofrios have been restoring paintings in Rome for generations. Certainly since the early nineteenth century. A good, artisanal trade, you know. Very respectable.'

'Not always,' Flavia murmured.

'It can be misused,' Bartolo conceded, 'I'm glad to say. But the skill involved, the training, that's the thing. A *ménage à trois*, if you see what I mean, between painter, canvas and restorer. Very delicate; each must get its due, and the restorer must be delicate, and discreet, and never thrust himself forward. It's like an old marriage that has broken down. The restorer is there merely to restore harmony between the partners, what the painter intended and his achievement. To bring back that balance. Not to impose his own. Never to get in the way. Always to be the loyal servant, not the master.'

'Uh-huh.'

'Now, old Giovanni, the father, he was perfect. The ideal restorer. Never a dab of paint too much. Never doing anything too much, lest he make a mistake. Always augmenting the painter's work, never replacing it. You see? It was his character as well; a very mild-mannered, charming man, so modest about his abilities. I always thought of him as a sort of artistic family doctor. When I gave him a painting, he'd just have it in his studio for months on end, simply to look at and get the feel of it. And when he worked, it was with such reverence and honesty.'

'That must have been tiresome,' Flavia said.

'Umm? Oh, I don't mean that, although he was that sort of honest as well. He could have been the finest forger of his generation, had he been so minded. Many a time I dropped a little hint – you know, take him an old copy and say, "Wouldn't it be nice if this Maratta could be brought back to its full glory?" Just a hint, you see, and he'd shake his head and apologize and say that he really didn't think it was a Maratta. He knew what I wanted, of course, but he was quite incorruptible.'

'And the son? Is he different?'

'Young Gianni? Oh, no. Not at all. Not any more, anyway. In his youth, twenty years ago, he did a little, ah, improving, but no more than most people. Once he got on his feet, and the excess zeal of youth faded, then he became so like his father it is frightening. Sometimes when I see him, I have to blink and remind myself of the passage of the years. They even paint in the same way. He worked his way up through skill and quiet competence. Unlike some people.'

'And here you are referring to Dan Menzies again, are you?'

'I am. While Gianni tries to bring a picture back to life, Menzies is an executioner, administering the *coup de grâce* to a master's vision. He paints himself. Whatever the subject. Dan Menzies's Sistine Chapel, previously attributed to Michelangelo, now in an improved version; although, thank God, they were too sensible to let him near the project. Dan Menzies's Virgin with St John, previously attributed to Raphael. That's his line. Give me a forger any day. At least they're honest.'

'You think he overdoes it?'

'Overdoes it? Listen, if some lunatic walked in off the street and sprayed acid all over some of the most beautiful pictures in the world, then daubed paint all over them, your boss

Bottando would steam and rage until the offender was locked up. Menzies does that all the time. The man is a licensed vandal. Do you know, I went to New York a few months ago and saw a Martini St Veronica he'd just finished with. I could have wept, I tell you. It looked like something out of *Playboy*. All the subtleties of light, all the toning, all the glazes; everything that made it into a sublime masterpiece rather than merely a decent painting, all gone, and replaced by Menzies's crudities. I was speechless, I tell you.'

'You seem to be making up for it now.'

'We've got to stop him,' Bartolo repeated. 'If he gets his hands on the Farnesina it will be the biggest atrocity since the Sack of Rome.'

'We?'

'Listen, Flavia, over the years I have never asked you for anything.'

'No?'

'Not very much, anyway, and I've given you lots of information in return.'

Flavia, who was now getting an uncomfortable feeling, nodded reluctantly.

'Help us.'

'How?'

'Oh, you know how. Is there anything on this man? Is there anything we can use to stop him?'

She gulped. 'Not as far as I know. And I wouldn't tell you anyway. It would only turn up in the papers tomorrow.'

Bartolo looked distinctly displeased by this. 'You expect me to dig up information for you . . .' he began.

'I do. And you expect me to tip you the wink about certain things as well, and I do that. But this is asking too much. And you know it is, as well.'

'I'm very disappointed.' And he sounded as though he meant it.

'You don't even know whether Menzies will get the job.'

'No,' he conceded reluctantly.

'I suppose there would be no harm in my asking my contacts how the candidates are running.'

Bartolo smiled. 'That is kind of you,' he said.

'You're welcome.' She paused for a moment. 'Tell me, it wasn't you who phoned us up to tell us about a burglary at San Giovanni, was it? To focus our attention on the place?'

Bartolo looked shocked. 'Certainly not,' he said robustly. 'I wouldn't be at all surprised if Menzies did it himself to generate some publicity. That's just the sort of thing he does. I wonder, though . . .'

Flavia held up her hands. 'No,' she said.

'No what?'

'No, I don't want to hear.'

'Very well,' he said, with the faintest flicker of glee in his eyes. 'Thank you so much. I'm so glad you came.'

'What for?'

'Wait and see.'

5

The following morning, Flavia had not even managed to get out of the shower before the meaning of Bartolo's words began to dawn on her. Bottando rang.

'Could you go down to that monastery and see this Menzies man?' He sounded irritated.

'Why?'

'He'll meet you there. I've just had a load of abuse hurled at me down the telephone; he's extremely annoyed and blaming us.'

'But what for?'

'In between the shouting, I gather that some paper has published an article about him, saying the police are investigating his activities.'

'What?'

'And that he's been wasting police time by planting fake stories about thefts to generate publicity. Do you know anything about this?'

'Ah.'

'You do. You haven't been talking to *journalists*, have you?' He said it with a slightly incredulous inflection in his voice. In Bottando's list of human sin, talking to journalists came somewhere between infanticide and arson.

'No. But I probably know who has. Leave it to me. I'll go and sort it all out.'

'Don't tell him who's responsible,' Bottando said. 'We don't want a murder on our hands. And deal with it quickly, will you? I don't have time for this sort of nonsense at the moment. And I don't want complaints being made, either.'

There was obviously no point in going to San Giovanni via

61

the office; and no point in going too early and still less in trying to take a bus or taxi. So she and Argyll, in peaceful harmony for the first time in days after a successfully restful and uninterrupted evening together the previous night, had a quiet breakfast on their little terrace, watching the sun beginning to heat up the stones of the city, then walked off together in the direction of the Aventino just before eight. The gentle start successfully soothed Flavia's irritation about Bartolo, who had obviously had the bright idea of using her to attack Menzies.

Argyll accompanied her because he had nothing to do until a lecture on the early Borromini at noon, but had given up the guilty pleasure of sitting around doing nothing all morning. Very Roman, very agreeable; but not the best way of cutting a dash in the world. Slogging in a dark and sunless archive in the search for that vital publication, alas, was. Especially as Father Jean, when he'd asked, had seemed more than happy to let him have free run of the archives to see what he could find out about St Catherine.

When breakfast was followed by a gentle stroll, walking arm-in-arm through the little back streets of the city, she arrived at their destination feeling totally, if only temporarily, at peace with the world. So what, she thought, if pictures got stolen? What was that in comparison to the morning sun on a crumbling Roman inscription set into a garden wall, half covered in ivy? Who cared about forgers, when she could distract herself with a pigeon that had made its roost in the mouth of an old statue? And who was really interested in irate restorers and their private battles?

'What a lovely place,' she said appreciatively when Father Paul had responded to the doorbell and let them both in. She also found Father Paul quite something as well.

'It is,' said Argyll. 'No doubt because it's under the special protection of the Virgin. So I'm told.'

Rather than smiling at the very idea, Father Paul nodded seriously, and Flavia, who had these turns sometimes, also looked appreciative.

'You've heard about that, have you?' said Father Paul. 'It's one of those stories we don't really know what to do with these days.'

'What is the story?'

'I thought you knew,' he said as he led them towards the block of buildings containing the offices and archives. 'How there was a plague in the city, and the monks prayed for help, and an angel flew down bringing the icon. He told them that if they treated it properly, then they would be forever under Our Lady's protection. So they prayed for its help, and the plague abated and not a single one of them died. As you can see from the building, she got us through the Sack of Rome, World War Two and so far has fended off the property developers as well. But of course, they tend to find that sort of thing awkward nowadays.'

'They?'

'Ah, you caught me,' he said with a faint smile. 'Where I come from we have no trouble at all with things like that. Here they are all very Vatican Two and rational, you see, and have a great deal of trouble dealing with the miraculous. Considering that they are all priests, I find that strange, don't you? After all, everything we believe in is based on a miracle. If you doubt them, what's left?'

'So you believe it?'

He nodded. 'I am prepared to. Otherwise you have to attribute everything to chance, and I find that much too far-fetched. It's the one thing in this place I wouldn't part with, I think. And the local population are fond of it. Were, in any case, until Father Xavier closed the doors. We still get scowls over that.'

'Has Mr Menzies arrived yet?' This was the voice of Father Jean, who came through the door with a worried frown on his face. 'I think I should talk to him.'

'Not seen him,' said Argyll, then introduced Flavia.

'Good morning, signorina. I'm very concerned about this. I think Mr Menzies will be very angry.'

'This' was a copy of a newspaper in his hand, opened at the arts pages.

'Ah, yes,' Flavia said, scanning it quickly. 'In fact, I can tell you he is very angry. That's why I'm here. To tell him it's nothing to do with us.'

It was short, but effective. Menzies, greatly criticized for some of his past restorations, was a shameless publicist being investigated for wasting police time. They suspected him of making bogus phone calls to drum up publicity as part of his campaign to get the job to clean the Farnesina. It remained to be seen whether a corrupt and barbaric government would sink so low as to allow one of the nation's greatest master-pieces to fall into the hands of such a latter-day Visigoth. Or, at least, that was the general line communicated without ever stooping so low as to make any direct accusations.

Argyll tutted as he read, Father Paul looked unconcerned, and Father Jean seemed upset, but more for the way the order was being dragged into public controversy than anything else.

'I do think it was a mistake to let Mr Menzies in here, you know.'

'This is hardly his fault,' Father Paul said gently. 'Perhaps we'd better go and talk to him now?'

Such was the awe in which Menzies's anger was held that, safety in numbers, a sort of unofficial delegation was formed, with all of them shuffling off nervously in the direction of the church, so the reaction could be absorbed collectively.

They never got there; the bell rang again and Father Paul headed off to see who it was. As he seemed to be the sort of person whose natural calm and authority might best deal with an irate restorer, the rest waited for him to return. He came back with someone Flavia recognized. Father Paul also had a look of vague alarm about him as well.

'Hello, Alberto,' Flavia said with surprise. 'What are you doing here?'

She introduced her colleague from the carabinieri, a tall, thin man who managed to have an air of vague perplexity about him all the time. Strange, she thought; he always looked like that. At the moment he also looked like someone who knew full well he was wasting his time when he could be getting on with his paperwork.

'I don't know,' he said. 'The emergency services had an anonymous call . . .'

Flavia scowled. 'Another one? What in God's name is going on here?'

'I have no idea. But this call was to say someone had been injured. They're a bit short of ambulances and get really pissed off with cranks wasting their time, so it was passed on to us. And here I am. Nothing going on, is there?'

He was unsurprised when Father Jean assured him that, as far as they knew, all was well. No illness, injury or death all night.

Flavia was puzzled, though. And a little alarmed. 'This is the second time in a few days,' she said. 'We'd better have a look around. What exactly did this call say?'

'Just that. Nothing else. It came in an hour or so ago. We've just heard about it.'

Fathers Jean and Paul exchanged looks, and then the group, augmented by one, resumed their collective move. There was no sign of Menzies; the door of the church was still firmly closed.

So they unlocked it and went in to check. It was unlit, and there was not a sound, certainly none of the grunting and scuffling and whistling that normally accompanied Menzies's labours. They went over to the transept that Menzies was using for his studio, but that again was empty; the Caravaggio stood there, still a mess but undoubtedly otherwise safe. That was one less thing to be concerned about at least.

Then they stood around, wondering what to do next. 'I suppose we just wait. He'll turn up eventually.'

Both Father Jean and Father Paul were just coming up with very good reasons why they had to go about their business, Alberto was becoming ever more convinced that the perverted sense of humour of some Italians had wasted his time, and the three were preparing to leave Flavia with the task of dealing with Menzies.

From the other side of the church there came a hideous scream, made all the worse by the resounding echo in the building, which made the high-pitched wail and strangled sob, and repeated ululations reverberate all around, seemingly growing louder and louder rather than fading away.

'Jesus . . .' Argyll began. All of them turned and began to

run the short distance to where the scream seemed to have come from, and Father Paul, with more practical sense than all the rest of them put together, walked purposefully in the opposite direction and began switching on all the lights, so that one by one, the gloom receded and they could see what the noise was about.

It was perfectly obvious. The cleaning lady, with her broom tangled in her legs, knelt frantically in front of the bank of candles, scrabbling desperately at the wall in supplication as she continued to cry and scream. The bucket of dirty water was upturned where she had dropped it and flowing all over the floor; the wet broom had fallen against a bank of extinguished candles and knocked them flying and the woman's old pink slippers, with pom-poms, rested in the thick, sticky blood that had flowed so horrifyingly freely from the broken skull of Father Xavier Münster, thirty-ninth superior general of the order of St John the Pietist.

It took another quarter of an hour before anyone noticed that the little painting of the Virgin to which Argyll had given a candle had been taken out of its frame and had vanished.

6

'Is there any chance that this might be kept private? Until we know what happened?' Father Jean asked humbly of Flavia. 'Must the newspapers know?'

Everybody was slowly calming down after the frenzy of activity that had followed the moment of stunned silence that the sight had caused in all of them. Father Paul, with impeccable resourcefulness, was the first to recover and, as Father Jean said later, had probably saved the superior's life – if, indeed, it could be saved. He staunched the flow of blood, organized blankets to keep the man warm, summoned the first aid kit and called the ambulance from the hospital which, as it was only a mile or two down the road, arrived with unusual speed. Everybody else more or less stood around as the old man was given emergency treatment, loaded on a stretcher and then rushed to the hospital.

His chances were not great, one of the ambulance men said. But it was a miracle he was alive. He must be a tough old bird even to be still breathing.

Flavia shook her head at Father Jean's question. 'Not a chance, I'm afraid. Somebody will tell a reporter. And it will look very much worse if we try to hide it. I'm afraid you'll just have to keep your heads down.'

'Will you be investigating, Signorina?'

'That depends. Assault is not normally our line of business. On the other hand, it looks as though Father Xavier might have been attacked trying to prevent someone stealing that painting.'

'And that would help? If that's what happened?'

'We would be involved, certainly.'

'That's good.'

'Why does it matter?' Flavia asked, curious that he should be so concerned with such matters which, in comparison to Father Xavier, seemed almost trivial even to her.

'It's always best to have someone who is delicate, and tactful, I think. Obviously, the attacker must be apprehended. That must be the first priority. But Father Xavier, I feel sure, would not want his misfortune to bring dishonour upon us.'

'Being attacked is hardly a dishonour.'

Father Jean nodded, and seemed about to say something, but decided not to, just at the moment.

'Do you have any idea . . . ?'

'What happened? None. And I know enough not even to think of it yet. We'll see later on. You certainly know more than I do at the moment. Now, if you could show me to a telephone . . .'

She walked off with the priest so she could telephone Bottando, and Argyll watched her go, rather abandoned, sitting on a pew. It always gave him something of a shock, watching her at work. She was so very calm and good at it. While he had felt almost weak at the knees at the sight of the blood, Flavia had shown no reaction at all, once the paleness caused by the initial shock had passed. In fact, he had even noticed her stifle a yawn at one point.

For his part, he needed a drink, early though it was. So he walked out of the building and down the road to the nearest bar. A gaggle of locals, men having their coffee and roll before going off to work, eyed him curiously.

'Ambulance at the monastery, I see,' one said conversationally.

'And police,' agreed another. 'I know those number plates.'

'You wouldn't know what it was about?' added a third, looking at Argyll.

'Well . . .' he began.

'Body being taken out? What's been going on?'

'I think there has been a theft. The superior was attacked. He's still alive, though.'

A lot of tutting and shaking of heads at this. The way of the world, what are we coming to? Still, what do you expect?

'What they take, then?' said one of the more jovial ones.

'Oh, not much, as far as they know,' he said reassuringly. 'Only a picture. They didn't even take the valuable one. They lifted a little Madonna instead.'

One of the men put his coffee cup down on the counter and looked Argyll firmly in the eye.

'A Madonna? Not My Lady?'

'A little icon.' Argyll gestured to indicate the size. 'Very dirty.'

'In the side chapel?'

'That's the one, I think.'

There was a lot of muttering at this, and Argyll noticed one of the men surreptitiously pull out a handkerchief from his jacket and dab his eye.

'Oh, no,' one of the others cried. 'Surely not?'

As is usual in such cases, Argyll glanced at the barman to get an indication of what exactly was going on. He, he thought, would be reliable. A youngish man, with fashionably cut hair and the sort of casual air of someone who had never been troubled by a sombre thought in his life. He also had turned grim-faced, and was drying a beer glass with an unusual intensity.

'The bastards,' this man said. 'The *bastards*.'

A chord had been struck. The cheerful atmosphere of the bar dissolved under the impact of Argyll's words like an ice cream in the July sun. In its place was genuine anger and, he thought, real distress. Almost worry.

'I'm sorry to bring bad news,' he said, trying to back pedal from his insouciant approach of a few seconds ago and adopt a more fitting demeanour. 'I didn't realize you would mind so much. No one ever goes in there, do they?'

'It was locked. By that man.'

'But still . . .'

'She was there. That's what counted.'

'I see.' Then he saw, with profound relief, the reassuring figure of Father Paul come through the door. Could he come back? Signorina di Stefano wanted to talk to him.

'Was Father Xavier in the chapel all night, do you think?' he asked the priest as they walked back to the monastery.

Father Paul shrugged. 'I really don't know, Mr Argyll. I really don't know. It was my job to do the rounds and make sure everything was locked up, and I didn't notice anything wrong then.'

'When was that?'

'Just after eleven. We have evening prayers, we are allowed an hour to ourselves, and the lights go off at ten. Then the person on duty goes round and checks everything is closed. It was something introduced after the last burglary.'

'And you saw nothing?'

A shake of the head.

There were five cars parked outside the monastery, which Argyll assumed contained all those specialists who emerge from under stones on these occasions. Flavia was standing in the courtyard, arguing fiercely with Alberto.

'Look, I don't want to argue with you,' she was saying, clearly not telling the truth at all. 'It's not my concern whether this is investigated by you or by me.' Another blatant fib. 'I was asked to come here about a possible theft, and I proposed to find out what was going on. I don't want to take on anything else if I can help it . . .'

Extraordinary how she could string together so many untruths and look so convincing. The other man was grumbling, but seemed prepared to retreat and let other people fight for his department's honour. They agreed that the entire matter should be passed on to their respective superiors and, that little bit of necessary posturing over, seemed quite content to resume normal relations.

'Jonathan!' She called him over. 'You'll have to give a statement, you know. This is the man who'll be taking it.'

Argyll nodded. 'Fine. Although it'll be short and less than helpful. Do you want it now?'

Alberto shook his head. 'No, I don't think so. We'll let the experts do their stuff and clear out. Then everything might get a little bit calmer.'

'Waiting around all day?'

'I'm afraid so.'

'Would it matter if I waited somewhere else? I was only

70

going to be here for an hour or so, and then I'm meant to be delivering a lecture.'

Alberto puffed and blew but, what are friends for? Flavia vouched for his good behaviour and he was let out with a promise that he come back immediately afterwards. He wasn't entirely certain whether he felt glad or not.

By the time he returned, a certain amount of progress had been made. The first information from the hospital said that Father Xavier was still alive, if only barely, and in intensive care. He had obviously been hit on the head, and was lucky to be alive at all. But he was unconscious, and liable to stay that way for some time. What was more, no blunt instrument of any shape or variety was in the area of the attack. Not with blood on, anyway.

So the police, both branches of it acting in harmony for once, began the task of asking questions and taking statements.

Menzies was useless, even when he had been weaned off his own problems and persuaded to concentrate on what, to the police at least, were more important matters.

He had left about six, gone home, changed and gone to a reception at which he had hoped to collar several influential members of the Beni Artistici. Said members had not been there, so he'd left early, eaten in a restaurant and gone home. He produced the bill from the restaurant, agreed readily that his movements were unaccounted for from the hours of half past ten to eight in the morning, when he'd gone for a coffee in the bar round the corner from his apartment, but seemed very unconcerned about the fact.

'If you can find me a good reason for assaulting Father Xavier, I'd be very interested to hear it. This affair is obviously an attack on me.'

Flavia looked puzzled. How on earth could he conclude that?

'Be reasonable,' he snapped. 'I am being attacked left and right, and by people who are completely unscrupulous. Did you see that scurrilous article this morning? It's a disgrace.

For which I hold you responsible. You obviously fed a story to the newspaper out of sheer xenophobic malice.'

'I assure you I did nothing of the sort. Are you suggesting I also attacked Xavier?' Flavia asked stiffly.

'The people behind this did,' he proceeded illogically. 'Clearly they came into the church at night to damage the painting I'm restoring. Father Xavier surprised them and they attacked him. It's obvious.'

'And the icon?'

Menzies waved his hand dismissively. 'Second-rate rubbish. Taken to put you off the scent. So you'd think it was a burglary and not pursue the real culprits. I tell you, this is to stop me getting the Farnesina job. And I intend to make sure that doesn't happen. I will hold you personally responsible . . .'

'Are you suggesting . . . ?'

'I am suggesting that the very fact that I am sitting here accounting for my movements will be all over the newspapers tomorrow. I've no doubt you will ring up your newspaper friends the moment you have the opportunity. No doubt they pay you well for this sort of malicious gossip.'

'I think I resent that.'

'I don't care one way or the other. I want a full statement from you that you have no suspicions of me whatsoever, and that this was part of a campaign by my enemies against me.'

'Do you?'

'And in the meantime,' he went on, levering his bulk out of the chair, 'I will go to the embassy. I'm a personal friend of the ambassador, and he'll want to hear about this. Do you have any idea how much money generous people in my country pour into conservation in Italy? Have you any idea?'

Without waiting for an answer, he stumped out, looking very much in combative mood.

Flavia sighed a little.

'Going to be one of those cases,' she said. 'Feel it in my bones.'

Father Paul was next in line, and had an even more commanding appearance as he moved into the room and sat down in front of them. He was sober and serious and upset but not at all frightened or cautious, unlike almost everyone else that Flavia ever interviewed.

Once the preliminaries were over, they had established that he was thirty-seven, from the Cameroon, a priest and had been brought to Rome to study at the Gregorian University.

'It's part of a programme to unify the church at the grass roots,' he explained. 'I come here, priests from Italy go to Africa. So we can study conditions and appreciate the meaning of cultural differences at first hand.'

'Has it worked? In your case?'

He looked uncertain. 'I would have preferred to have been sent to an inner-city parish where I could have done some real work, rather than sitting in a library,' he said. 'But of course I am happy to obey the directions I am given.'

'And you want to go back?'

'Of course. I hope to return fairly soon. Or had hoped to.'

'Why the change?'

'It depends on getting the permission of the superior general. He had refused my request, unfortunately . . .'

'And now?'

Father Paul smiled. 'And now, when he recovers, he will refuse it again.'

'And if he doesn't recover?'

'Then I will withdraw my request, lest it be thought I have taken advantage of this tragedy. But I am convinced he will get better.'

'Faith?'

'Nothing so elevated. I trained for a while in medicine before I found my vocation. He is badly hurt, but not fatally, I think.'

Pretty impenetrable there, Flavia thought. Not even so much as a hint of indignation at her implication. 'How long does it take to elect a new superior? Or do you appoint a deputy?'

Father Paul shrugged. 'I'm not certain. This is uncharted territory. I think that Father Jean, as the oldest member, takes over for the time being; he used to be the official deputy when Father Charles ruled us.'

'Oh. Now, last night, you went for your walk . . .'

'About ten o'clock. I walked down the street, around one or two blocks, and came back at half past. I let myself in with the key, then locked and bolted the main door. Then checked the other side doors, which were all locked as they should be, then the library block, making sure the building was empty, the windows closed and the door locked when I left. The accommodation wing is always open, because of the risk of fire.'

'And you went into the church?'

'Yes. I switched on all the lights, checked quickly and locked the door when I left.'

'And how many keys are there?'

'Lots. Everyone living here has one, of course. And Mr Menzies, Signora Graziani, the man who does the gardening, the nuns who come in and cook for us, and so on.'

'And the church?'

'The entrance key fits the door from the courtyard.'

'So Father Xavier could have gone into the church without having to ask anyone for a key.'

'Of course.'

'There's no other way into it?'

'There's a door on to the street. But that has been closed for the last three years. It was used by ordinary people who wanted to come in to pray. There were not many any more, I'm afraid, and it was a practice that was disapproved of.'

'Why?'

'The local parish church didn't like it, and the icon was rather against the spirit of the times. The local priest of the parish is a very modern man. When the burglars struck a few years back, it was felt that this was a good time for change. We mended our fences with the parish and obeyed police strictures about security. And Father Xavier felt that as so few people used the church any more, it would not be noticed.'

'I see,' said Flavia. 'And was it?'

'There was a surprising amount of disquiet. It's still very much a neighbourhood around here, with people who've been in the quarter for generations, and they rather regarded that Madonna as their patroness and protector. They never

74

paid any attention to it while the church was open, of course, but they were upset when it was closed. Young girls used to come before they got married, and even the most hardened of boys found themselves in front of her before examinations.'

'I see. Now, you get up when?'

'At half past five. Normally there is a service, then an hour of meditation before breakfast. Usually, that's when the church is opened. But because of Mr Menzies making such a mess in there, we've been using the library recently.'

'So the church wasn't opened until nine.'

'That's right. Either Signora Graziani, or Mr Menzies, opens it up.'

'Tell us about the signora.'

Father Paul shrugged. 'I know little about her. You'd have to ask Father Jean, I think. She works on a food stall on market days. When she does she comes early to clean. Every day, rain or shine; it's some sort of vow, I believe. She is pious in a way which is rare nowadays. Probably always rare, in fact.'

Like Father Paul, Father Jean provided a brief biographical sketch, and told them that he was in effect the librarian of the community, and had stopped acting as deputy superior when Father Charles had stepped down three years previously.

'I would have retired, as that is theoretically now possible,' he said with a faint smile. 'But alas, permission was denied me.'

'How old are you?'

'Seventy-four.'

'Too young, eh?'

'No, it's because there are so few of us left. The average age of the order is about sixty now. There are no vocations any more. When I was young, there was competition to get in; the order offered useful work and an unparalleled education. Now the state provides the education, and no one believes in the work. So they need me.'

'Father Paul . . .'

'Is, as you may have noticed, from Africa. And a very fine

75

young man. The Third World is the only place we get vocations now. Unless we do something, I wouldn't be at all surprised . . . still, this is not what you want to ask me about.'

'I suppose not. Tell me about Father Xavier. Is he popular? Well-liked?'

Father Jean hesitated. 'I'm not so sure what you're asking.'

'Does he have enemies?'

'You mean . . . ?' The old man looked pale with horror as it dawned on him what Flavia was asking. 'Surely, he was trying to prevent a burglary. This was nothing to do with him personally.'

'We do have to cover all options. Of course, it was almost certainly a burglary. But please answer the question anyway.'

'This is terribly distressing, in the circumstances.'

'Tell me anyway.'

Father Jean nodded and sighed heavily. 'I suppose I must. As far as I know he has no family; none close, anyway. And virtually no friends, inside or outside the order.'

'Enemies?'

'He is not a popular leader, and has been controversial ever since he took over, although it would have been difficult for anyone to fill the shoes of Father Charles.'

'In what way, controversial?'

'We are at a difficult stage,' he began eventually, after a long search for the best way to phrase it. 'And Father Xavier was the man forced to confront that. I am convinced he was on entirely the wrong track, but I suppose I must give him credit for trying. Many others would merely have swept all our problems under the carpet, and left them until they became too difficult to solve.'

'What precisely?'

'We have to decide what we are for, if you see what I mean. It is no longer enough to pray, and other people, it seems, can do good works better than us. So what are we doing? We have some money and we have good people. Are we doing God's work with either?'

'Some of you wanted to give it away?'

'Oh, no. Hardly that.' Father Jean permitted himself a faint, ironic smile. 'It was more a question of how best to use what we had. And for some of us, how to get more. For the best possible reasons, of course.'

'Of course.'

'The church as a whole is in a certain amount of turmoil; you may have noticed. And being the church, it goes on for a long time. We think in centuries, so a convulsion lasting fifty years is a mere nothing. But that essentially is the problem. Do we guard the old ways or alter completely our approach? Do we try to change the world, or allow the world to change us? That is the basic problem facing all traditional religions, it seems.'

Flavia nodded. 'I still don't see . . .'

'We have no new vocations,' Father Jean continued. 'Except from the Third World, as I said. Thirty priests under the age of thirty-five, and all but five come from Africa or South America. Yet all our officers are Italian or French – mainly French – most are over sixty, our headquarters are in Rome and most of our expenditure is in Europe. A significant number want to recognize the changes; an equally significant number want to keep things as they are. That, if you like, is the problem in a nutshell. The debate has caused much bitterness in our ranks.'

'What were Father Xavier's proposals?'

'They don't have much relevance . . .'

'Tell me anyway.'

'Father Xavier, and those who supported him, wanted to rebuild us into an aid and teaching order. Raise money, and pour it all into development and missionary projects in Africa. And to raise money, he wanted to sell off assets. I was totally opposed to the scheme but was not certain that my views would prevail.'

'I see. And which assets are we talking about here? Wouldn't be the Caravaggio, would it?'

'Unfortunately, it would. Although that was only a start. We had a meeting to discuss the principle a few days ago. Fortunately the proposal was defeated.'

'Meaning what?'

'Meaning that we decided as a body to refuse permission for anything to be sold at all.'

77

'Are you short of money?'

'I don't know. We are not a rich order, but two years ago, when I was in a position to know such things, we were not desperately poor.'

'Was this proposal caused by any offers? Had someone said they wanted to buy the Caravaggio?'

'Not that I am aware of, no.'

There was a pause, as Father Jean realized that perhaps he had allowed the outside world too much of an insight into private business.

'So who runs things now?'

'Until such time as the situation becomes clear – whether Xavier will be returning to his post or not – then we are in limbo. And, as far as I understand it, the most senior available member takes charge.'

'You?'

He nodded. 'It is a burden I do not wish to fall on my aged shoulders. But I have given my life to this order and now, in the time of its crisis, is not the moment to shirk my responsibilities.'

Flavia nodded. He wouldn't have much trouble becoming a politician, she thought. He already speaks like one. And she thought she saw the bright glint of opportunity in his eye. 'OK. Let's leave that. What were your movements last night and this morning?'

Father Jean said he had had an unexceptional evening. He had worked in the library until six, attended the evening service, had dinner, read for an hour, gone to chapel again then gone to bed at ten.

'In the morning I got up, attended chapel, spent an hour in prayer, ate and began work at seven. I stayed in the library until Father Paul came to say that there had been a terrible tragedy.'

'You sleep well?'

He shrugged. 'Well enough, I think. I need little sleep; we old men don't, you know. I normally wake at about three and read.'

'And you did that last night?'

'Yes.'

78

'What were you reading?'

Father Jean looked a little sheepish. 'Adventure stories,' he said. Flavia kept a straight face. 'They are very entertaining, in the small hours. My nephew sends me them. Then I pass them on to all the other people here. We read them avidly.'

'Is that . . . ah . . . ?' Flavia knew she shouldn't ask, but the vision of this community of old priests, up late at night reading varieties of bodice-rippers was too irresistible to let go.

'Allowed?' Father Jean asked with a smile. 'You think we should spend all our time reading St John of the Cross or a light Vatican encyclical? Oh, yes. It used not to be permitted, of course, but we are now allowed to keep in touch with the outside world. Even encouraged, as long as it doesn't go too far.'

'Yes. Right.' Flavia paused a while to remember what line she had been pursuing before this unlikely diversion had cropped up. 'Now,' she continued, when it came back to her. 'Where is your, ah, cell? Is that what you call them?'

'It faces the main courtyard. Opposite the church. Where I would have been in a good position to hear any shouting or screaming had any occurred.'

'And it didn't?'

He shook his head. 'Nothing. And as I'm such a light sleeper, I feel certain I would have heard anything at all during the night. A bird singing is often enough to wake me up.'

Flavia paused. Why was it that she did not believe him? He was sitting quietly, hands folded in his lap as though he was attending a long church service. There was nothing suspicious or hesitant about him at all, and yet she knew, as sure as anything, that at the very least he was concealing something.

'Tell me, Father, how did Mr Menzies get the commission to clean the paintings?'

'He didn't,' the old man replied. 'He offered. We weren't paying him. That was the only reason we accepted.'

'He was working for nothing?'

'Yes. I believe there was a grant from some American charity. We had to pay only the expenses, although that amounted to a substantial sum.'

'That's unusual, isn't it?'

'I suppose. He said he wanted to clean the pictures and was prepared to do it for nothing. Who were we to question his generosity?'

Flavia thanked him, and let him go, then turned to Alberto. 'Well?'

'What?'

'You have a look on your face. Crazed monks beating each other's heads in.'

'No, I don't,' he protested lazily, wondering whether you were allowed to smoke in monasteries. 'I'm just sitting here quietly taking it all in, that's all. I never prejudge things, not even when priests are concerned. My look of scepticism was merely to indicate my feeling that we aren't getting anywhere. That's all.'

'Oh. That's all right, then. Shall we see Signora Graziani next? And stop for lunch?'

Alberto agreed that an early lunch was by far the most professional way of proceeding. Signora Graziani was ushered in and sat down nervously. Flavia looked at her with satisfaction. No likelihood that this one would keep anything back, she thought. And as she discovered the attack, had a key and also seemed to have something of an obsession with the icon, she had a certain amount of convincing to do.

She said that she had arrived and was just beginning to clean the church as usual when she saw Father Xavier. And screamed. There wasn't much else to add, really. She lapsed readily back into a shocked silence.

So Flavia established that she had been at home until leaving for the church, saw and heard nothing suspicious. Her daughter and granddaughter, who lived with her ever since that beast of a husband had left the poor dears destitute by running off with some floozy – may God forgive him, although she, Signora Graziani, wasn't going to – would vouch for that.

'You must remember, signora, that anything which can help might be of enormous importance here.'

But she shook her head. She'd come into the church, collected her bucket of water and cleaning equipment, and walked down the aisle to close the main door when she saw . . .

'To close the what?'

The main door, she said, which was slightly ajar. Surely they must have noticed that it was unlocked? She'd closed it and locked it just before she noticed . . .

'Jesus,' Flavia swore under her breath.

'Fine, great,' she said hurriedly. 'I think that will do. Thank you so much, signora.'

'Is there anything else?' asked Alberto, speaking for almost the first time. 'I believe there is. What is it, signora? Do you know who attacked him or something?'

She nodded again. 'Yes,' she said. 'I do.'

There was a slight clunk as the front two legs of his chair came back to earth, and he leant forward on the table.

'Well?'

'She did,' Signora Graziani said. Alberto, who thought for a moment the woman was referring to Flavia, looked surprised.

'What?'

'My Lady. She did.'

'Ah . . .'

'She is as harsh in her punishments of sin as she is gracious and forgiving with those who make amends. The Father was wicked, and turned from her. So he was punished.'

'Well . . .'

'He stopped her receiving supplicants, and took her away from the people who loved her. And he was going to hurt her.'

'Just a minute,' Flavia said, suddenly realizing what the woman was talking about. 'Do you mean that painting?'

Signora Graziani looked puzzled for a moment. 'Of course,' she said simply.

'And you think Father Xavier was attacked by a painting?'

'My Lady,' she corrected gravely, 'punished him. A priest without belief is no man of God.'

'Yes. Right. Thank you very much,' Alberto said. 'That's very illuminating. So kind of you to spare the time to talk to us.'

'Will you want a statement?' she asked placidly.

'Not just yet, I think. Maybe in a day or so,' he replied, holding open the door.

Signora Graziani bowed slightly as she left. 'You don't believe me,' she said. 'But you'll see I'm right.'

'Damnation,' he said when he'd shut the door on her. 'I thought for a moment . . .'

Flavia laughed. 'You should have seen the look on your face when you realized what she was talking about.'

He snorted. 'I suppose we'd better check that door. Quite a big thing to have missed, don't you think?'

She nodded. 'I imagine she will have wiped any fingerprints off, mind you.'

'Probably. But we do have the problem of finding out who unlocked it in the first place.'

7

Argyll's lecture, a moronically simple canter through the more ostentatious church commissions of the seventeenth century, had gone tolerably well, so he thought. That is to say, there had been forty people in the room when he started, and still more than twenty when he'd ended. Such wastage would have alarmed him, but his head of department assured him that it was pretty good, considering. Considering what? he'd asked. Considering that it was a morning lecture, was the reply. Not early risers, these people. As they, or their parents, were paying a fortune, they generally imagined that lectures should be scheduled for their convenience. Just as they seemed to think that the level of grade should vary in direct proportion to the size of the fees.

'And,' this wiseacre continued. 'You didn't show many pictures. Risky. They like looking at pictures. You don't show pictures, they've not got anything to do. Except listen, and think. And lectures. Dear me. A bit authoritarian, you know? Don't you think a group interaction module might be better?'

'What's that?'

'It's where you break down hierarchy. They teach themselves.'

'But they don't know anything,' Argyll protested. 'How can you teach yourself if you don't know anything to start off with?'

'Ah. You've spotted the snag. However, that one is easily solved. You are confusing knowledge with creativity. You are meant to be encouraging their self-expression. Not stifling it by the imposition of factualities over which you deny them control.'

'Factualities?'

The other man sighed. 'I'm afraid so. Don't look at me like that. It's not my fault.'

'I don't have to do that, do I?' asked a newly anxious Argyll.

'I exaggerate greatly. Just for the pleasure of watching the blood drain from your head. But you do have to watch it. Do you want to have lunch?' he asked. Amazing how a bit of idle chat can make some people friendly. The man had scarcely talked to him before, although as almost no one in the entire department had acknowledged his existence as yet this hardly marked him out.

'No. That's kind. But I have to get back to San Giovanni.'

'Oh-ho. That's courageous of you. Did you know Menzies is working there?'

'I did.'

'The Al Capone of restoration? I'd be careful. There was a terribly funny article about him in the paper this morning . . .'

'I saw it.'

'Did you? Goodness, how I laughed. I wonder who wrote it. You saw it was anonymous, I suppose.'

'Yes.'

'I'd steer clear if I were you. I wouldn't like to be the person who supplied all that information to the press, either. He has a violent streak, has Menzies. Did you hear of the time he was addressing the art restorers' annual bash in Toronto? About four years ago?'

'Can't say I did,' Argyll replied cautiously.

'Burckhardt had the temerity to question a fluid he was using. Very polite, merely in the spirit of enquiry. They came to blows, in fact, Menzies threw a glass at him.'

'During the conference?'

'Not *in* the actual hall, no. That would have been entertaining. But in the bar afterwards. Very dramatic. I'm sorry I missed it, really; probably the high point of the evening. Vicious bunch, art restorers. Cut-throat, you know. They had a return match the other day. Didn't actually hit each other, alas.'

'Oh?'

'He was gawping at his restoring, and Menzies all but threw him out. Amazing. He told me about it at dinner. That's why I thought of it.'

'Who did?'

'Burckhardt.'

'Who is this Burckhardt?'

'Burckhardt? *The* Burckhardt.'

Argyll shook his head.

'And I thought you were once an art dealer. Peter Burckhardt. Of Galéries Burckhardt.'

'Oh,' said Argyll humbly. '*That* Burckhardt.'

He told Flavia about it over the minestrone.

'Who?'

Argyll looked at her scornfully. 'And I thought you were meant to keep your finger on the pulse. *The* Peter Burckhardt. Only the oldest and canniest icon man in the business. He virtually sets prices. Icons are worth what he says they're worth.'

'You know this man?'

He shook his head. 'Only by reputation. Which is very good. He's an Alsatian, I think. French, really.'

'Where does he hang out?'

'Paris. He operates in the Faubourg St-Honoré. Has done for decades, I think.'

'And he's in Rome.'

'Apparently. So this man I was talking to said. And had a run in with Menzies. They had a spat a year or so ago and it still rankles. Something about fluids.'

Flavia ate a spoonful of soup and thought it over. 'So we have a dealer who specializes in icons in the church a day or so ago. The order decides not to sell any of its possessions and the icon gets stolen. What does that indicate to you?'

'That you should forget Caravaggio and think Orthodox. And ask Menzies why he didn't mention this. And examine Peter Burckhardt's luggage. On the other hand, he is terribly respectable. I mean seriously. It's *possible* he might turn a blind eye to an icon with a dubious past; he'd have to. It's almost impossible to get hold of any which aren't a bit shady. But actually stealing things himself . . .'

Flavia nodded thoughtfully. 'I wonder if he knows Mary Verney.'

'He tries to buy it, is turned down, so goes on to his reserve line of attack?'

'That sort of thing.'

'I thought you said they hadn't received any offers?'

'So I did. What a pity. Nonetheless, I suppose I'd better find this man. Give me something to do. Thank you.'

'You're welcome. Don't want you to get bored, after all. Any other progress?'

She grinned. 'Thanks to Alberto's persistent questioning, yes. We have our culprit. A pity she's on the run.'

Alberto smiled back, a little half-heartedly.

'Well done,' Argyll said enthusiastically. 'Who was it?'

'The Virgin Mary. We have a witness.'

'What?'

Flavia explained. Argyll shook his head seriously.

'No. It doesn't sound right to me. I mean, the face. You can always tell by the face. Does that painting have a violent face? It does not. I think,' Argyll said definitively, 'that someone is trying to stitch her up.'

'You reckon?'

'I do. Have you figured out what Father Xavier was doing in the chapel?'

'Do priests need a reason? Probably keeping a late-night vigil to pray for guidance, or something. There seem to be squalls. Not a happy little order, in fact. Either that or I frightened him so much about the possible raid that he was keeping a vigil.'

'Have you considered Mary Verney here?'

She nodded. 'How could I not? But he was hit with some force, and that doesn't really seem like her, somehow. But I may be wrong, so we'll have her in anyway, see what she's been up to. Where are you going now?'

'Back to work.'

'You couldn't get some shopping, could you? I'm not going to have a minute.'

Argyll sighed. 'Do you promise to eat it this time?'

She nodded. 'Promise.'

'In that case, I suppose I could manage. As long as you don't expect anything complicated.'

8

Mary Verney spent the hours before lunch looking at paintings; it was a way of calming herself down after an alarming morning. Now she had largely given up stealing them, she discovered she quite liked the things, although old habits, she found, died hard. When she came across a particularly delightful specimen, such as the small Fra Angelico she was looking at now, she was hard put to avoid checking for wiring, and wondering how securely the windows were fastened. But, as it was now three – no, nearly four – years since she had worked, such thoughts were becoming more abstract; she liked retirement and had no desire whatsoever to emerge from it. She disliked intensely those foolish people – thieves or football players, politicians or boxers – who could not believe the world could survive without them and who refused to acknowledge that they, like everyone else, were at the mercy of time. No fool like an old fool, and Mary Verney had never, ever, been a fool.

But perhaps she was turning into one. She hadn't slept either, although she explained this by the fact that she really needed to be careful over the next few days. She needed to examine San Giovanni, but simply couldn't run the risk of being seen there.

It was for this reason that she not only left the hotel by the back entrance, but also did so at six in the morning. Nothing to do with not being able to sleep. The principle was sound: firstly she doubted that the police would keep up an all-night vigil for her sake; secondly she had a very much greater chance of spotting someone following her when the streets were all but deserted.

On the other hand, the buses were few and far between and she didn't want to take a taxi. So she had to walk. A lovely walk; one she would have greatly enjoyed in other circumstances, but this morning her mind wasn't on the dawn coming up over the Forum, or the Palatine dark against the lightening sky. Another beautiful day, it seemed, but so what? She was busy. All she wanted to do was examine the street, the locks on the building, side alleys and so on. Nothing fancy or detailed. A preliminary survey only, for the moment next week when she'd have to go to work.

So, like Argyll and Flavia before her, she walked slowly up the road leading to the monastery, checking distances, mentally noting which side streets were one way, which led nowhere and which gave out on to main roads. Noted the refuse collectors up the road, and made a note to see if they always turned up at the same time. Then the monastery itself; the high wall, the carefully locked door. Round the back there was a grim little alley with only a few, small windows, and these with thick bars over them. Burglary was nothing new in Rome, it seemed. They may not have had alarms and searchlights in the sixteenth century, but they did their best. And quite effective it was too. However she was going to get this picture for that damnable man, it wasn't going to be by athletic means. Just as well. She hated that sort of thing. Her original scheme would have to stand.

But as she walked back to the main street and walked past the monastery one last time, she began to revise her plans. Luckily she was on the opposite side of the road, otherwise she might have been seen. It wouldn't have mattered as he didn't know who she was, but best to keep things simple. She tucked herself away in the entrance of a block of flats and watched carefully.

He was hurrying along, dressed unremarkably but carrying over his right shoulder a brown canvas bag, which he clutched tightly to his body. Mary Verney observed this with interest, and saw with some alarm that he walked straight up the steps to the main entrance of the church itself, pushed on the door and went in. A compact man, with dark curly hair, sports jacket, glasses.

It didn't take a great genius to realize that he was not there by chance, and that he knew the door would be open. Which it surely shouldn't be; who leaves doors open all night these days? Mary Verney was seized with a wave of panic. Something else was beginning to go badly wrong. She felt it in her bones. If it did, then all her plans would collapse. And Mikis would carry out his threat about her granddaughter. She knew him well enough for that. She had managed to keep it at the back of her mind most of the time, but this sudden development brought it all painfully close. She walked forward quickly, crossed the road and began mounting the steps to the church. She had no idea what she was going to do in there, but she had to do something.

She was almost at the door and a few seconds later would have bumped into the man coming out again. He was pale and nervous, and looked as though he had had a bad fright. He almost ran down the steps, half tripped and dropped the bag. It fell on the hard stone with a soft thud, and he scooped it up quickly before hurrying off up the street.

She thought quickly, then decided. Something wasn't right. She quickly walked into the church and looked around. It took a few seconds for her eyes to get used to the darkness, and then she saw a figure lying on the ground. It was an old man, a priest, with a bad wound to his head; the blood was dripping out of the cut.

He was conscious, but only barely. She kneeled down beside him. 'What happened?'

He moaned softly, and tried to shake his head. With surprising gentleness, she stopped him, cradling him gently in her hands. 'What happened?'

'The picture . . . He . . .'

'Who? Who is he?'

'Burckhardt. He'll . . .'

Then he was unconscious. She knelt down to look at him more closely, then stood up to avoid getting blood on her. 'Don't struggle or move,' she said softly as she loosened his clothing and tried to staunch the bleeding. 'It'll be all right. I'll make sure.'

And nothing else to be done for him at the moment. She

glanced up and saw the empty frame of the icon, and ran out of the church again. She was afraid she'd lost him, but after a few minutes saw his distinctive figure standing still, consulting a map.

Thank God for irrational Roman street-planning, she thought as she slowed down and took up her station a hundred yards or so behind him.

'We are nervous, aren't we?' she thought. 'But make up your mind. Where are you going, little man?'

Then he was off, down the via Albina, then crossed the little park leading to the pyramid and the Porta San Paolo. Here he consulted his map again, then crossed the square into the little railway station. Mary followed at a discreet distance. It had finally clicked; should have done the minute she heard the name. Eggs and Bacon. Icons and Burckhardt. Of course.

But again, he changed his mind, came out and started walking round the back and into the Ostiense station which was already disgorging the first commuters of the day on to the streets. This time he was more decisive. He walked into the grim entrance, and straight across to the left-luggage compartments. Fumbled in his pockets for some coins, and threw his bag into one of the lockers. Shut it, removed the key, and put it in his pocket.

He found a taxi outside and she let him go; there was no point in following him any more, and walked across the road to a bar. Half an hour should do it, she thought, just to be safe. But first, a little humanitarianism. She rang for an ambulance.

Not the police and not the Art Squad; that would have been too obvious. Doing as good an impression as she could manage of a Roman accent, she reported an accident in the church of San Giovanni and rang off before they could ask any more questions. Seven-forty. Conscience salved. Time for a large, frothy cappuccino and a pastry, sitting down at the back. She was certain that in that bag, in that left-luggage compartment, lay the solution to her problem. She might even be on the plane home this afternoon.

At ten past eight she walked back to the station, straight over to the manager's office.

'*Bon jorno*,' she said in an execrable accent. 'Ho un problem.

Difficulty. Understand?' She smiled inanely as she twittered. The man on duty, used to the occasional idiocies of tourists, sighed heavily and smiled pleasantly. He was in a good mood. One more shift and he was off on holiday. It was something he'd been planning all year, and he was eager to get going. The challenge of a lifetime.

'Yes?'

'Baggage? Left luggage. Um, *Consigno*? Lost the key.' She made suitable movements with her hand to indicate someone turning a key in a lock. 'Big problem.' And smiled sweetly again.

The man frowned, and bit by bit they worked out between them what was the matter, he straining to understand the verbal nonsense she spouted, she trying to avoid using the Italian words she knew all too well.

'Ah. You have lost the key to your left-luggage locker. Is that it?'

She nodded enthusiastically, took out a piece of paper and scribbled the number to hold up to him. 'C37,' she said.

'What's in it? You have to say. Otherwise how do we know it's yours?'

She delayed a reasonable time about understanding this, waving what she hoped would be mistaken for a plane ticket to indicate how desperately late she was for a flight. Eventually she condescended to understand and, successfully giving the impression that she was outraged at anyone doubting her honesty in the matter, waved her hands some more.

'Bag,' she said. 'Case. Sack?'

'*Sacco, si.*'

'Lovely. Light brown. Shoulder strap. Zipper.'

Then she prattled away, describing spurious contents so quickly that she knew he wouldn't have a chance of understanding a single word, until he held up his hands. 'OK,' he said. 'OK.'

He opened a drawer and took out a key and led her across the forecourt. Mary pointed at the box, and he opened it.

'There we are,' she said delightedly, taking possession. 'Oh, thank you, signor. You're so very kind.' She pumped his hand up and down with fervent gratitude.

'*Niente*,' he said. 'Be more careful next time.' He was in too relaxed a mood to make the report that regulations required, but reminded himself to tell the appropriate people to dig out a new key. But not at the moment. There was too much to do. He'd get around to it later.

And Mary Verney went off to the toilet, locking herself into a cubicle and putting the bag on her knee. Journey's end. Thank God for that. Well wrapped up, she thought as she unzipped it. Her heart was beating fast with excitement.

Then she stared inside with complete dismay and incomprehension. There was no icon. Just money, a whole lot of it. But who was interested in that?

Damnation, she thought. It's not there. Where the hell is it?

She flipped through the piles, to see how much there was. Stack after stack of deutsche marks. Big ones, little ones, all wrapped up in elastic bands. Nothing else at all.

She counted quickly. Must be about two hundred thousand dollars' worth, she guessed. She zipped the bag shut again, and sat and thought.

This did not make sense. Didn't make sense at all.

Still, first things first. Better get rid of this bag. She left the toilet and walked on to the platform, then hopped on to a crammed commuter train that lumbered in a few moments later. She knew that no one in their right minds would try to collect a ticket from her, especially as it was only another five-minute run to the end of the line. So she stood there, clutching the bag with only slightly less nervousness than Burckhardt had shown, and waited patiently until the train creaked into the main terminus and disgorged her along with several hundred others.

She repeated his tactic of leaving the bag in the left luggage at the terminus then rang Mikis at his hotel. It took some time to wake him.

'We've got another problem,' she said quickly once she had his attention. 'The icon's gone. Someone went in there and beat the hell out of an old priest and took it.'

'I don't know who it was,' she continued. 'But a man called Burckhardt was there. Do you know him?'

Strangely, although no great connoisseur, he did seem to know who Burckhardt was. 'Yes,' she went on. 'The French icon man. That's the one. He's in Rome and I assume he's after the icon as well. I don't think he attacked the priest. But he went and put something in a left-luggage compartment. Ostiense. C37.'

Another pause. 'Certainly not. I am damned if I'm going to spend a day hanging around a train station. Go and ask Burckhardt. He must be in a hotel somewhere.'

'That's your problem,' she went on. 'Call his gallery in Paris and ask where he is. Even you should be able to manage that. But I can't steal a picture if someone's already stolen it. We'll have to meet later on. I can't see what else you expect me to do.'

Might work, she thought. Even he couldn't expect miracles from her.

Then she went back to her hotel, emerging from her room ten minutes after she arrived through the back door again.

She'd slept wonderfully, she told the waiter who brought her breakfast. Must be the Roman air. A day in an art gallery today, she thought. Which one did he recommend?

9

When Argyll had gone off to investigate the market for dinner, and Alberto returned to his paperwork – love to help, but it's the end of the month, could you manage without me until tomorrow? – Flavia hit the beat, leaving a message for Giulia, if ever she came back from lunch, to join her. A tiresome business, knocking on doors time after time, asking the same questions and getting the same answers, but it had to be done. When Giulia finally appeared, she sent her to start at one end of the street, she took the other, and they methodically worked their way through the apartment blocks, floor by floor, occupant by occupant, until they met in the middle.

'Did you see or hear anything at about five o'clock this morning?'

'Of course not. I was asleep.'

'No. My bedroom is at the back.'

'Pardon? You'll have to speak up. I'm a little deaf.'

'The only thing I heard was the refuse collectors. They do it deliberately, you know, making such a noise, trying to stop respectable people from sleeping. Do you know . . . ?'

'What do you think I am, a Peeping Tom?'

'Go away. I'm busy. The baby's just thrown up on the floor.'

And so on. An entire street and, as far as Flavia could discover, the desired combination of a nosy insomniac with good hearing and a bedroom facing in the direction of the monastery did not exist.

'Complete bloody waste of time. And my feet are killing me,' Flavia said when she got home afterwards, proud at least of coming home in time for dinner and an evening pretending to be normal and civilized. She took off her shoes and waggled her toes in Argyll's direction to show him what she meant. They looked perfectly fine to him.

'What you need is a nice quiet desk job.'

'What I need is a glass of gin. Do you know anything about icons?'

Argyll paused as he unscrewed the bottle. 'Nothing.'

'You must know something.'

'No. Zilch. Zero. Very specialist trade, icons. I couldn't tell a medieval one from a modern one. It's shameful to admit it, but they all look a bit the same to me.'

'You never sold any?'

'Not likely. It's bad enough trying to make money dealing when you do know what you're doing. Besides, there hasn't been much money in them in the last few years. There's a decent market now, of course. Prices are beginning to go up again, now that the old Soviet Union has virtually been cleaned out.'

'What do you mean?'

'Supply and demand. Icons have been a terrible drudge recently. Once Russia opened up, almost every icon in the country was pinched in a matter of months. The dealers in the west were virtually knee deep in them. Some amazing quality, as well. The sort of thing major museums would have fought over ten years back, you could scarcely give away.'

'So what sort of price are we dealing with here?'

'Depends. How good was this?'

'I've no idea. But the maximum possible? What's the highest price you could imagine?'

'Biggest I've heard of is a quarter of a million dollars.'

'I see. And was this one in the monastery in that category?'

'Not a clue. I doubt it very much. It seemed a bit sad.'

'Sad?'

'Hmm. Neglected. Unloved. Not the sort of thing collectors fight over. I gave it a candle.'

Flavia yawned mightily. Jonathan's opinions were frequently a little wayward, but he had good instincts; far better than hers ever were. When people were concerned, of course, it was the other way around, but he had a sensitivity for paintings which he rarely managed for real human beings.

'A candle,' she said sleepily. 'Why did you do that?'

'It seemed appropriate. And it thanked me.'

'What?'

'Well, not the painting, of course, but the cleaning lady. A sort of displaced thanks, if you like.'

'I see. Why did it seem lonely?'

'Well, it was set up to have a lot of people around it,' he explained. 'There was room for hundreds of candles, and enough space to have lots of people praying. As there was no one there, and no candles, it had this air of having fallen on hard times. It was obviously once considered of greater importance. Probably these legends.'

'Could you do me a favour and find out something a bit more concrete about it?'

'You've heard the story?'

'About an angel bringing it?'

'That's the one.'

'I have. And you may find me unduly hard-headed, but I'm a bit sceptical. Besides, when did these angels bring it?'

'Only one angel,' Argyll said. 'Only one.'

'My apologies.'

'I can go and find out if you like. Or try to. And when I can't find anything, I'll ask our Orthodox and Islamic man.'

'Does he know about icons?'

'Written enough on them. How did you get on today?'

Flavia waved her hand and yawned again. 'Don't ask. It's been enormously frustrating. I got the address of Burckhardt's hotel, but he's nowhere to be seen. Oh, damnation.'

'What's the matter?'

'I've just had an idea. One of the people I talked to this afternoon said the only thing they heard early this morning was the refuse collectors.'

'So?'

'So they might have seen something. Which means I have to go down to the central depot tomorrow morning and find the gang that did the road. I have a feeling they start early, as well.'

'You'd better get an early night, then.'

96

Flavia didn't answer. She was already halfway to the bedroom, yawning so much she didn't hear. The conversation had lasted ten minutes. Not much for an entire evening.

10

The depot was a bleak parking lot for sleeping trucks on the outskirts of Rome where, every morning at dawn, several hundred men gathered to go forth in the unending and frustrating attempt to keep the city moderately tidy and halfway hygienic. Every day, they drove off in a billowing cloud of exhaust fumes, only to return many hours later covered in dust and the smell of rotting vegetables, groaning with the weight of discarded paper, plastic sacks, potato peelings and old newspapers. Every day they had a few hours after they disgorged their aromatic load to rest and restore their energies, before setting out again; they had done so since before the days of Augustus, and would do so until the Second Coming. Maybe beyond as well.

The depot was dimly lit by floodlights, most of which were out of action, and Flavia dimly saw dozens upon dozens of men, standing round like tank crews before going into battle, chatting away, smoking and taking the occasional sip of alcohol to fortify themselves for the day's battle against the forces of chaos. She picked out a man who looked as though he might be in charge of something, and asked for information.

Not a talkative man. He squinted at her identification, then pointed her in the direction of a small and grubby bar, outside and on the other side of the road. It presumably lived off the refuse as well, feeding up the crews before they went off, and watering them down again when they came back. Certainly, there was nothing else around to provide it with any business.

Flavia went in, looked at the crowd of men in blue overalls crammed against the bar, and picked one at random.

'Aventino three,' she said.

Another point. Not a talkative lot, she thought, but who is at this time of day?

She ended up with a small, thin little man who looked as though he could barely carry a shopping bag, let alone the hefty weight of one of the huge, apartment-size bins that the city provides for collective cleanliness.

'Aventino three?' she asked again.

He didn't say no, so she continued. 'Did you collect in the via San Giovanni yesterday?'

He looked at her suspiciously, as though she might be a city official about to relay a complaint from a resident about noise or leaving piles of rubbish in the street.

'Maybe we did,' he said.

She again pulled out her identification. 'There was a robbery with violence there, probably before seven,' she said.

'Oh, yes?'

'In the monastery. The superior had his head cracked.'

'Uh-huh.'

'And a painting was stolen. Did you see anything?'

He thought for a moment, his lined brow puckering with concentration. Suddenly, enlightenment dawned.

'No,' he said.

Flavia sighed. 'Are you sure? You didn't see anyone coming out of San Giovanni? Going in? Did you hear anything?'

He shook his head, and walked off to the bar. Flavia cursed silently to herself. She might as well have stayed in bed. Then she yawned, and realized that the early rise, the coffee on an empty stomach and the faint air of rotting vegetables that came off the clothes of everyone in the place was making her feel slightly sick. No, she thought. Make that very sick.

'He did it.'

She tried briefly to keep her stomach under control and saw that the little man had come back, this time with another figure, as big as he was short, and as powerful as he seemed weak.

'What?'

'Giacomo did that end of the street. Yesterday.'

She concentrated hard, and managed a faint smile at Giacomo. He grinned, nervously and foolishly, back at her, showing his stained teeth. She caught a whiff of stale alcohol and cigarette on his breath, mingled with rot, and hoped desperately she could keep upright for long enough to question him.

'Did you see anything? At six? Or thereabouts?'

'Nothing in particular,' he said. He had a slow, stupid voice.

'No unusual noises?'

'No.' Every time she asked a question, Giacomo paused, and looked up at the ceiling, and thought hard. Hurry it up, she thought. I'm not asking you to perform calculus. He shook his head slowly, as though that gave added weight to his words.

'Did you see anyone in the monastery?'

'No.'

'Nothing?'

'No.'

She paused and thought. Waste of time.

'I saw a man come out of the church.'

She looked up at him urgently. 'When?'

'I don't know. Six-thirty? Something like that. No. I tell a lie. It must have been before, because we stopped for a break a bit after. We always stop at six-thirty.'

'Wonderful,' Flavia said heartily and insincerely. 'Now, what did you see?'

'Like I say, a man came out of the church.'

'And?'

'And nothing. I only noticed because the door is always locked. I've never seen it open. So I thought, hello, the door's open.'

'Yes,' she said patiently. 'Now, this man, was he holding anything? A package?'

He shook his head, slowly, from side to side, then thought some more. 'No.'

'You're sure?'

'Yes. He had a bag, though.'

'A bag?'

'That's right.' He held out his hands to show the size. 'I noticed because he dropped it.'

'Did it make a noise? Did he seem worried that he dropped it?'

He shook his head. 'He just picked it up by the shoulder strap, and hurried away.'

'Hurried?'

'Oh, yes. That's why I noticed. Another reason, you see, apart from the door being open, that is. He ran down the steps very fast, dropped the bag, then walked off very fast.'

'I see. Now,' she said urgently, partly because she wanted to know and partly because she knew her stomach was running out of time, 'what did he look like?'

There followed an adequate description of a short, mild-looking man. Flavia took out the photographs that Giulia had taken that first afternoon when she'd been put on to the task of watching the monastery. Menzies leading someone out of the church, bidding him a fond farewell. So it seemed.

Giacomo peered at it carefully, and sucked his dentures in careful thought. 'Oh, yes,' he said. 'That's the one.'

'You're sure? The man on the right is the man you saw coming out of the church yesterday morning?'

He nodded. She thanked him and turned to go, her stomach heaving from the aroma in the bar, the bitterness of her coffee and the lack of anything to eat. She told him he'd have to come to the station to give a statement at some time. He seemed disappointed.

'I'm sorry, but it really is necessary,' she said as patiently as she could manage.

'That doesn't bother me. I just wondered whether you wanted to hear about the woman.'

'What woman?'

'The one who went into the church after this man. I saw her.'

'Oh,' she said. 'Yes. Maybe I do want to hear about her.'

All in all, Flavia thought with some satisfaction and an odd sense of disappointment, pretty conclusive. The refuse collector had given a description of Mary Verney which was passable and would undoubtedly identify her properly when called on to do so.

But they didn't yet have an explanation. The more she thought, the more she realized this awkward little fact. Someone had left the church with a bag which was just about big enough for a small icon. Mary Verney had left empty-handed. Their witness was sure of that. She had only been in the church for a minute or two; not long enough to hit Father Xavier, steal the icon and hide it somewhere. They'd have to search the church again, just to be sure. This Burckhardt was almost certainly the one who took the picture, and also the man who attacked Father Xavier.

Stood to reason. Icon and icon man. Bit of a coincidence otherwise.

But why steal it? Obviously because he wanted it. But a distinguished man like him? Stealing in person? Very unusual. Unheard of. Even the stupidest dealer would sub-contract something like that. To a specialist. Like Mrs Verney. So what was he doing leaving before she got there? And surely someone like Mrs Verney wouldn't do a job and take her employer along for the ride?

This stumped her, so she punished her stomach some more by smoking another cigarette and having another coffee and staring at the ceiling in the hope that something would occur to her.

It didn't. And then, before she could take that precious half hour off for something to eat she'd been promising herself since five o'clock, Alberto rang. He had news, he said. They'd found someone floating in the Tiber. Did she want to come and have a look? She might be interested.

Why? she asked. Nothing novel about that.

'Ah, well, you see. His name was Burckhardt. He had identification on him saying he was an art dealer. From Paris. So I thought . . .'

'I'm on my way.' She picked up her jacket, calmed her stomach and walked out.

11

Whoever was responsible hadn't tried very hard to conceal what they'd done; the body would have surfaced and floated ashore sooner or later anyway, even if one of the ancient, slow dredgers that pursue the thankless task of scooping up silt from the bottom of the river hadn't sucked him up bodily and spat him out into the cavernous hold of the boat.

On the other hand, it was lucky that anyone had noticed. Had one of the crew not been new to the job, and been leaning over the railing watching because he was not yet experienced enough to have lost interest, the body might have been instantly buried under several tons of sand, taken out to sea and dumped four kilometres or so in the Mediterranean. Equally, had the new recruit not been the son of the captain, it is likely that his alarm would have been ignored anyway.

Either way, it was only by mere chance that the corpse of Peter Burckhardt was discovered so quickly, allowing the police to avoid a considerable waste of time in their less than urgent desire to talk to him. Time which they were instantly able to divert to the more urgent task of discovering who had taken him a couple of miles down river, shot him in the head, then tipped his body in.

And why, of course. He had nothing on him which helped in any way, except for an address book containing several hundred numbers which the unfortunate Giulia was told to ring up, one by one, in search of stray information. Certainly, there was nothing which instantly made the enquiry progress by leaps and bounds. The information lay in the existence of the corpse itself. But even that was relatively uncommunicative, offering no help over when it got there or who put it there.

And, so the pathologist assured Flavia morosely, it probably wouldn't. Not even a bullet, which had gone straight through and out the other side.

'So whoever it was shot him was standing close? Is that fair?'

'Maybe. Depends on the gun, doesn't it? If you want a guess . . .'

'Why not?'

'I'd say small pistol, fired close. Less than a metre. More I cannot say. Certainly not at the moment.'

Great. She had expected no less, and certainly no more.

'There is one thing, though,' Alberto said as she was about to leave.

'What?'

'In his pocket.' He held out a piece of paper in the palm of his hand. 'We found this.'

'So?'

'It's a key for a left-luggage deposit.'

'Can I borrow that for a while?'

'If you sign for it and give it back.'

'So fussy you are.'

'Can't trust anyone these days, you know. Do you have any ideas?'

She shook her head. 'None that make sense. What about you?'

'We thought we'd have that restorer in for a chat. Menzies.'

She looked puzzled.

'They were enemies,' he pointed out. 'So your friend says. Came to blows. Had another squabble a couple of days ago. You're the one who says art restoring is a vicious business.'

'Not *that* vicious. Had someone pulled his head off, then Menzies would be your man. But shooting him?' She shook her head.

Alberto shrugged. 'We've got to do something to pass the time. Unless you can suggest something better . . . ?'

She couldn't, so she signed a receipt, put the key in her pocket, and walked slowly away.

There are well-established ways of finding out where keys

come from, but they are enormously tedious and often take a long time, even when you are fairly sure that what you are looking for is a left-luggage locker. Nonetheless, Flavia put the machinery into action, and herself sat at the desk in her office and tried to hurry things up a little.

Let us assume, she thought, that this is important. Let us assume that it will get us somewhere.

She got out her old and much-used map of Rome, spread it on her desk and considered. The twin stations of Ostia Lido and Ostiense were the most likely, although there was also the metro station at the Colosseum. If it had lockers.

Keys, she thought as she walked to the taxi rank and pushed her way to the front of the queue. The Romans accepted it; the tourists looked daggers at her. Keys, she thought as the taxi inched its way into the traffic. Lots of keys. To lockers and to church doors. Tiresome. But, you never know. Journey's end might be just around the corner. With a bit of luck.

Not today. Not with that key, anyway. The Colosseum was a dud; Ostia Lido was a dud; Ostiense was a bit of a poser.

For a brief moment she had a surge of hope. The station had its bank of lockers, and a few moments' examination led her to one labelled C37. It was locked. With a tremor of anticipation, she put the key in, and smiled as it turned in the lock.

There was a bag inside. But not a canvas one. A suitcase, covered in American airline stickers.

She pulled it out, still hoping but already half suspicious that something wasn't right, put it on the floor and opened it up.

Socks. Underpants. T-shirts. A tag identifying the case as the possession of Walter Matthews, 2238 Willow, Indianapolis 07143. USA.

Totally perplexing. She frowned as she sat cross-legged in front of the scattered contents, oblivious to the passengers skirting round her, trying to figure out the connection. She didn't understand. She was just about to start putting all the bits and pieces back into the case when she vaguely heard a footstep from behind. She ignored it, but was forced to be a bit more attentive when this was followed up with a loud cry

105

of triumph as she was put into a neck lock by a large, sun-burned, muscular and American arm.

'Gotcha!' screamed Walter Matthews of Indianapolis.

'Oh, for God's sake . . .'

'Thief! Police!'

An interested circle of passengers gathered round to watch this little drama, and Flavia was pinned to the ground by the outraged tourist for several minutes until the station manager put in an appearance. Followed by two passing carabinieri who attempted to arrest her while the manager tried to calm the situation down.

'Look, guys . . .' Flavia said.

'Shut up. You're under arrest.'

'I am not under arrest.'

'Oh yes? That's what you think.'

She reached for her identification, and was instantly pinned to the ground again.

'Jesus Christ! I am *in* the police. Let me go, you stupid morons.'

It was said with sufficient force to make them hesitate long enough for her to drag the identification out of her back pocket. Her colleagues in law enforcement looked at it, twitched with embarrassment, then let go of her arms, pro-ducing a bellow of outrage from Walter Matthews.

'Oh, be quiet,' Flavia snapped, conscious that she wasn't exactly enhancing Rome's international image but not really caring either. 'Take your bloody bag and be grateful we don't confiscate it.'

Not that he understood a word, of course, until she calmed down long enough to translate a slightly calmer version. Crime. Murder. Locker involved. Police investigation. No damage. Thanks for your cooperation which is greatly appreciated. Etcetera.

All this in English, which the station master did not under-stand. Which was a pity. If he had, he might have been more sympathetic; as it was, he was more indignant about the smooth running of his station and was distinctly cool about answering Flavia's questions.

He couldn't go into details, he told her, because he was

merely a stand-in while the real station manager was on holiday.

'Where?'

'Vienna. The State Railway choir. They're going on tour in Austria. Verdi's *Requiem*. And some Palestrina. Signor Landini is a tenor.'

'Good for him. How is it that there are two keys? I have one, this American had one.'

He shrugged. Evidently one had been reported lost and replaced.

'When?'

Another shrug. Such matters are always put in the book.

'Get the book.'

Reluctantly, he did. Flavia examined it with care. Nothing.

'You would have cut the new key sometime. Is there a record of that?'

There was always a duplicate set, he explained. People lose keys all the time, and get very upset.

'So you have no idea when the second key came into operation? When the original went missing?'

'No.'

'Can you tell if this is the original?' She handed over the key found in Burckhardt's pocket. The station master looked at it and nodded. It was the original. You could tell by the numbering. She retrieved it, and looked so discouraged the man finally took pity on her, and picked up the phone.

'Lockers? Did Signor Landini ask you to get out any replacement keys in the past few days?'

There was a pause. 'Yesterday? The number? Good. No, everything's in order. He forgot to note it in the book, that's all. Holiday spirit, I suppose. He didn't say anything about who lost the key? I thought not.'

He put the phone down. 'Yesterday,' he said. 'Someone came saying they'd lost the key yesterday.'

'I heard. They didn't say when yesterday?'

'No. Signor Landini reported it just before he left.'

Getting the necessary permissions to go into Burckhardt's hotel room took the usual length of time. That is to say hours;

107

he was on his own, there was no one to ask and official permission had to be sought from some legal nook and cranny. Left to her own devices, Flavia might well have just let herself in with a picklock, but the carabinieri were involved and they were terribly fussy about that sort of thing these days. They used not to be, but what with enquiries and investigations and assessments and all that, everyone was being awfully careful and punctilious about following the rules. Partly to avoid trouble, and partly to show to the powers-that-be that following rules was time-consuming and expensive.

So while they fussed around magistrates, and pathologists fussed around Burckhardt's body, and Paolo went chasing after Mary Verney, Flavia was left temporarily with nothing to do. Instead she went back to San Giovanni, to see if Alberto had collared Menzies yet. There was no one around, so she saw Father Jean instead.

'What are all the flowers for? On the steps to the church?'

The old man frowned. 'They're from the local population. Trying to persuade their Lady to return and forgive them.'

'What for?'

'For neglecting her.'

Flavia thought back to her schooldays, and scratched her head. 'Does that make good theology?'

He smiled, and shook his head slowly. 'It makes appalling theology. But what's that got to do with it? They think she is displeased, and has withdrawn her protection. Frankly, it teeters on paganism. And, of course, we are being blamed. If we hadn't cut her off by closing the doors . . . Do you know, one of us, Father Luc, was shouted at in a tobacconist yesterday? Told he was bringing disaster on the quarter? Can you believe it in this day and age?'

'Hard.'

'Staggering. Father Xavier's idea, you know. To shut the church. But none of us realized she was held in such affection. Anyway, the flowers and baskets of fruit are to woo her back. If it goes on, we're going to be visited.'

'Who by?'

'The parish overseer, and our Cardinal supervisor. This

could cause trouble for us, you know. We will get criticized for shutting the church, and criticized for encouraging superstition. I know it. Signorina, you know, I'm too old for this.'

Flavia looked at his old and lined face, and the slump in his shoulders and couldn't do anything but agree. Fortunately, it was outside her province, although she thought Bottando would probably give useful, worldly advice. But he was fat and sixty, and could do things like that. She had her work cut out doing her own job, let alone telling other people how to do theirs.

'It's about keys,' she said, to get the subject back on to more comfortable territory. Then paused for a long while. Father Jean sat patiently, waiting for her to elaborate.

'A man was seen coming out of the door of the church at six-thirty. Somebody on the inside must have opened it. How many keys are there? Who has them?'

'To the big door? The one on to the street?'

She nodded.

'There is only one,' Father Jean said.

'Can I see it?'

'By all means. It hangs on a hook just inside the door.'

'I'd better check it's there.'

He smiled. 'There is no need, although you are more than welcome to do so if you wish. I saw it myself this morning. Have you arrested this man? It may be uncharitable, but if he attacked Father Xavier I will find it very hard to forgive him.'

She grimaced. Evidently no one had yet told them. 'I'm afraid that this case is becoming rather complicated,' she said. 'Mr Burckhardt was found in the Tiber this morning. He had been shot.'

'Oh, my goodness. The poor soul.'

'Indeed.'

'I'm afraid I don't understand what all this is about.'

She looked at him sadly. 'You are not the only one, Father, believe me. This is becoming very much more than the theft of a not very important work of art. It's a nightmare. I hope that Father Xavier will help. Assuming we're allowed to talk to him tomorrow.'

'You don't think that he is in any danger?'

She shrugged her shoulders. 'I didn't think anybody was. I was evidently wrong. I've had a guard put over him.'

'For some reason, I am not as reassured as I might be.'

'No,' she agreed flatly. 'Nor am I.'

'I would like to send one of our more muscular brothers down to sit by him.'

'I'm sure that would be fine. What is it?'

Father Jean was looking suddenly ill at ease, very much like someone who felt the need to say something but was too delicate to begin.

'Come on, you can't surprise me. Nothing can surprise me today.'

'I was wondering when we would be seeing the General. I'm sure, of course, that you are more than experienced enough. Please don't think that. But as General Bottando knows us from the last time . . . I like to think he and I struck up a rapport, you see, and I was looking forward to seeing him.'

'I'm afraid that's unlikely,' she said. 'I have been put in charge of the case. General Bottando is too – ah – preoccupied at the moment.' She did her best to avoid being irritated, and just about managed. It was, after all, something she was going to have to get used to.

'I am sorry. I mean, I didn't wish to imply for a moment . . .'

'I know. But there it is. So if there is anything to say, you'll have to tell me, I'm afraid.'

'Oh, dear. I don't wish to seem doubtful. It's not about you, but simply because I don't know you, you see.'

Flavia gave him an exasperated look. So much dithering. It was obvious he'd disgorge eventually. Why couldn't he just get on with it?

'I'm afraid that in the last day or so I have discovered certain things which I find deeply distressing.'

'And which you don't want anyone else to know about?'

He nodded sadly.

'I'm quite able to forget something if it is not directly relevant,' she said. 'My job is to find a thief and a murderer. Not to spread other people's dirty laundry around the world.'

He grunted, took a deep breath, then began. Or almost began. A few circumlocutions to warm up first.

'You've gathered, perhaps, that Father Xavier and I did not always see eye to eye on many matters?'

She nodded. 'Something like that.'

'Not very long ago, I was effectively the second in command here to the superior general, Father Charles. He was probably the best leader this order ever had. That's not just loyalty on my part; he kept us going through the rough times of Vatican Two and its aftermath, and had a way of quelling arguments and gently persuading people. It is a rare skill. I'd known him all my life, virtually. He was a few years older than me, and I loved him like a brother. A real brother, you understand.'

She nodded.

'And he got ill. He was old, had a good life and got ill and could no longer discharge his duties. We elected Father Xavier to replace him. You may think it unfair of me, but I think he is a weak man; he has little certainty in his soul, so borrows the appearance of it, if you see what I mean.'

He glanced at her, and she shook her head. Not a clue.

'When he decides to do something he doesn't *feel* he is right, in the way that Charles did. He persuades himself, and because he is so doubtful, he presents his ideas with much more dogmatism and fervour than if he was really convinced. When he has an idea, he is determined to stick to it, for fear of revealing his own weakness to himself. He confronts rather than persuades, and angers rather than conciliates.

'He wishes to rebuild the order from top to bottom. He is probably right; we can't go on like this. Something has to change. But, you see, I hated him, and even though I knew it was wicked of me, I could do nothing about it. He is an easy person to dislike. He was not Father Charles, and his urgency was an implicit criticism of what Charles did. He had replaced the irreplaceable. He was not as wise, or as kind or as saintly.

'So every time he has proposed something, I have found myself opposing it. He wanted to raise money, to build up our teaching in the Third World, and I voted against simply because it was not his place to propose changes to what Father

Charles had done. And when he proposed selling some of our possessions, I was the one who led the opposition again, and had the sale voted down. Do you understand what I am saying?'

Flavia nodded.

'You may think it is simply the silly games of a group of old men, but it is more than this. We have the opportunity of doing good work, and I stopped it. And it ended in disaster.'

'Well, hardly . . .'

'I see. But I don't understand . . .'

'As I've been running this place for the past few days, I have had occasion to go through the files. And what I have found shocks me. And concerns me deeply. A moment.'

He got up and walked over to the desk, where he fumbled with a key ring and opened a drawer. 'Here,' he said, handing Flavia a thin manila file. 'The first letter arrived yesterday morning.'

Flavia opened it and looked at the letter. It was from a firm of stockbrokers in Milan. She frowned as she read. It didn't make a whole lot of sense to her.

'I phoned them, of course, to ask exactly what it meant.'

'So why not tell me?'

'Xavier always had this notion of being modern; using the techniques and opportunities of the real world – he always called it that – to help us in our work. I fear he was terribly naive about it, and convinced himself that making money was easy. So he used these people – without ever mentioning it to anyone – and, as far as I can see, gambled with what money we had. That's not the phrase these people use. Exploiting investment opportunities, I believe is how they phrased it.'

'And?'

'And like an innocent lamb to the slaughter, he has lost us a fortune. I don't understand the process at all, but I do understand the result. Instead of having a reasonable sum in assets, we now owe these people a quarter of a million dollars. Xavier has gambled the rest away.'

'Which presumably is why he wanted to get on with selling things.'

'I imagine. And I suspect we will have to do so now, barring a miracle. We will have to pay his debts. Our debts. It came as a great shock.'

'I can believe it. How long has this been going on?'

He shrugged. 'More or less from the moment he took over from Charles, I believe. I don't know. I do very much wish it hadn't fallen to me to discover this.'

'Why?'

'Because it confirms my worst fears about him. And I find myself deriving too much satisfaction from being correct. I should now institute proceedings against him as our rule provides, but I doubt my motives too much. And because it is partly my fault. Had I not opposed him so much and so unreasonably, he might not have felt obliged to resort to such measures. I led the opposition. Why? Because I think bringing health care and education to the Third World is a bad idea? Not at all; I am a fervent admirer of Father Paul, and that is his whole existence, and why he is pining away here in Rome when he should be back in his own country doing what he does best. No; it was because Father Xavier was in favour. That was all. You see what I mean? My foolishness made a bad situation worse, until it ended in disaster. I thank the Lord that Xavier was not killed, although I grieve for Signor Burckhardt.'

She nodded. 'I see. So what do you do now?'

He shook his head. 'I don't know. Where do you get money from in a hurry? That is not an area where I have a great deal of experience.'

Flavia stood up and smiled faintly. 'Nor me.'

He nodded as she got up to go, and rose to open the door for her.

12

'Good day so far?'

Which just showed how sensitive he could be on occasions.

'Hardly.'

Flavia had arrived at Jonathan's little cubbyhole, taken a chocolate biscuit from the secret hoard, specially imported from England, he kept behind the reference books and then decided she didn't feel all that hungry.

'Just asking. Why don't you tell me what's wrong? You've been looking as cheerful as a funeral ever since you got here.'

'Rough day.'

'Go on. Tell me.'

'Later,' she said brusquely, impatient at his cheerful unconcern for once.

'Please yourself. What are you here for, if not to unburden the troubles of the world?'

'Why should I be here for anything?'

'You don't often turn up for no reason.'

True enough. What was she here for? Reluctantly, she made herself concentrate on the practicalities of the case, and forced its complications into the background.

'You said you might be able to find out something about the icon. Have you?'

'Not yet. It's been a busy day.'

'Listen, Jonathan. I don't have time for your busy days. This is important.'

He frowned. 'And it's police business, not mine. I've been working since I got here. You never said it was so very urgent.'

'I'm sorry.'

114

'Look, what is the matter with you? What did you come here for? Did you just want to snap my head off?'

'I said I'm sorry. I know you're busy, but I need to find out about that picture. I've been up since five, this man Burckhardt has been murdered . . .'

'*What*?'

'He was shot. There is evidently much more to that picture than we thought. I need to know what. And for obvious reasons it's becoming pressing.'

Argyll gaped at her in astonishment for a second, then shook himself, got up and walked out of the room. He came back a few moments later with a bearded man in his mid-forties.

'This is Mario di Angelo. He's the head of the department. Tell him about Burckhardt.'

So she did. Di Angelo's face registered firstly astonishment, then genuine shock and distress. 'And I had dinner with him only a few days ago. Who would have thought?' he said, shaking his head sadly. 'Poor man. Poor, poor man. A really nice, companionable fellow. Very learned as well. He'll be badly missed, you know.'

Flavia nodded. 'At this dinner, he didn't mention being in Rome to buy an icon, did he?'

A shaken head. 'No. I assumed that he was here for some such reason, of course. We knew each other as scholars, and never talked about his business.'

'Nothing at all?'

'No. He said he was going to finish off some research and had this wonderful idea. Such as he told me was quite interesting. All about the theological aspects of icons. Their changing role in the liturgy of the early church. The connection between the uses of icons and the uses of statues to local gods before Christianity.'

'Eh?'

'You know, ancient Greek cities had their protecting deity, with Athens and Athena, and so on. Christian Greek cities and towns had their own saint or particular representation of Christ or the Virgin or whoever, which also had a protecting role. Now, was this a mere transference of old patterns of worship and belief on to new forms, or was it more complicated than that? Fascinating subject, really. He published a small note in the *Journal of Byzantine Studies* a year or so ago. He sent me a copy. I'd be happy to let you have it, if it would help.'

He was beginning to get into second gear here, and Flavia had this feeling that he might go on for a long time unless diverted. Not that she didn't find it interesting, but . . .

'Thank you. Jonathan? Could you look through this stuff? Try and find out what Burckhardt was after?'

'Apart from icons?'

She nodded.

Argyll cocked his head and put his hand to his ear.

'Please?' she said.

'My pleasure.'

It was half past four, it had been a long day and it was far from over. Flavia had to see Mrs Verney at six and somehow she felt it wasn't going to be an easy meeting. At the moment there wasn't anything urgent to do, and she felt suddenly exhausted again. Once back in her office, she considered doing some paperwork, then the call of the sofa became loud and insistent. She lay down for a few seconds, curled up, and fell fast asleep.

One of those deep, drugged sleeps as well, where you are aware of being all but dead, know you should wake up but can't do anything about it. And where you wake up sluggish and disoriented, especially if it is sudden and unexpected. Such as when you are brought round by someone shouting loudly and furiously in your ear.

'Go away,' she murmured, wanting nothing in the entire world except to be left alone to sleep some more.

'I will not,' she heard. 'I want some answers and I want them damn fast. And as there's no real policeman here, you'll have to do.'

She forced open an eye, focused vaguely and after her brain had clanked ineffectually for a few seconds not only recognized Dan Menzies, but even recalled something about him.

Waking herself and pulling herself upright was one of the bravest things she had ever done.

'Now listen . . .' Menzies said, pointing aggressively at her.

She couldn't even feel annoyed yet. Instead, she waved her hand vaguely and staggered out into the corridor and to the coffee machine where she downed an espresso in a gulp. Then she went and stole one of the strong cigarettes Paolo habitually smoked, lit it, hacked away at the sudden shock to her throat, and felt human again.

'Now,' she said when she got back to her office. 'What can I do for you, Mr Menzies?'

Oddly, she had behaved perfectly. Menzies had worked himself into a fit of indignation before he arrived, but being treated so dismissively by someone who seemed not at all alarmed by his rage threw him off his stride. In truth, Flavia would, in other circumstances, have been a little more sympathetic. She took it for granted that Alberto had found him. It is not pleasant, if you are quietly restoring away, to be hauled off for questioning about a murder. A less volatile person than Menzies might well be annoyed.

He thrust a copy of the latest paper at her, and waggled it under her nose. She dutifully took it and read. It was another attack, containing details of the robbery in San Giovanni and vaguely suggesting that if you let American restorers into your house then naturally you'd expect to find bits of cutlery missing from the cabinet. Bartolo at it again. She'd phoned him to complain about what he was doing, but he had denied all knowledge of it. Lying through his teeth. She half considered dusting off his file to dig out one or two little matters to confront him with. A warning shot to indicate her displeasure. But she didn't have time. He would have to wait until this was cleared up.

She did wish Bottando was around. He'd been spending his time on the phone and sloping around embassies seeing what, if any, real support there was for this project he'd been put in charge of. Normally he would have dealt with someone like Menzies. One of the aspects of his job she didn't welcome taking on. Perhaps she should go with him after all. There are advantages to being subordinate.

'Hmm,' she said usefully. What else was she meant to say?

'And what do you imagine will be in there tomorrow, eh? Once you've rung them up? They'll accuse me of murder next. I know it.'

'Well . . .'

They wouldn't, of course. All they'd do was link the various bits together. Menzies has a reputation for assaulting people. Menzies sees Burckhardt two days before the murder. Burckhardt dies. No other suspects. Leave it to the reader to decide. Bartolo would make sure all the right people at the Beni Artistici saw it.

Menzies was not impressed. 'I've spent the last three hours being asked stupid questions. Did I shoot Peter Burckhardt? Good God, it's disgraceful. What are you going to do about it?'

She blinked a couple of times and yawned. 'What am I meant to do?'

'Stop it, of course. I tell you, if you don't . . .'

'Free press, Mr Menzies,' she said wearily. 'I can't stop anything. You should see what they say about us on occasion.'

'You can stop feeding them the information.'

'Oh, not again . . .'

'Look,' he said, jabbing his finger at the article. '"Police sources say . . ." That's you, isn't it? How else could they know all these details? They must have come from you.'

'I'm sorry, but . . .'

'They didn't come from me, and Father Jean assures me no one in San Giovanni has talked to the press. That leaves you. And I'm telling you to stop.'

'I can assure you as well, if you like. I have not said a word to any journalist, about this or anything else. And I'd be very surprised if anyone else has either.'

'You think they got all this detail by inspired guesswork?' he shouted, getting redder in the face and beginning to work himself into his old frenzy again. 'Don't give me that. I'm not a complete fool. I'm going to complain –'

'To your old friend the ambassador. I know. If you must, you must. I can't stop you. But it won't do any good. We

118

never give details of a case to the press if we can help it. And we haven't in this case either.'

'Who did, then?'

'I've no idea, and frankly, at the moment, I couldn't care less. I would suggest someone from the carabinieri; they're talkative, but . . .'

'There you are then.'

'But,' she continued. 'If I remember rightly the first story appeared before the carabinieri had anything to do with the place. So it can't be them.'

'So what are you going to do?'

'Nothing,' she said. 'You're on your own, I'm afraid.'

'Thank you very much.'

'What do you expect? The only thing I can do is find out what's been going on. And to help with that I might as well ask you a few questions, as you're here. Sit down.'

'I'll do no such thing . . .'

'Sit down!' she shouted suddenly, her patience snapping. Menzies, completely taken by surprise, did as he was told.

'Thank you,' she said. Then summoned Giulia from next door.

'What's she here for?'

'To take notes. Now, let's go through this stage by stage, shall we? Why didn't you mention Burckhardt when we interviewed you the day before.'

He squirmed a little. 'Why should I have done?'

'Icon dealer in a church the day before an icon is stolen? That didn't strike you as being important?'

'At the time, no.'

'Why not?'

'Because I didn't know who he was.'

Flavia looked scornful. 'You beat him up in Toronto.'

'I did not. I simply threw a little water at him.'

'It was still in the glass.'

'I didn't mean to. I got carried away.'

'Exactly my point. And, no doubt, the point the papers will be making.'

'I saw him for five minutes. And I didn't remember who he was until later.'

'Come now.'

'It's true. I don't know anything about icons or icon dealers. I didn't know who Burckhardt was. In Toronto, all I knew was that some little squirt in the audience dared to criticize me from a standpoint of total ignorance, and renewed his attack afterwards. Maybe I had had a little too much to drink. But it was such a minor incident, I forgot all about it. I vaguely recognized him in the church. But I only remembered when the carabinieri told me he was dead and showed me a photograph.'

Flavia grunted. There was such a combination of injury, anger and embarrassment coming from the man she doubted anyone could fake such a cocktail. She didn't necessarily believe him, but there was nothing to be done about it at the moment.

'When Burckhardt appeared in the church, did he walk straight up to you?'

'I don't know. I was concentrating. I only noticed him when I heard him behind me.'

'He didn't look at anything in particular?'

He shook his head. 'I wasn't paying attention. I think he was down at the far end of the church, by the main door, but I'm not sure.'

'Did he seem in a good mood?'

Menzies thought. 'It's difficult to say with someone you don't know. But, yes, he seemed OK. Seemed quite happy.'

'Had you examined the picture? The icon. You were going to clean it.'

'I'd looked it over.'

'And?'

'And decided it would take longer to clean than it probably merited. As far as I could see it was very old, hadn't been looked after well and was in terrible condition. It had had woodworm at some stage and had been treated, by immersion. A long time ago. The treatment had put a thick brown coating over the painting so you could barely see it. It would have been phenomenally difficult to get that off without destroying the painting entirely. Some of it had gone anyway. For all my reputation, I don't believe in doing things unnecessarily or unless I'm sure I can do it safely. In this case I was simply going to clean the surface, treat it again for rot and reinforce it. It would have been something of a risk just taking it out of the frame.'

'Which someone has now done.'

'Hmm? Oh no. I mean the inner frame. There were two. The outer one of gold and silver laid on wood, and an inner supporting frame. The second one was taken as well.'

'Does that surprise you?'

'Not at all. The outer frame came off easily. The inner one was fixed much more securely. It would have been difficult to remove it, and much safer not to.'

'I see. Now, how did Burckhardt get in? Was the main door open?'

'No. It never is. He must have come in through the usual entrance.'

'Which means ringing the bell and someone letting him in?'

'I suppose. Unless he arrived with someone who has a key. Everyone in the place has a key.'

'No one we've talked to let him in or heard him ring.'

Menzies shrugged. 'Must have pole-vaulted over the wall, then.'

'Thank you, Mr Menzies.' She stood up and showed him to the door before he could begin to move the conversation back to newspapers and journalists. 'I may very well need to talk to you again in the next few days. I'll come and see you at the monastery if need be.'

Surprisingly, he walked out quite meekly, and left her alone. She sighed heavily, shook her head, then glanced at her watch. Her heart sank. Menzies had distracted her from her real business. It was ten to six. Time for Mrs Verney. She was not looking forward to it.

Flavia had persuaded Paolo to pick Mary Verney up from her hotel and bring her in, then had her kept in a small room in the basement for a couple of hours to meditate on her sins, whatever they were. She did not think Mrs Verney had stolen the picture. She didn't know what Mrs Verney had done. She merely knew that she had done something, and hoped that a spot of peace and quiet in a dank and airless room would persuade her to explain. Somehow, though, she doubted it.

For all that she was on the verge of panic, Mrs Verney seemed perfectly unconcerned on the surface. She did not relish the idea of jail; she resented the fact that pressure from others had landed her in this position and, above all, she was terrified that unless she delivered the goods, her granddaughter would suffer. And at the moment, she was completely at a loss. The picture had gone, and all she had to show for it was a hefty stash of money found in a left-luggage box. While Flavia wanted the interview to bring some enlightenment, Mrs Verney awaited the conversation with very similar hopes.

Like a good prisoner, though, she sat quietly as Flavia came in and waited for her to begin the questioning.

'Now then, I have to tell you that you are in serious trouble.'

'Really? Why is that?'

'Let me summarize. Yesterday morning, a painting was stolen from the monastery of San Giovanni on the Aventino. Do you know the building?'

A smile of the sort that indicated that she thought setting such an easy trap was, well, a bit insulting, really.

'Of course I do. Which painting was stolen? The Caravaggio, or the little icon in the corner? I saw them for the first time some twenty years ago. I lived in Rome briefly and was a very assiduous tourist.'

'The icon.'

'Goodness,' she said, then offered no more.

'Do you know anything about it?'

'Should I?'

'I'm asking you.'

'So you are.'

'Are early-morning walks a speciality?'

Mrs Verney gave a brief twitch of a smile as she spotted the clue she'd been waiting for. She now had a measure of how much the police had found out.

'When I can't sleep, they are. To be up at six o'clock is a privilege of age. Especially in Rome. And, since that is what you seem to be getting at, yes, I was walking on the Aventino. Do you want the whole story?'

'What do you think?'

'As I say, I went for an early-morning walk. And – just by chance – found myself walking past the monastery.'

'Oh, come now,' Flavia said. 'You expect me to believe that?'

'It's true,' she said with a fine mixture of surprise and indignation at being doubted. 'Anyway, I saw a man come down the steps from the church. The door was open, so I thought that maybe they had early-morning services, or something like that.'

'And you felt a burst of piety come over you?'

'More like nostalgia, I think. As I say, I'd visited the place many years ago, when I was young and fancy-free. And what could be more natural than to revisit it?'

'What indeed?'

'So I did. And found this poor man lying on the ground, with blood streaming out of his head. Now, I'm a good citizen, most of the time. I did what I could for the poor soul, then went straight away to phone the police for assistance. How is he, by the way?'

'He'll recover, we think.'

'There you are then. And rather than being thanked, here I am being interrogated as some sort of suspect. I must say, I am not happy about it.'

'Dear me. I suppose you can explain why you were so modest about receiving thanks for your considerate act?'

'Do I need to? Heaven only knows what Jonathan has told you about me. But naturally I thought you would be suspicious if I was found there, however innocently, at such an early hour. In the circumstances. So I thought it best not to complicate the issue.'

'I see. Now, what time was this?'

She grew vague. 'I couldn't really say. After six, before seven. Maybe.'

'We have witnesses that it was about six-forty-five.'

'Must have been, then.'

'And the phone call was logged at seven-forty. That's a long time to find a phone.'

She shook her head evenly. 'Not really. There aren't any bars open, and there aren't many public phones in Rome. I went as fast as I could.'

'I see. Now, this man, did you recognize him?'

'No. Why should I have done? Who is he?'

'Was. A man called Peter Burckhardt. A dealer.'

'Was?'

'He's dead. Someone shot him.'

For the first time the unconcerned mask slipped. She hadn't known that, and doesn't like it, Flavia thought. How very interesting. What is she up to?

'Dear me.'

'Dear me, indeed. We are now investigating a murder, an assault and a theft. And you are right in the middle of the investigation.'

'You think I had something to do with this? When was the poor man killed?'

'We think yesterday. About midday, give or take an hour. I suppose you can tell me where you were?'

'Absolutely. I was in the Barberini, then I had lunch at my hotel, and then I went shopping. I can give you all the receipts, which I imagine have time stamps on them. They usually do, nowadays.'

'We'll check them.' Not that there was much point. She knew they'd stand up.

'Can I go?'

'No.'

'What more do you want from me?'

'Answers.'

'I've answered everything you've asked so far.'

'I have a problem.'

'I'll happily listen if it will help.'

'Perhaps it will. You see, I know that you are a thief. What's more, I know that you are one of the most accomplished thieves I've ever come across. What was it? Thirty or so major thefts, and never a hint of suspicion.'

'If you say so.'

'I do. Now, all of a sudden, you turn up in Rome. We get phone calls saying where the theft will take place. We notice you and question you. It worries me. From your past track record, you've been meticulous about planning. Never put a foot wrong. If you were involved in the theft of that icon I would have expected it to vanish without trace and without warning. And without violence. And I would have also expected that, when something went wrong, you would abandon everything and go home. Instead we were alerted in advance, there's blood everywhere and you are still here. As I say, it makes me think.'

'The obvious conclusion, surely, is that I am telling the truth, and that none of this has anything to do with me at all.'

Flavia snorted. 'I don't think so.'

'But you can't come up with anything better.'

'We'll see.'

'You're going to have to let me go, then.'

'Oh, yes. We never thought of holding on to you. This was just a friendly chat. The first, I suspect, of many.'

Mary Verney stood up, waves of relief passing through her, drenched with sweat and her heart still pounding. Appalling performance, she thought. Gave too much away to that damnable policewoman. She was getting too close for comfort. Besides, she was right; this was a disaster from beginning to end.

Flavia even opened the door for her, marvelling at the woman's utter calm and insouciance as she walked out. Didn't budge an inch. Leaving her as much in the dark as she was at the start.

Progress, however, was being made at the duller and more routine end of the enquiry; Peter Burckhardt was seen leaving his hotel on the morning of his death with a man in his late thirties and getting into a car. Flavia's heart had a little skip when she heard this; because Burckhardt, bless him, had been staying in a hotel in the via Cactani. An ordinary street, a bit noisy from too much traffic, but less busy than the large, polluted thoroughfares all around it. It was a no-parking zone, and there was no obvious reason why anyone should pay any more attention to such trivialities in that quarter than they did anywhere else in the city.

Except for historical circumstance, of which Flavia fervently hoped the murderer of Burckhardt was unaware. Because just around one corner of the street was the via delle Botteghe Oscure, containing the headquarters of what had once been the Christian Democrat Party, and close to that was the place where terrorists dumped the body of Aldo Moro. It was all many years ago now; the Christian Democrats had fallen on hard times and the only memento of the former prime minister was the occasional ragged bunch of flowers left at the site where he was found.

But the police still kept close watch, fearful lest those dark days should suddenly come again. Perhaps they were more concerned now that angry voters would come to take revenge on the politicians who had deceived them for so many years, or perhaps it was simply because standing orders, once given, tend to get forgotten. All over Europe, perhaps, policemen stand and guard things for no reason except that their predecessors, and their predecessors' predecessors, stood and guarded in exactly the same place. It was no doubt apocryphal, but a colleague in Paris had once told him of a building in Neuilly-sur-Seine, the residence of a minor ambassador, which had received round-the-clock surveillance for years after the embassy moved to other accommodation and the building was turned into a brothel.

So policemen patrolled regularly, and the camera, once installed, was perhaps too expensive to take down again. It was Alberto who pointed this out to her, and suggested she came round immediately for a video show.

She got there in fifteen minutes, and was treated to the most encouraging sight she had seen for days. A terrible picture, taken at long range, and certainly not good enough for use in a court, should it ever come to that. But enough to give them an idea, to identify the type of car used, and three letters of a registration number.

'Let's see it again,' Flavia said, and they sat and watched as once more Peter Burckhardt and a man several inches taller

126

than him came down the street from the direction of the hotel and got into a Lancia.

'Doesn't look under great duress. No gun pointed at him. Nothing like that.'

'No.'

'Got the car?'

'Still checking. It should be here any moment. Have you made any progress?'

'Not really. That is, I have someone I'm desperately interested in, but I can't find any way in to her.'

'Her?'

'An Englishwoman. Who is more interested in art than she should be. The trouble is, I'm fairly certain she didn't steal the picture.'

'I thought we'd established Burckhardt did.'

'Have we? I'm not so sure. He didn't break into the place, after all. Someone opened that door from the inside for him. What's more, I'm not sure he hit Father Xavier, either.'

Flavia didn't want to go into any more details, and didn't have to, as she was interrupted by the arrival of a computer print-out. 'Bingo,' Alberto said. 'A run of luck for once.'

'What do you mean?'

'It's a rented car. Picked up at the airport last Friday by one M. K. Charanis. Greek passport, staying at the Hassler.'

'Better go and get him then. Can you rustle up some manpower?'

Flavia got home at ten, more tired than she could believe, starving to death and with a blinding headache. Argyll took one look at her, suppressed a desire to mutter about how late it was, and instead ran a bath and fetched some food. She was so exhausted she could barely eat but, after he had given her a broadside of tender loving care, she began to lose the feeling that her neck muscles were tied in knots. The bath helped too.

'We were close,' she said after telling Argyll about the hunt for Charanis, waving a sponge in the air for emphasis. 'If we'd only had a little bit of luck . . .'

It had been gruelling. The result would have been the same

whatever they'd done but, while spotting this man showed the carabinieri at their best, trying to arrest him brought out all their worst characteristics. Too many anti-terrorist training courses, that was the problem. Rather than Flavia and Alberto, with a couple of supporters, going round and knocking on the door of his hotel room, someone, somewhere – and Flavia suspected Alberto's immediate superior, who was a man with a flair for the unnecessarily melodramatic – decided now was the time to give their Los Angeles-style rapid response unit a whirl.

The result had been total chaos which – quite apart from enraging the management of one of the most expensive hotels in the country and creating a very bad impression among a large number of its guests – probably served only to warn Charanis that he had been noticed, assuming he watched the news on the television station which sent along a crew to film an entertaining display of official muscle. At least Flavia persuaded Alberto to put out some vague story about drug smugglers to try and keep them away, although she doubted it would do much good.

As for the rest of it, she had watched appalled as truck after truck of heavily armed idiots ran around waving guns, shouting into radios, getting into position so that they could interdict, negativize or otherwise arrest and render harmless a man who had, in fact, checked out of the hotel the previous evening and was nowhere to be seen.

And all they had to do was ask in the first place. May the Good Lord defend us from such imbecilities.

'That's a pity,' Argyll said when she finished and he offered her a towel.

'You can say that again.'

'Is he a regular customer?'

She shook her head. 'Not that I know of, no. Never heard of him before. We've put out enquiries to the Greek police, to see if they know anything about him. God only knows how long that will take. Last time we asked them anything the man we were interested in died of old age before we got a reply.'

'Sort of makes the case for Bottando's international bureau, doesn't it?'

'Sort of makes the case for people answering enquiries. I don't think you need set up huge expensive organizations.'

'What do you do now?'

'Go to bed, I think.'

'I mean about this icon.'

'Sit and wait. The carabinieri can look for this Charanis character; I can't do much with Mary Verney at the moment. Apart from talking to Father Xavier tomorrow there's not a lot to do.'

She dried herself, with Argyll helping, and breathed a sigh of relief. 'Human again,' she said. 'You didn't find anything interesting, did you?'

'Depends.'

'Depends on what?'

'On what you think is interesting, of course. Hang on.'

He walked out of the bathroom, letting a draught of cool night air blow in as he went, and came back a few minutes later.

'Look.' He held up a Xerox, then flicked it over to show a mass of scribbling on the other side which indicated how hard he'd been working on her behalf.

'Spirits,' he said. 'Visitations by. Anthropological study of. Structure and meaning in the magical appearance of gifts. It's an article Burckhardt published three years ago.'

'So?'

'That icon was brought by angels, remember?'

'What does it say?'

'According to this, it's a common enough story. Angels seem to have worked overtime as delivery boys in the Middle Ages. Forever running around with paintings and statues, even whole houses in the case of Loretto, and leaving them in unlikely places. The general argument is that it is often enough a folk memory with some substantial foundation.'

'Such as what?'

'The example he quotes here is a church in Spain, near the Pyrenees, which has a miraculous statue. Also delivered by an angel, according to the legend. He reckons it was donated

129

by a generous benefactor who distributed money to the poor to mark the occasion. This got confused as the generations passed and the gift of the statue became associated with the money, then it was thought that it was the statue which gave the money, so naturally it became a miracle. And the person who gave it turned into a delivering angel.'

'San Giovanni is associated with a cure for the plague.'

He nodded. 'Better food, more resistance to disease. I suppose it fits.'

'Does it say that?'

'No. That's me making it up. However, there is one reference to San Giovanni; nothing relevant, but he was obviously in the archive there once. That's interesting, don't you think?'

She nodded dubiously. 'Not much to go on, though.'

'I'm doing my best. There's a lot of stuff to digest here, you know. It's hard when you're starting from scratch.'

'And I can't think of anyone better to scratch away. Would you mind keeping on going? See if you can dig up anything more specific?'

He nodded. 'All right. But only for one reason.'

'What's that?'

He grinned at her. 'I quite enjoy it.'

13

Flavia barely got into the office the following morning when a dire message came through from Alberto. Foreign ministry, please. Now. Heavy-duty stuff indeed, the sort of thing Bottando would do. But he was not around and she was in charge. She had never been in the building before, let alone been summoned to a meeting headed by a full-blown, senior smoothie.

He also, it seemed, was not used to dealing with members of the police and managed to convey the impression very swiftly that he strongly suspected that all such people had sweaty hands and probably did not bathe all that frequently. He sat behind his desk for all the world like someone preparing to make a last stand against the barbarian hordes, and made polite but condescending conversation until the distinguished visitor was ushered in.

This was, oddly enough, a trade representative from the Greek embassy, which caused confusion all round until it was explained that just because he was a trade representative, it didn't mean he had anything to do with trade, you see.

'May I ask why the head of the department is not here, as I ordered?' the Italian said. Flavia bristled slightly, and she noticed an amused look from Alberto.

'I *am* the head of the department,' she said, and noticed how well and easily the words rolled off her tongue. 'And you ordered nothing. You asked me to come, and I agreed. Now, do I gather that you, sir, are a spy, and we're playing silly games here?' she continued, ignoring the Italian completely.

'Exactly, dear lady,' he enthused. 'Silly games. Exactly

131

that.' He gave her a large stage wink as he nodded approvingly.

'Good. I'm glad we've got all that sorted out,' said the Italian in a suit. 'Perhaps we might proceed. I don't have all day, and Signor Fostiropoulos is a busy man as well.'

'That's a pity,' Flavia said. 'We have all the time in the world. What's a murder or two, after all?'

'That's what we're here for, is it not?' Fostiropoulos said.

'I don't know. Why are we here?'

'You have been making enquiries, about a Signor Charanis.'

'We have.'

'And I am here to inform you that you have made a bad mistake. The idea that he could be in any way involved in any disreputable activity is quite ludicrous.'

'I don't even know who he is.'

'He is a very wealthy man. Huge interests, all absolutely above board. He is a greatly respected man.'

'And a powerful one, if he sends you along to defend him.'

'Don't be flippant. Or rude, signorina,' said the Italian diplomat.

Fostiropoulos nodded. 'Quite all right. He is indeed powerful. I have come along merely to save you from wasting your time on a fruitless line of enquiry.'

'He wouldn't collect paintings, would he?'

'Very much so. But that is hardly a crime.'

'You still haven't told me why you are so sure it's fruitless.'

'Firstly because Signor Charanis is at this moment in Athens, and has been since last week. Secondly because the man you are interested in is in his thirties while Signor Charanis is seventy-two. And thirdly because it is simply absurd to consider the idea that he would ever consider doing such a ridiculous thing. He could buy this picture – could buy the entire monastery, in fact – out of his small change.'

'I see. Nonetheless, we do have a rented car with our victim getting into it, and it was rented in the name of Charanis.'

'Criminals have been known to use pseudonyms in the past.'

'Have you seen his photograph?' Flavia handed over the grainy reproduction taken from the video machine.

Fostiropoulos took it and, she noted, kept it. The difference between a spy telling the truth and a spy telling a lie was, she supposed, difficult to detect; and Fostiropoulos had probably had years of practice. Flavia's instincts, more than her observation, told her the man instantly began covering something.

'I don't recognize him. Certainly not Signor Charanis, who is over seventy.'

'I see.'

The Greek stood up. 'That's my contribution done, then. I must be going. I do very much hope that you find this man, whoever he may be. And that you will find that I have been of assistance to you. I'm sorry to bring this meeting to an end so swiftly, but I think there is nothing else to say on the subject. It was a pleasure to meet you, signorina.'

He nodded to Alberto, who had not been successful in saying anything at all, and did the same to the diplomat, who showed him out with all due ceremony, then shut the door and breathed a sigh of relief.

'Goodness,' he said. 'That was close.'

'What was?'

'We very nearly had a major incident on our hands there. Do you have any idea how powerful this man is? Fortunately, swift action avoided it.'

'What major incident? Come to think of it, what swift action? I didn't notice anything.'

'He was very upset.'

'No, he wasn't.'

'I hope you appreciate his consideration in coming here.'

'No one has thanked us for our consideration in coming here yet,' she snapped. 'We're not responsible to you, you know. Besides, he didn't say anything at all.'

The diplomat eyed her coldly. Flavia eyed him back. She didn't understand why she was behaving like this, but she undoubtedly enjoyed it. Did Bottando enjoy being obstreperous so much? Was it one of the hidden perks of the job?

'What could he say? You go around levelling baseless accusations which turn out to be a tissue of nonsense to conceal the gross mistakes you've committed, and you expect him to help? A lesser man than Fostiropoulos would have lodged a complaint at ministerial level and left it at that.'

'In that case you people are complete idiots.'

'I beg your pardon?'

'And you are a bigger idiot than most. We make a routine enquiry – which normally takes weeks to process – and within twenty-four hours we have a top-level meeting with some Greek spook, who comes round here like a bat out of hell to point us in another direction. Doesn't that strike even you as a bit odd?'

'No.'

'I'm quite prepared to accept that our thirty-ish suspect is not a seventy-two-year-old millionaire. So ready to accept it that this meeting was unnecessary. So what was it in aid of? Eh?'

A shrug, and the meeting ended. A few seconds later, Flavia and Alberto found themselves once more in the empty corridor outside.

'Moron,' she said when the door to the office had shut. 'What a waste of time.'

'Do you believe him or not? Fostiropoulos, I mean,' Alberto asked.

'I believe what he said. It's what he didn't say that bothers me. Still, we're just not going to get any help from that quarter, I'm afraid. Back to work.'

They walked down the stairs, and queued at the desk in the lobby to hand in their security passes and sign out. The receptionist checked the passes, ticked them off and said, 'This was left for you, signorina.'

She handed Flavia a small envelope; she opened it and read:

'Dear Signorina di Stefano,
'I trust you will do me the great honour of joining me for a drink at Castello this evening at six p.m.
'Fostiropoulos.'

She groaned. 'Of all the luck. Not only do I not get any useful information, I have to spend the evening being oozed over.'

'Don't go,' suggested Alberto.

'I'd better. You never know. I might squeeze something out of him. If I don't, I might risk another international incident. I must say, I do hate the personal touch. Especially when touch is likely to be the operative word.'

'It's a tough life in the police. Now you know why they paid Bottando so much.'

'You heard about that, did you?'

'Oh, yes. Word travels, you know. I hope it doesn't mean too many changes. What happens to you?'

'I've been offered the job of acting chief.'

'I'm impressed. Ma'am.' He bowed politely.

She grinned. 'What do you think? Could I do it well?'

He thought carefully.

'Oh, come on,' she said.

'Of course you could. Although if you become as rude to everyone as you were to that diplomat man they'll go begging for Bottando to come back.'

'Was I that rude?'

'Not diplomatic, no.'

'Oh. I was a bit nervous.'

'Try smiling coquettishly next time you tell people they're contemptible morons with brains the size of a pea.'

'You think?'

'It might help.'

She nodded. 'Maybe you're right. I need to practise.'

'You'll get the hang of it.'

'Now, tell me. What are you up to today?'

Alberto groaned. 'What do you think? Miserable routine, checking hotels and airports and credit cards, mixed in liberally with miserable enquiries, explaining how it is that we ended up deploying thirty-five people in six vans with enough weaponry to fight a civil war in an attempt to arrest someone who wasn't there. And, what's more, telling it all to a large group of people who make their career out of telling other people how things should be done. Largely because they were so bad at doing it themselves that they had to be taken off active work to safeguard the public.'

Flavia nodded. 'I thought so.'

'What about you?'

'Do you know, I'm not entirely certain. I'll go to the hospital to see whether Father Xavier has come round and can talk. If he has, I'll see what he has to say. If not, I have a horrible feeling I'll spend the day sitting at my desk twiddling my thumbs hoping something will turn up.'

Jonathan Argyll, in contrast to Flavia's mood of vacillation, set off the same morning with high hopes of accomplishing something useful. He had never been very interested in the nuts and bolts of Flavia's type of crime, the how and the who of policing. Like all people who did not have the task of actually locking people up, he found the why of it all very much more interesting. In his view, everything else should be subordinated to that, and it would make crime a far more fascinating prospect. Of course, it wouldn't result in many arrests, but that was not his concern. How the painting of the icon was stolen was simple enough, after all. Someone went in and took it. Easy. Who stole it was more interesting but offered only a couple of possibilities, judging by what Flavia had told him. *Why* they stole it, on the other hand – now that was a bit of a puzzle, as far as he could see. Just the sort of thing for a subtle, complex mind.

This flying painting, borne by angels, had not excited over-much interest in the past few centuries; he had woken up that morning with the task of discovering why that situation had changed as his project for the day. For the week, if necessary, as he had given his charges a long essay to write which should keep their brows furrowed for several days.

He hadn't told Flavia, being someone who liked to spring his surprises fully formed, but he reckoned he had an idea already. Not a big one, but something. It was a question, he thought, of what triggered Burckhardt into action. Whether that would help in getting the picture back was another matter, of course.

He explained his quest to Father Jean when he arrived at San Giovanni.

'You may look with pleasure, if you think it will help in any way,' the old man said.

'Do you have a record of what this man looked at?'

'Which man?'

'Burckhardt. The dead man. The one in the river. He cited some of your archives in an article, so unless he was a total fraud, he must have used them. I thought it might be useful to know what he looked at.'

Luck was not with him. Father Jean shook his head. 'I'm sorry.'

'You don't keep records?'

'Oh, no. On the rare occasions someone comes here, we just give them a key to the archive room.'

'Is there a catalogue of the documents?'

Father Jean smiled. 'After a fashion, but it's not very satisfactory. In fact, it's unusable.'

'Still useful.'

'I'm afraid not.'

'Why's that?'

'Because it was all in the head of Father Charles, who knew the papers backwards and forwards.'

'And he's dead, I suppose.'

'Oh, no. Full of life, but he is over eighty and his mind is not what it was.'

'You mean he's senile?'

'I'm afraid so. He has his lucid moments, but they are becoming more and more rare.'

'And he never made a catalogue?'

'No. We planned to get it all down, and would have done so except that Father Charles had a stroke and was put out of commission. If we ever get a catalogue, we'll be starting from scratch. And I'm afraid it is not a very high priority.'

'That makes life more difficult. Is there any chance of seeing him anyway? Just in case?'

'Probably. But I can't take you to him myself. We have our latest crisis to deal with.'

'What's that?'

137

Father Jean shook his head. 'We seem to have a popular religious revival on our hands.'

'Isn't that good?'

'Do you know, I'm not sure. I'm afraid the order spends so much time running hospitals and schools that we are no longer sure what to do with religious feeling. Especially when there are signs that it is superstitious and idolatrous.'

'I'm not with you.'

'That icon. You heard, no doubt, that it was a sort of local protector. Guarding the quarter against plague and bombs?'

Argyll nodded.

'All that had died out, of course. Except for a few old people like Signora Graziani, it was hardly remembered. So I thought, anyway. For some reason the theft has brought it all to the surface again. They're like that, the Romans. However much you may think they have become brash and material-istic, scratch the surface . . .'

'So what's going on?'

'Everything. Late-night vigils asking the icon to return. Genuine fear, it seems, that the quarter is exposed to danger by its absence. Confessions tagged to the locked door hoping that a genuine show of contrition will make it relent and come back . . .'

'But it was stolen.'

Father Jean shook his head. 'It seems not. It seems that in the minds of a surprising number of people here, it got up and walked out on its own to indicate Our Lady's displeasure. And will not return until she is satisfied everybody is in a properly repentant frame of mind. Obviously, I've read about phenomena like this in history books, but I never thought that I'd witness such a thing. It's genuine, you know; absolutely genuine. The trouble is, that the order is being blamed.'

'What for?'

'For cutting Our Lady off from her people. Closing the doors. It's all General Bottando's fault, in fact, as he was the one who told us to lock the doors.'

'That's his job.'

'Yes. And I'm coming to believe that it should have been

138

our job to ignore him. So you see, we have to discuss this, and work out what to do.'

'Of course. Perhaps if you could tell me where this Father Charles is? If there's any chance of getting something out of him . . .'

'Oh, that's easy enough. He's here. We look after our own, you know.'

Father Jean looked at his old watch, and grunted. 'I can take you to him quickly. If he's alert, I'll leave you. Then you'll have to fend for yourself.'

Very quickly, he headed off down corridors, up stairs, mounting higher and higher in the building until the decorations gave way and was replaced by older, blistered and peeling paint. The windows got smaller and smaller, and the ever more narrow doors became looser on their hinges.

'Not lavish, I'm afraid,' Father Jean observed. 'But he refused to move.'

'He wants to live here?'

'He has done for sixty years and refused to budge even when he was the superior. We wanted to give him a lighter room on the ground floor. It would have made it easier for him to get around, and the doctors thought that more cheerful surroundings might help his mind. But he wouldn't have it. He never did like change.'

He knocked on the door, waited for a moment then pushed it open.

'Charles?' he said softly into the gloom. 'Are you awake?'

'I am,' an old voice said. 'I am awake.'

'I have a visitor for you. He wants to ask about the archives.'

There was a long pause and a creaking of a chair from the other side of the darkened room. Argyll noticed the strong, musty smell of underventilation and extreme old age in the air, and braced himself for a difficult and unrewarding encounter.

'Show him in, then.'

'Are you able to talk to him?'

'What have I just been doing?'

'You're in luck,' Father Jean whispered. 'He'll probably lapse after a while, but you might get something out of him.'

139

'Don't whisper, Jean,' came the voice, cross now. 'Send me this visitor, and get him to open the shutters so I can see what I have to deal with. And leave me in peace.'

Father Jean gave an affectionate smile and padded softly out of the room, leaving Argyll, oddly nervous, alone. He stumbled across the room to reach the wall and opened both windows and shutters. The morning sunlight streamed in with such intensity it was almost like being hit.

The light revealed a sparse, austere room, with a bed, two chairs, a desk and a shelf of books. On the wall was a crucifix, and from the ceiling hung a light with a single, unshaded light bulb. In one of the chairs sat Father Charles, looking at him calmly and with the infinite patience of age. Argyll stood still while the inspection was on, not daring to sit down until invited.

He was surprised by what he saw. He had half expected an wizened little man, as pitiful as old age can be, doddering and pathetic. Instead, the sight presented to him could hardly have been more different. Father Charles was still big, and must have been enormous when young. Barrel-chested, powerful and tall, even in ill-health, he dominated the room and made the chair he was sitting on seem far too small. More important still was his expression, which flickered with interest as it studied Argyll's face with care, taking all the time he wanted, conscious that nothing would happen until he was ready to allow the interview to proceed.

After a while, and having established through his silence who was in control, Father Charles nodded to himself.

'And you are . . . ?'

Argyll introduced himself, speaking loudly and clearly.

'Sit down, Signor Argyll. And there is no need to talk like that. I am neither deaf nor stupid.'

Argyll looked embarrassed.

'And don't look embarrassed, either. I am, as Father Jean has no doubt told you, not what I was. But much of the time I am perfectly *compos mentis*. If I feel myself slipping I will tell you, and bring the conversation to an end. I am too proud, I'm afraid, to relish people seeing me in the state such deterioration brings. You would not enjoy it either.'

'By all means,' Argyll said.

'So, young man, tell me what you want.'

Argyll began to explain.

'Ah, yes, Our Lady from the East. Would you mind telling me why you are interested?'

Argyll explained about the theft. As he talked, the old man shook his head with interest.

'No,' he said. 'It cannot be.'

'I'm afraid it is.'

'Then you are wrong. She cannot – will not – leave this house. It is impossible, unless' – here he smiled to himself – 'unless world politics has changed markedly since I read the newspaper. And that was only yesterday, you know.'

So much for his *mentis*. More *composted* than *compos*.

'She will reveal herself in her own good time. Have no fear.'

There was no point arguing about it. Argyll tried a more oblique approach. 'Nonetheless, your colleagues are very concerned, and want me to help. For their sake, even if it is unnecessary . . .'

Charles's face twitched with a little smile. 'I am not mad, sir. I talk perfect sense.'

'Of course you do,' Argyll agreed heartily.

'And don't patronize me. You are much too young for that.'

'Sorry.'

Father Charles leaned forward and studied Argyll's face. 'Yes. I remember you. I have little time, I fear, sir. You had better tell me your business so that I can answer when I am able.'

Argyll explained about Burckhardt, and how he thought the dealer had come in pursuit because of something he'd been told which might have come from the monastery archives.

'I know it's a long shot. But if I can discover what it was, then I might be able to find out why he was so interested, you see,' he said.

Father Charles nodded to himself awhile, and Argyll was afraid he was disappearing into his own mind. Then he looked up with a faint smile on his face. 'Mr Burckhardt, yes. I remember him. He was here last year. I'm afraid I was a little wicked with him.'

'How was that?'

'A mechanic, if you see what I mean.'

Argyll shook his head. He didn't see at all.

'Interested in style only and concerned to explain everything. No appreciation of the power of these images. If people pray to her, then he saw it as a quaint example of outmoded superstition. If legends were attached to her, then he wanted to find a rational explanation which took away all the miraculous. He was cruel to other people's beliefs. And above all he used them to make money for himself. So I'm afraid I was not as open with him as I should have been. He had to do his own work, and missed very much.'

'Oh.'

'In your case, I believe I will perhaps let you find what he did not. Do you know why?'

'Because the painting has vanished and I might help to get it back?'

He shook his head. 'Oh, no. I have told you; she does not need your help. She will return when she wants.'

Argyll smiled.

'It is because you are kind, and you do not wish people to know it always. Often, when I am able, I go to the church to pray. I have done so several times a day for more than half a century and I like the quiet. I was there a few days ago, and I saw you come in and light a candle to her. And look embarrassed when Signora Graziani thanked you. It gave her great pleasure.'

'My Protestant conscience,' Argyll said. 'It doesn't always approve.'

'It was kind, nonetheless. To Signora Graziani as much as anyone.'

It was a long time since anyone had accused Argyll to his face of being kind, and he wasn't entirely certain how to react. He thought that saying 'thank you' might be appropriate; so he did.

'I don't intend to compliment. I merely state a fact which

makes me believe I can trust you with some of the documents I decided not to give to Burckhardt.'

'I'm very grateful.'

'Now, give me a piece of paper and a pen, and I will tell you what to look for. I would help, but I am afraid that my mind is beginning to play tricks on me again. You must leave me now, I'm afraid.'

Argyll did as he was told, and Father Charles wrote quickly on it, and handed the paper back. 'Fourth cabinet, third drawer down. At the back. Now, leave me, please.'

'It's very kind of you . . .'

He waved his arm impatiently. 'Leave me now. Please, go away quickly.'

Argyll spent the next eight hours reading with painful slowness; all the documents were in Latin, and he had always been painfully bad at Latin. But he felt obliged to do it himself and not call in help, and so he sweated his way through gerunds and gerundives, dictionary by his side, moving forward word by word and phrase by phrase, until he was sure he was getting the translation right.

The trouble was the documents were in no particular order; they had been gathered together almost at random, as far as he could see. A page of inductions into the monastery; pages from the daily record of events; transcripts from the papal ports, bills of loading and unloading of ships from the year 1453. A record of a papal address. A note of a nobleman's landholdings. Remarks on religious festivals, mainly to do with the festivals of the Virgin. Argyll was out of his depth. It was obvious that it was all important and relevant; Father Charles had done everything except spell it out to him word by word. But he still couldn't figure it out.

But he felt captured by the old man's spirit, and would have felt it a betrayal to call in some expert from the classics department, or a medievalist who would have been able to run through the manuscripts in a matter of minutes and tell him exactly what they contained. This had been given to him and him alone, and it was surely not too much to ask that he work it out by himself. Even if it took today, tomorrow and the entire weekend as well.

He had a cigarette break, sitting in the sun on a stone in the courtyard, thinking absently about what he had read so far, trying but failing to make sense of it. Perhaps the second or third bundles would give a clue. He noticed Menzies coming and going in the church. He waved, but didn't feel like talking. Father Jean came out of the building and drove away in a tiny little Fiat. And from the outside he dimly heard the sound of singing.

Such was his mood that it took several minutes before he realized that this was strange, and even more before he got up to see what was happening. Going out of the door, he looked up the street to the church entrance, and saw a group of twenty people, mostly women, mainly old, standing and chanting. Some were holding crosses, or rosaries, and around them was a second group, this time of onlookers, among them a photographer and a man Argyll vaguely recognized as a reporter. He walked over and asked what was going on.

'They say it's a vigil,' the reporter said with a faint smile of bemusement.

'Goodness.'

'They are going to stay until the painting is brought back.'

'It may be a long wait.'

The reporter nodded, and stared glumly at the crowd, wondering how he should angle his story. Touching tale of piety? Or whimsical story of Roman superstition, played for laughs. A tough one.

Argyll left him to his dilemma and wandered back into the monastery in case the reporter thought that he might have some inside knowledge.

Flavia had anticipated having to wait for Fostiropoulos in Castello's that evening, and wasn't disappointed. She was on her third cigarette and second bowl of nuts before he bounced in, beaming happily. He kissed her enthusiastically on each cheek, twice, for all the world as though she was his closest friend, and ordered champagne. Here we go, she thought. One of those evenings. Still, it was good champagne.

144

'What do you think of our mutual friend di Antonio?' he asked as he concentrated on filling the glasses.

'Who?'

'The man who organized the meeting this morning.'

'Oh. Him. Not a lot.'

'A fusspot. A major fusspot. All diplomatic services have them, I'm afraid. File marked, "not to be allowed out of Rome". A pity, but there you are. That's government for you. Over the years, it accumulates all sorts of strange people. The fusspots, the incompetents, the downright malevolent. Don't you think? They silt up the works, but for some reason no one ever thinks of getting rid of them.'

'You speak from experience.'

He smiled. 'Believe me. Personally, I think there should be a revolution every twenty-five years. Clear everyone out, and start again. Mao was right, although it's a bit unfashionable to say that nowadays.'

'From my experience, you always end up with the same people in charge again,' Flavia said, vaguely aware that there might be a sort of under-conversation going on here. 'However much you try to get rid of them.'

'Of course. But not all. And you can always recognize them. The style remains the same. Take my line of business.'

'Spying.'

'Trade, Flavia, trade. You don't mind if I call you Flavia?'

'Not at all.'

'Gyorgos. Anyway, you see, in the good old days, we were worried about spies and communists and all that sort of thing. We knew what we were doing and why we were doing it. Guarding the flanks of Europe, I think. Then, pouf! All change. Strange things start to happen.'

'Such as?'

'It's a bit odd. People lose their sense of orientation. The old certainties vanish, so they go back to even older ones. A traditional enemy vanishes, so they concentrate on one which is even more traditional. Do you see what I mean?'

'Not a clue.'

'Really? You surprise me.'

'Have another go.'

145

'Old Charanis. A strange man. What do you know about him?'

'Not much; I've only ever heard of him as an art collector and man about the galleries, although I thought he'd given that up. I remember a dealer complaining about it once. Didn't he announce he'd more pictures than he knew what to do with?'

Fostiropoulos smiled. 'That's correct. He got old, began to think about mortality and became pious. And gave up old masters and has turned instead to donating works of art to churches. Such as icons. But he's even given that up now.'

'Still, even you must admit it is something more than a coincidence.'

'Perhaps. He's an odd man. The strangest thing about him is that he is a fervent democrat.'

'Why is that strange?'

'When we had the coup back in the sixties, he was against the colonels. About the only member of the hundred families who own Greece who was. Admittedly it was because he thought it was bad for business, but also because in his soul he's a romantic. Greece the cradle of democracy. Virulently anti-communist, but no supporter of these nationalistic thugs who took over.'

'So he's as pure as the driven snow.'

'Used to be an obsessive collector, so they say. With magnificent results, as well. The national museum is trying to get his collection left to them in his will. It's a hard slog, not least because old habits die hard in someone like him. He wants so many tax breaks and concessions and contracts in return that it's not yet certain it'll work. On top of that, so I'm told, the director of the museum is balking a little at one or two pieces he owns.'

'Oh, yes?'

'Origins a bit doubtful. No one knows where they came from, or how they got there. Still, that's irrelevant.'

'Is it?'

'It is. Because he hasn't bought anything for five years or more and refuses absolutely even to consider buying more.'

'What a pity.'

'He spends all his time in retreat. Of course, because he's a bit of a megalomaniac he has his own monastery, and a cell for meditation which is equipped with a satellite link and fax machine, but his heart is in the right place, as much as he has one.'

'Where is this?'

'Near Mount Athos. He spends more and more of his time there. Even dresses like something out of the Middle Ages. Rumour has it that he is repenting for his sins. He's got a big job on his hands.'

'So we can forget him? Is that what you're telling me? Same as this morning? So why this meeting?'

'For the selfish delight of your beautiful company, dear signorina. And to point out that you might, as computers tell us to do these days, refine your search a little.'

'I know I'm being obtuse . . .'

'Not at all. Not at all. You have been looking for someone called Charanis.'

'Oh, I see. Brother, son, daughter, cousin?'

'He has difficulties with his children, poor man, although I can't imagine he was much fun to have as a father. Smothered them with material goods but, unfortunately, expected them to deserve it. He is absurdly competitive himself and, so it is said, took particular delight in winning, even when playing a little kid. When the poor boy was four, he used to try hard to beat him at table tennis. Of course, popular gossip says there are good – or at least understandable - reasons for this.'

'And? What does popular gossip say?'

'It says that nine months before Mikis was born his wife was more than a little indiscreet. Charanis at the time was having a passionate affair with some woman, and his wife did the same. Now, this is a great dilemma. To admit your wife is unfaithful is a shaming thing. To preserve your pride and bring up a cuckoo in your nest is as bad.'

'He did the latter and made the son pay for it?'

'Correct. Even after he divorced he kept the boy, largely, I suspect, to teach her a lesson. And Mikis has grown up with a very unfortunate personality and an unpleasant attitude towards authority. Of late, this has found its expression in politics.'

'Public service,' Flavia said. 'Could be worse.'

Gyorgos grimaced. 'I doubt it, unfortunately. He took up with the most venomous bunch of right-wing nationalists there are. The sort of people who make our old military junta seem like milksop liberals. Common pattern, I believe. A desire to impose order and discipline on the entire country and beat up foreigners to show you're tougher than your father.'

'Lot of them about, these days. What does it mean in Greek terms?'

'As you'd expect. Don't like Slavs, don't like Arabs, don't like immigrants of any form. A fervent desire to discipline the country and bring it back to true patriotism and order. The usual brew, but in his case, of course, it's allied to our glorious historical past.'

'Athens?'

''Fraid not,' he said as he swept a bowl of nuts into his huge hand and thrust them into his mouth.

'Don't tell me. Alexander the Great. He wants to conquer Persia.'

'A bit ambitious, even for someone as extreme as young Charanis,' Gyorgos continued after he had washed the remnants away with a large swallow of champagne and refilled his glass. 'No; his past is the Christian empire. Byzantium, in other words. He and the motley collection of lunatics he associates with want to take back Istanbul. If Leningrad can become St Petersburg, why should Istanbul not become Constantinople again?'

Fostiropoulos picked up another fistful of nuts, then changed his mind and poured the entire bowlful into his palm and swept them all into his mouth and sat there chewing noisily and smiling at Flavia to reassure himself that she had got the point.

'He's got a big project, then.'

'As I say, you go back to the old certainties. Don't underestimate them. Religion, history and dreams of glory make a heady brew for some people.'

148

'You're not concerned about this, are you?'

'Officially, no. Not least because he is still protected by his father, and he is not a man to annoy. Unofficially, five Muslims were burned to death in Thessaloniki a few months back, and we're sure these people had something to do with it. There's not many of them, they're not powerful, but they are getting stronger. And yes, we are concerned.'

'Do you know where he is?'

He shook his head. 'Not in Greece, that's for sure. We know he was, that he made a three-day trip to London three weeks ago, came back to Athens and then vanished. No one's seen him for over a week.'

'Went to London, did he?'

He nodded. 'Does that concern you? Why?'

'Just an idea. Could you do me a favour?'

'Of course.'

'These pictures that alarmed the director of your museum. In Charanis's collection. Could you find out what they are?'

'A pleasure,' he said, looking at his watch. 'Anything else?'

'I wouldn't mind a decent photograph of this man as well. One which isn't so hazy.'

Gyorgos smiled, and reached into his pocket. 'Nothing easier,' he said handing over an envelope. Flavia opened it up. 'If you meet him again, do let me know. We are very interested in him, you know.'

'I will.'

'Now I must go. It has been a delight meeting you, signorina.'

And then he left, leaving Flavia with the remains of the nuts and just enough champagne in the bottle for another glass. What the hell, she thought, and poured it out.

14

Buoyed up by a pep talk of thanks and encouragement over breakfast from Flavia – who thought she might start learning the business of man-management with an easy target – Argyll returned to do battle with the intricacies of medieval handwriting and the complexities of dog Latin in a more determined frame of mind than he had managed the previous day.

He had, after all, something to work on. Previously, all he had known about the icon was that it was old and eastern. Now, from Fostiropoulos via Flavia, he had a bit more focus. Byzantine icons. Those travelling scholars and exiles the records had referred to so elliptically; they were the place to start, he felt sure, especially as the reference to the plague the painting fended off placed its arrival in the middle fifteenth century.

Constantinople falls to the Ottoman empire, and those who get away on western ships do so at the last moment. They bring what they can with them. Many are given pensions by the pope, or sympathetic monarchs in the west, guilty at not having gone to the aid of the Byzantines before it was too late. Some plan to launch a counter-offensive against the infidel, and travel the world, begging for help. Others realize it is all over, that all hope died when wave after wave of Turks swept through breaches and brought two thousand years of Roman history to a violent end. These souls live out their lives as best they can, teaching if they cannot abandon the Orthodox faith, or entering monasteries if they can. They could at least console themselves in their exile that it all ended courageously, and that the last emperor, Constantine, had lived and died in the finest traditions of Rome, leading his dwindling band of troops until he was cut down by the enemy, and his body so dismembered it was never identified.

It was a gripping and poignant story, and Argyll felt a faint ripple of pleasure at the prospect of getting to grips with even the smallest fragment of it. Some of these lost and shocked exiles came to the monastery of San Giovanni. He was prepared to bet that one of them brought the icon as well. But so what? Many of these people brought lots of booty with them; some of them almost shameful amounts, the boats stuffed with valuables when they could have brought out citizens who were left behind. What was one picture amongst hundreds? How did it connect the end of the second Rome, and those who wanted to raise the third back to its traditional place?

The vigil had grown greater overnight. The number of flowers and prayers tagged to the door had grown, so that scarcely any of the old wood could be seen for as high as an arm could reach. Instead of a small handful of people encamped outside the door of the church, there was now a couple of dozen, and the sleeping bags suggested they were serious. A surprising number of them were young, as well. Yesterday nearly all had been old women, brought by sentiment and a feeling that yet another part of their universe had been forcibly taken away from them. Now ten or fifteen were young, some with the intense air of theology students, others drifting Europeans in search of something and hoping to find it on the steps of this old monastery. Argyll talked to them for a few moments; one seemed conventional in religion, another talked vaguely but intensely about the Great Mother. Two at least had thought it was a good place to spend the night. All appeared to have passed by and sat down for reasons which even they did not understand. They seemed perfectly tranquil and certain about it all, but Argyll felt very uneasy. He noticed Signora Graziani sitting on her own, and said hello to her. She smiled at him, and seemed uninterested when he said that the police were still at work. She didn't appear to think it was necessary for the police to do anything, but was grateful for their efforts.

A little unnerved, Argyll went into the monastery, to find

151

that the members of the order were even more jittery than he was. They had divided into two camps; one group regarded the show of piety on the steps as a nuisance that would have to be endured until it faded away of its own accord. The others felt that the whole business was an absurd display of sentimentalism and were inclined to employ more positive action to shoo people away. Only Father Paul, in fact, seemed perfectly tranquil and even quite pleased at what was going on outside.

'It's real,' he said softly as he stood by the gate and placidly regarded the group on the steps outside. 'This is how great movements have started, from simple, popular piety. Do you know, I think I am the only person here to have considered the possibility that this might be the work of God? Don't you think that is strange?'

'I suppose it is. I don't really know. I was brought up an Anglican; I've never really had much to do with religion.'

Father Paul smiled at what he took to be a joke, closed the door and made sure that Argyll had everything he wanted.

'I suggested that maybe the doors of the church should be flung open, to allow people inside in case it rains,' he said as he prepared to go off. 'The idea was turned down for fear of disturbing Mr Menzies.' He shook his head and left Argyll to his labours.

The file was just as thick, and almost as impenetrable; with the sort of intense concentration that ultimately produces a raging headache, Argyll laboured in silence, translating, reading, thinking and noting. At least he made progress. In 1454, the monastery admitted two people; both, irritatingly if predictably, took new names for the occasion – Brother Felix and Brother Angelus – and neither was referred to by any other name. But, given the date, and the fact that there was a note that baptism was especially waived for them, it was reasonable to assume that they were fresh off the boat from the ruins of Constantinople, especially as one was in late middle age, and the other was described as a widower.

So, two new monks, and it would surely have been unusual for them not to have made the usual contribution to the order's coffers when admitted. Where, Argyll thought, was the ledger of deeds and goods? And had they brought that icon, anyway? He leaned back in his chair and tapped his teeth with the end of his pencil, then smiled broadly. Like a crossword puzzle, he thought. Obvious when you know the answer. He bent over and crossed Brother Felix from the list. No point worrying about him. The picture had been brought by an angel, and here was Brother Angel himself, in the right place at the right moment. You could almost hear the wings flapping.

So, Brother Angel, he thought. Where did you get this fine piece of work? Did you pick it up on the way to the port, looting it from some church as it went up in flames and you dodged through the back streets to avoid the enemy soldiers? Was it an old family heirloom you'd sent on ahead, realizing disaster was looming? Did you steal it even from one of your fellow exiles so you could buy your way into a comfortable monastery when you reached journey's end? What sort of person were you? Priest, nobleman or simple subject?

All good questions, which the documents in front of him did not answer. He didn't even know who had arranged the collection. A strange assemblage it was, as well, different sorts of papers, dating from the fifteenth to the eighteenth centuries, brought together without rhyme or reason. But somebody, and not too long ago, had collected them. Father Charles, perhaps, before he'd taken to running the order. If it had been him, he had then locked them all away in this special file, and allowed no one to see them. There seemed little point; there was nothing even remotely terrible, or even interesting, so far.

He eyed the next brown paper folder warily; perhaps in here? Somehow he hoped not; seventy-five miscellaneous pages of Latin in varieties of bad handwriting. It could take him weeks to get through that, if he was being careful. He really should have paid more attention during his Latin lessons. How was he to know it would ever come in useful, after all? He flipped through the pages, hoping that by some miracle there would be passages in Italian to make his life easier, and groaned as he found exactly the opposite. Greek, for heaven's sake. Ten pages in Greek. Life is very unfair, sometimes.

It was no good. He simply couldn't do it. He stared moodily at the pages again, then shook himself. Nothing for it. He'd just have to hope that Father Charles was operational this morning. And willing to help.

The Gemelli hospital, where all the best religious illnesses are treated, was a mixture of the antiquated in architecture and the advanced in equipment. Merely because the nurses were nuns did not mean they were any less ferocious than their counterparts in more secular institutions; the sick threaten to disrupt the smooth running of the hospital, and visitors were a lower form of pond life whose mere existence was an affront to anyone seriously interested in health care. Getting in to see Father Xavier was, therefore, slightly more difficult than Flavia had anticipated; by the time she had battled her way through three floors of obstruction to Father Xavier's floor, she was feeling both punch-drunk and irritated. At least he was finally conscious.

The last stage was easier, though not because of the nurses in charge; rather, the priest Father Jean had sent down to watch over the superior came forward and offered his protection; he held very much greater authority than a mere member of the police could ever have.

'Thank you,' Flavia said gratefully when the last nurse had pulled in her fangs and retreated.

'They are very protective, I find,' he said mildly. 'And you are the third visitor today. They are concerned he may be tired out too easily.'

'Who else has been?'

'Father Paul, to see how he is doing. And another man from the police. That is why the nurses were cross, I think. They expect you to coordinate things better . . .'

'Somebody else from the police . . . ? Who?'

'I don't know. A very kind gentleman, very gentle indeed with Father Xavier.'

Flavia's irritation was growing apace. It must have been one of Alberto's minions – probably his sidekick called Francesco – and she thought she had a clear agreement that questioning the old priest would be her job. Alberto hadn't even wanted to send anyone. He was quite within his rights to change his mind, of course, but he could have told her in advance. That was only fair.

'Late forties, stout, balding, permanent sweat, slightly smelly?' she said, knowing that her description of her colleague would be recognized.

'Oh, no,' he said. 'Not at all. He was in his thirties, I'd say. Very well-dressed, but a lot of stubble. But a very assured air about him, you know. Looked unusually chic for a policeman, in my view. But, of course, I'm not Italian myself . . .'

Flavia handed him a photograph of Mikis Charanis.

'Yes. That's him.'

Flavia closed her eyes in despair as the details sank in. 'When was he here?'

'About fifteen minutes ago. That's when he left. He was only here for ten minutes.'

'And have you seen Father Xavier since?'

'No. I just sat out here . . .'

Flavia walked quickly to the door, brushed aside the remaining nurse guarding it and walked straight into the room, hoping desperately that her worst nightmares were not about to come true.

Father Xavier peered at her with mild interest from his bed. 'Good morning, signorina,' he said, as alive and as well as could be expected in the circumstances. Certainly, he had not acquired a bullet in the brain recently. And for that, Flavia was profoundly grateful. The fact that it was mere luck, that Charanis could quite easily have killed the man had he been minded to do so, did not make her feel any better at all. Damn it, wasn't Alberto meant to have put a man on the door?

She sat down heavily on the only chair available, and breathed deeply as she recovered herself. No point, she decided, in causing unnecessary alarm, or advertising your incompetence.

'I understand you have just had a visit from a colleague in a rival department,' she said with as much of a smile as she could manage. 'I'm with the Art Squad, investigating the theft

155

of your icon. Perhaps you could just tell me what you told him? That way I can stop bothering you.'

'By all means. All he wanted to know was what happened, and where the icon was. Which, alas, I could not tell him.'

Flavia frowned. 'He asked you where it was?'

'Yes.' Father Xavier smiled. 'I see you feel that is your job, not his. Not that it matters. I can't tell either of you. I was in the church, to pray, and that was the last I remember.'

'You didn't see your attacker?'

He shook his head. 'No. He must have come up from behind.'

'And was the icon in its place? Did you notice it?'

He shook his head. 'I didn't look. I'm afraid I'm not much of a help to either of you.'

'And you were in the church to pray.'

'Yes.'

'Is that usual? I mean, do you do that often?'

'I *am* a priest. Of course.'

'At six in the morning?'

'When I was a mere novice, signorina, we had to get up at three as well as at five. I like to continue that old way, even though I don't think it right any more to impose it on anyone else.'

'I see. And while you were praying, did you hear anyone? See anyone? Speak to anyone?'

'No.'

'Nothing unusual at all?'

'No.'

Flavia nodded. 'Father, it pains me to say so, but I'm afraid you are not only a liar, you are a bad one.'

'Your colleague did not have the effrontery to say so.'

'I'm glad to hear it. But I do, I'm afraid. You were in that church to meet Burckhardt. Even though your order had voted not to sell anything, you decided to go ahead anyway because you were desperate to raise money to cover your losses at your stockbrokers. You rang him, and agreed to meet him at six in the morning. You went to the church, took the key, and unlocked the main door so he could come in. Then you waited for him to turn up. That is perfectly clear; so much

156

so that you needn't even bother to confirm it. There can be no other explanation.'

She stopped and looked at him, to see whether she had hit home. His total silence convinced her she was absolutely right. It had been perfectly obvious, anyway. She let him stew for a while before continuing with a new idea that had just popped into her head.

'And to avoid trouble with your order, you tried to organize things so that it looked like a robbery. You were the person who left the anonymous tip-off saying there was going to be a theft.

'Now,' she said, before he could waste his breath with a denial, 'your relations with your order are not my concern, thank goodness. I don't have a clue whether you had the right to do it or not. And for the sake of simplicity, I might even be prepared to forget about the way you wasted our time with false reports. I could file a charge on that. But we have more important things at the moment. And I want whatever help you can offer me.'

'Or else?'

'Or else. That's right. You note that I do you the credit of assuming that you wanted the money for the good of the order, and not to keep for yourself.'

'Of course not,' he said, almost angrily. 'I have spent my entire adult life in it. I would never hurt it. Do you think I want money? For myself? I have never had any and wouldn't know what to do with it anyway. But the order needed it. There is so much to do, and it costs a fortune. And I have been blocked time and again by that band of recalcitrant, obstructive old fools.'

'Fine. So if you care about your order that much, you had better tell me everything. Otherwise, I will make sure it is embroiled in so much distasteful scandal that they will rue the day they ever let you through their doors.'

She peered at him, to see how this went down. To her alarm, when she craned her head to look at his face, she saw a large tear running down his cheek.

'Come on,' she said softly. 'Get it over with. You'll feel better.'

She stood up and fetched some tissue, then handed them brusquely to him and waited while he dabbed his eyes, pretending not to see just as much as he pretended there was nothing wrong.

'I suppose I have to,' he began eventually. 'God knows I have reproached myself enough; I can hardly pretend I have been anything but a stupid old man. About two years ago, soon after I became the head of the order, I received a letter from a company in Milan, making an extraordinary offer. That is, if we gave them the equivalent of a quarter of a million dollars, they would guarantee to double it within five years.'

Flavia nodded absent-mindedly, then paused, thought, and stared at him.

'You didn't give them it, did you?' she asked incredulously.

Father Xavier nodded. 'It seemed too good an opportunity. You see, with the money, I would be able to fund the new mission in Africa without disturbing anything else. Even Father Jean would not have been able to disapprove.'

'It didn't occur to you that there might be something fishy with anyone who offers such a thing? Risky?'

He shook his head sadly. 'They gave absolute guarantees. And said it was an offer they were only making to a few select investors.'

Flavia shook her head sadly. One born every minute.

'Last month I got a letter saying that, due to unforeseen circumstances, the progress of the investment had been slower than anticipated. I made enquiries, of course, and discovered that according to the contract I could not get back even the money that remained.'

'Who knew about this?'

'No one.'

'You didn't put it before the council, ask their permission, check with any outside advisors?'

He shook his head. 'No. And before you say it, I know now I was a complete fool.'

'In that case I won't say it. So, you gave these people a quarter of a million dollars. Exactly how much have they lost?'

He sighed heavily. 'Nearly all. They are reluctant to tell me.'

'I bet they are.'

'And about then I got a letter from Signor Burckhardt, offering to buy the icon. For nearly enough to make good the loss.'

'Good Lord! That's an absurd amount. Why was he prepared to pay that much?'

'He said he wanted to make sure we would accept, and didn't want to waste time in foolish negotiations. Of course, he didn't bank on Father Jean.'

Flavia thought. What dealer would offer nearly a quarter of a million when there was a reasonable chance it could be had for a fraction of that amount?

Answer, obviously, one who was working to commission. Five per cent of a quarter of a million is more than five per cent of fifty thousand. Burckhardt must have had a client lined up.

'Go on.'

'So we had a meeting to discuss the possibility of selling some of our possessions, and Jean made sure it was turned down flat.'

He paused to see whether this was being heard sympathetically. 'I was desperate, you see. I had to get hold of some money.'

'So you decided to sell the thing anyway.'

'Yes. I believe it was within my competence as head of the order. I arranged for him to come to the church to pick it up. He was going to bring the money, take the icon and go. And then, I suppose, I would have reported a burglary.'

'Just a second. What do you mean, he was going to bring the money with him? In *cash*?'

'I said I wanted the money. In cash. I'd had enough of being made a fool of.'

It got worse and worse. Flavia by now could barely believe what she was hearing. She had heard of some stupid operations in her time, but this set new standards.

'And then?' she asked. 'What went wrong?'

'I don't know. I went to the church just after six, unlocked the door and took the Virgin off the wall, and put it in a bag. Then I waited. And someone hit me. That's almost the last I remember.'

'And that was when someone took the Virgin?'

'No,' he said definitely.

'How do you know?'

'Because she was still there. I know.'

'How? You were unconscious.'

'She talked to me.'

'What?'

'I was dying, I know I was. And she saved me through her grace. She came to me and said, "Don't struggle, don't worry, it'll be all right. I'll make sure." Such a soft and gentle voice; full of compassion and care. Immediately I felt suffused with a warm glow of peace.'

The old Catholic in Flavia fought a momentary battle with the equally venerable old cynic, and decided to call it a draw. It had made Xavier cooperative; that in itself was truly something of a miracle. That didn't mean she was prepared to accept that the icon wasn't stolen by the man who hit him.

'It was a miracle,' Xavier went on. 'My skin goes cold just to think of it. I have acted badly, and deserve little favour, yet I am blessed with her forgiveness. Tell me, what are you going to do with me?'

She shook her head. 'I have no idea at all. Fortunately, other people decide that. I merely find out what happened. But you are in big trouble, believe me.'

Flavia walked from the Gemelli to the office; a long walk, right across the centre of town, taking her across the river and through the medieval quarters. By all reasonable standards it was absurd and a waste of time that could be much better spent. Stopping for twenty minutes at a quiet, back-street bar for a coffee and a glass of water was even more foolish. But she reckoned she needed time to think things through.

And besides, she thought she needed a little celebration. Not because of any achievement on her part, certainly. She realized she had come perilously close to having another murder on her hands. But she knew that Charanis had gone into the hospital, talked to Father Xavier and left. It established that Charanis was not only still in Rome, but also, it seemed, did not have the picture. He must have thought Burckhardt had it; then killed him when he refused – or couldn't – say where it was. And he's still trying. What makes him think there is any chance of getting hold of it now?

And there was the obvious point that if he didn't have it, who the hell did? That perhaps was the central problem, and, consequently, one that had to be put aside and forgotten about for a while. Mary Verney was the prime suspect, of course, except for the fact that she was still here.

Flavia sipped her drink, and watched the office workers and occasional tourist who had been lured down the street thinking they were on the way to somewhere, stopping frequently and looking with puzzlement at their maps, turning them upside down and then doing an about turn before heading back the way they came. Know how you feel, she thought as she paid her bill and stood up.

One final detail awaited her on her desk which clinched it. A note from Fostiropoulos, admirably swift. The director of the Athens museum negotiating for Charanis's pictures was concerned about one picture in particular. A Tintoretto with very dubious origins. Naturally the man hadn't mentioned it to anyone before because he didn't want to offend a vastly rich potential donor unfairly, but he was keen to know where it came from.

It took Flavia only twenty minutes to find out. The picture had vanished twenty-six years ago from a castle in Austria. Just like that, no warning, no clues and never seen again. Exactly the style of Mary Verney when she was on top form. One of the ones they hadn't found out about last year. Got her.

Half an hour later, she had Mary Verney arrested. No politeness, no personal touch this time. Just three large policemen with a car. She told them to bundle her in the back and bring her to a cell in the basement. Don't talk, don't say a word. No explanations. Make it seem as grim and intimidating as possible. Frighten the life out of her.

They did a good job of it. For all her life of crime, Mary Verney had never been in trouble with the police before. Even traffic wardens made her nervous, and the experience of the Italian police at their least charming rattled her considerably, as did the fact that she was left to stew on her own for three hours before Flavia decided the time had come for a conversation. When she walked in with a file of notes as a prop, the woman seemed properly chastened. Flavia adopted a world-weary, businesslike air. Another one to put in jail. Oh, dear.

'Now, then,' she began after she'd sat there for several minutes reading her notes and making marks in the margins with a pencil, 'I should tell you that we have enough for the magistrate to charge you on several counts. Firstly with leaving the scene of a crime. Secondly, conspiracy to commit theft, and thirdly – and most importantly – conspiracy to commit murder.'

'Murder?' Mary Verney said, her head jerking up in astonishment. 'What murder?'

'Peter Burckhardt.'

'That's absurd.'

'I don't think so. We will be arguing, with evidence, that you informed one Mikis Charanis of Burckhardt's presence in the church of San Giovanni on the morning that the icon was stolen and Father Xavier was attacked.'

'I'd never even heard of this Charanis before.'

'We will prove that twenty-six years ago you stole a Tintoretto for his father.'

'Nonsense.'

'Far from being retired, as you say, you came to Rome specifically to steal that icon, either for the father or the son. I don't care which one. Personally, I think you should have taken your own advice. You've lost your touch. Greed, Mrs Verney. I'm surprised at you. I would have thought you had enough sense to know when to stop. Now you've blown everything.'

There was a long pause, as Mary Verney considered how right Flavia was. She always knew in her bones this was going to be a disaster, so the fact that she was sitting here, quite probably facing a hefty jail sentence, should come as no surprise. And all because of that man, whom she had liked and trusted, and who didn't even have the courage to face her himself.

Was there any way out? If she kept quiet, she would undoubtedly go to jail. What's more it was unlikely Charanis would believe she would keep quiet, and so would carry out his threat. And if she told the truth? Surely the same result.

'How long are you going to take over this?' Flavia asked.

'I was wondering whether you might want to come to some accommodation.'

'No. I don't need to. So talk to me.'

'The question is whether you can help me.'

'The question is whether I am prepared to.'

This seemed to produce a stalemate, and Flavia was not in the mood for playing games today. There had been more than enough of those already. 'You seem to be wanting a deal. You give me something, I give you something. I'm not interested. I want the truth, full, whole and unabridged. I want a way of checking it. And I'm not going to offer you anything in advance at all. No promises, no deals and no assurances. Take it or leave it. I don't know why you're so desperate to steal this picture, and I don't care. That's your business. So, either get on with it, or forget it.'

A third long pause, then Mary shook her head. 'I know nothing about any icon or murder. I was walking on the Aventino that morning merely by coincidence. I haven't stolen anything or injured anyone. I am a little old tourist. That is all I have to say.'

And with a calm look very much at odds with what she felt, Mary folded her hands on her lap and gazed placidly at the policewoman sitting opposite to her.

Flavia glared at her angrily. 'I don't believe a word of it. You're in this up to your neck.'

She shook her head. 'How many times do I have to tell you? I do not have the icon.'

This time Flavia lost her temper. 'I know you don't. Menzies does,' she said angrily. 'He took the thing home to clean it. And won't let us have it back until tomorrow when he's finished. He might have told us, but he didn't, and it's not the point in any case. The point is that you came here to steal it and it went wrong. One man died and another was put in hospital. Now, tell me, what happened?'

A third shake of her head, although this time a slight glint in the eyes showed that she knew she'd won. She had kept her nerve; Flavia had gone too far. 'I have nothing to say on this matter at all. Charge me or let me go.'

Flavia slammed the file shut and strode out of the cell, then leant heavily against the cool of the concrete wall.

'Well?' the man on duty asked. 'What am I to do with her?'

'Keep her for another few hours, then let her go.' She marched back to her office to consider what she had done. Then she took a taxi to the monastery to see Dan Menzies.

Argyll's quest for an easy solution to his own Greek problem met an early reverse as he climbed the stairs to Father Charles's grim little room. He met Father Paul coming down, as calm and serene as ever.

'I'm afraid I do not feel that would be a good idea,' he said after Argyll had explained. 'He is not well at the moment.'

'I wouldn't detain him long. But he could save me an awful lot of time. He's given me a puzzle and as far as I can see he already knows what the answer is.'

Father Paul shook his head. 'You can try, of course. But I'm afraid the illness has overcome him again. It is difficult to get much sense out of him, and you would not be able to rely on anything you did hear. His dementia, when it comes, is overpowering.'

'How long does it last?'

'It depends. Sometimes a few hours, sometimes days.'

'I can't wait days.'

Father Paul looked helpless. 'I'm afraid there is nothing I can say to assist you. By all means go and see him; even if he doesn't understand I think that human company is a solace to him. I try to visit him myself whenever possible. He found me and brought me into the order, so I owe him a great deal and it is a pleasure. But I think you will get little from it.'

'I'll try anyway. He doesn't get, ah, aggressive, does he?'

'Oh no, not at all. Not physically.'

'He shouts? Just so I'm ready for it, you understand.'

'He can be very frightening. He says terrible things. And sometimes . . .'

'Sometimes what?'

'He speaks in tongues.'

Father Paul was obviously struck by this last manifestation of the old man's madness; Argyll found it the least alarming of all prospects.

As long as he gives a running translation, he thought to himself as he climbed the last few stairs after telling Father Paul he'd try anyway, he can do a mime act for all I care.

Still, dealing with madness was a slightly unnerving prospect; he had seen far too many gothic horror movies for him not to have a sense of trepidation as he knocked on the door and waited for a reply. There was none, so, after waiting a few minutes with his ear to the door, he quietly opened it, and peered in.

It was dark again, but this time he knew where to look and, through the thin slices of light coming through the closed shutters, he saw Father Charles on his knees in front of his chair. Praying. Bad manners to interrupt someone while they are praying. He started to back out.

Then Father Charles spoke, lifting his head, but not turning round. Greek, by the sound of it. Too fast for him, though.

Argyll stood there, wondering what to do next, then Father Charles turned and gestured for him to come in, repeating the phrase. Argyll was relieved; not only did the old man seem sufficiently aware to realize he was there, his face had little of the madness Argyll had expected. Total serenity and calmness, in fact, his eyes half closed, his gestures slow and almost languid. He looked at Argyll, held out his hand and waited.

Argyll walked over and took it, but the slight frown that crossed Father Charles's face indicated something else was expected from him. He didn't want it shaken, didn't want to be helped up . . .

With a burst of inspiration, and not a little audacity, he bent over and kissed it. Bingo. Father Charles nodded and allowed himself to be helped into his chair. He gestured for Argyll to sit down on the floor, at his feet. Argyll obeyed and watched carefully for a new clue.

More Greek; Argyll nodded as though he understood. Then what sounded like Latin, then a language which was way outside his range. What had the man specialized in? Sanskrit? Assyrian? Hebrew? Could be any of those. Father Charles looked concerned when he realized he wasn't getting through, and tried again. He swept through German and what sounded like Bulgarian before coming up with a sentence in French. Good enough. Argyll nodded furiously, and replied.

'It is your duty and privilege to remain quiet,' Father Charles said with a tone of regret in his voice at having to issue the reprimand. 'I may have fallen far and been forsaken, but you will give me the honours that are mine. So much was I promised.'

'Sorry. Sir.'

'And you will address me in the appropriate manner.'

'Forgive me,' Argyll said contritely. 'But what is that?'

'Your most Holy Majesty.'

'You're a monk,' Argyll said. 'Wouldn't "Father" be more appropriate?'

Father Charles paused, and peered at Argyll closely. 'I see my disguise works. Who are you, young man? I recognize you. I have seen you before. And you don't know?'

Not much to say to that. Argyll shook his head.

'Yes, I am a monk, so it is said. I dress in these clothes and pretend. But that is for the world; not for me. You come from his Holiness, Callixtus?'

Argyll smiled. He didn't know much about religion, but he knew who the pope was. And Callixtus he wasn't.

'And he never said,' Father Charles continued, sounding almost amused. 'Not even to you. How very like him. If you are to be my emissary, though, you must know. Otherwise you may make an error and ruin everything. But you must swear a vow of silence, that you will never reveal anything beyond this room, not even in the direst necessity. Do you so swear?'

What the hell? Completely potty, but strangely touching.

166

At least he had a considerable amount of grandeur in his madness. Argyll swore away.

Father Charles nodded. 'Know then the truth as I reveal it to your ears. I am Constantinos XI Paleologos Dragases, Emperor of Byzantium, Noblest soul, God's vicegerent on earth, heir to Augustus and Constantine.'

Pretty grand. Argyll gaped at him in astonishment.

The Emperor Constantine smiled condescendingly. 'I know. You thought me dead, yet here I sit. But how I am lost, ruler of half the earth, hiding and disguised in this place, pretending to be a monk and having to celebrate in secret, in a little back room so that no one will know of my continued life. Only two or three people know it, and now you are one of them. You must keep this secret, lest all be ruined. The Emperor died on the walls of Constantinople, falling to the infidel. So the world believes, and must continue to believe until all is ready. Then he will return, sweeping down under the protection of her likeness, to restore the faith. But surprise is of the essence. A little trick, but justifiable, in the circumstances, don't you think?'

Argyll nodded.

'It will take time, of course,' the old man said thoughtfully, but with a glint of battle in his eye as he plotted in his mind. 'But our situation is not as hopeless as it seems. The Venetians and Genoese will help; will have to help because of their commercial interests. George of Serbia will do the same, because he knows he is next. The knights of St John on Malta can be relied on, I think. And there is also the Morea.

'But,' he said, leaning forward intently, 'it must be done correctly, this time. Our forces are few, and we can make no mistakes. If I am to regain my throne, everyone must know what to do and when to do it. I figure a three-pronged attack. The knights land in Anatolia and pin down the forces there. George sweeps across the Balkans to the straits, and meets up with a seaborne fleet of Venetians and Genoese.'

'And yourself, your majesty?' Argyll said, almost forgetting this was simple madness and half seeing the pennants on the ships ready to sail. 'You must lead them.'

Father Charles smiled, nursing his secret. 'Of course. Of

course. Now, I shall tell you a secret. The greatest of them all. And show you God's goodness. Out of this disaster, this most bitter lesson, goodness shall come. Byzantium fell for a reason. It was His displeasure at our divisions. East and west, spending more time fighting each other than our common enemy.'

He stopped, and cocked his head to one side. 'Check the door, sir. I fear being overheard.'

Argyll dutifully got up from his sitting position, joints cracking from the strain of being so uncomfortable, and peered round the door. 'No one there,' he said quietly. 'We're not being overheard.'

He came back, and Father Charles, face suffused with excitement, leaned forward to whisper in his ear.

'For the past six months, I have been negotiating the reunification of Christianity. East and west will come together again and act as one. It is a miracle; Christendom will be stronger and more powerful than ever before. I had a sign that day, in the Church of Holy Wisdom, before the walls fell. It was too late then, our contrition, but I knew my task, and I am close to completing it. Callixtus and I, we have reached agreement; he will put his whole weight behind the enterprise. And the first the infidel know of this will be when I appear once more before the walls of Constantinople, at the head of an army of French and German and even English knights. They will be overpowered and swept away.'

'And until everything is ready, you will hide here, pretending to be Brother Angelus? Is that the idea?'

He nodded slyly. 'Good, eh? With only my servant Gratian, who would suspect I would live in such reduced circumstances? Lull them into a false sense of security. And all the while my secret emissaries and those of his Holiness cross Europe, weaving a net to catch the infidel in so tightly he will never escape until he is exterminated utterly. So, now you see the need for the utmost secrecy. Do you see?'

'Of course. But such a secret cannot last forever.'

'It won't have to. There is little time. His Holiness is behind the plan wholeheartedly, but he is old and sick. And a faction at his court is opposed, and want to exploit my weakness.

Another reason for secrecy. We must strike fast and hard.'

Argyll nodded. Made sense to him. 'But isn't there a bit of a problem here?'

'What problem?'

'You're dead, right? I mean, you're pretending to be dead. Killed on the walls, and all that. If you are suddenly resurrected, who's going to believe it? Won't everyone say you're just an impostor? And refuse to follow you? Following the Emperor is one thing; following a fake is another.'

Father Charles wagged his finger. 'Very astute, young man. But not as astute as I am. Believe me when I tell you; this has been planned well. They will believe I am who I am, but it wouldn't matter if they didn't.'

'Why?'

'Because they will follow her.'

'Who.'

'The Hodigitria.'

Argyll looked at him, and Father Charles chuckled, then turned deeply serious.

'You are stunned into silence. I thought you would be. Yes, young man. Yes. Rejoice at the news. She has survived. The holiest picture in all the wide empire, the Mother herself, painted by the hand of St Luke guided by God, and a true image of her likeness and that of her only begotten son. She lives and is here.' His voice fell to a hoarse whisper. 'In this very building. All true Christians will follow her. He who has her blessing is destined to hold the Christian empire in his hands. So it is believed and so it will be. Now, guard my secret until we are ready to act.'

By the time he left Father Charles's room, the return to sunlight and normality as sudden a shock as if he had suddenly been transported in a time machine across the centuries, Argyll was well off-track. He had found out what the picture was, or what it might be; that was all that was important. He should have got into a taxi and gone straight round to Flavia and told her.

But he didn't. He was so bemused by Father Charles that

he forgot all about what seemed to him now to be a somewhat parochial and trivial aspect of the whole business.

He didn't even doubt it, or not much. He headed back to the university library for one reason only: to confirm Father Charles's story. He knew it was true, or at least a reasonable interpretation of events. Father Charles was completely out of his mind, but he was still intelligent. Somewhere in his brain all sorts of connections had short-circuited, probably at the shock of the painting being stolen. The tale of the Emperor, the loss of the picture had all become jumbled up in his head, causing him to identify too much with those subjects he had studied in the past. But just because his method of telling it was a little unorthodox, didn't mean the tale was senseless; it had just come out in an odd way.

But first he could at least see if there was anything on record which contradicted the story. He collected piles of books; built himself a small fortress of volumes in one corner of the library before opening them and starting to read. Ouspensky on Icons. Runciman on the siege. Pastor on the Popes, Ducas for an eyewitness account of the fall. Then dictionaries and encyclopaedias and digests. Enough to be getting on with.

He read furiously, then got up for more, and started again, reading incredibly quickly and with a level of concentration he could rarely manage. An hour passed, then two, and still he found nothing, not a word, to make Father Charles's madness seem impossible. The Emperor was said to have fallen on the last day of the siege, but no one ever properly identified the body. The Turkish Sultan Mehmet II impaled a head on a stake, then stuffed it and sent it round the courts of the Middle East to show his victory, but there was never the slightest proof it was the right head. The Emperor Constantine vanished, and was never seen again. There was no body, no eyewitnesses to his death. That didn't mean that the Greek Brother Angelus was the Emperor, but it didn't prove that it could not be, either.

So what about the painting, the Hodigitria. It was easy to establish that this was the most venerated icon in the whole of the east; a Virgin, left hand outstretched, with a child on the right arm. Paraded around the walls in 1087 and credited

170

with saving the city from disaster, and brought out from the church in times of war and emergency. Traditionally said to have been painted, from the life, by St Luke. The special symbol uniting Emperor, city, empire and Christendom. The Turks had destroyed it, in the orgy of looting and violence that was their right when a city which resisted was taken by siege. But again, no witnesses. No one saw them do it. And on the evening before the final assault, the painting was not brought out and paraded around the walls as was the custom. If ever divine help was needed it was then. Her failure to appear would surely have demoralized the troops terribly. So why not? There could be no reason – unless it had already left the city, smuggled out on one of the Venetian galleys that were already slipping out of harbour and running the gauntlet of the Turkish siege to get to safety. Perhaps the Emperor had laid his plans well in advance, and realized that not even the Virgin Mary herself could save his city from its own foolishness. So he made sure she was safe, and set up his own last-minute escape, already thinking about his counter-attack. Then he came to Rome, to plot and wait.

But the counter-attack never happened. No massing of armies, no reunification of Christendom; nothing. Nobody lifted a finger, and Constantinople became and stayed Istanbul. Argyll began on his pile of books about the popes. The name was right, at least; Callixtus III was pope from 1455, and dedicated his papacy to recovering the east. But nothing came of it. The only attempt at reunifying Christendom had been years before, at the Council of Florence, and it fizzled out in mutual acrimony. And Callixtus himself died in 1458, to be replaced by a new pope more interested in building projects and artistic patronage. Certainly, if the Emperor had survived, then his chances of a *revanche* died with Callixtus.

One final question. Father Charles had talked of the last night in Santa Sophia, the Church of Holy Wisdom, before the final assault. Ducas had an account of it. How in the panic, the remaining population, knowing the end was near, went to the Church of Hagia Sophia to pray, and had to make do with whatever priests were around. Catholics submitted to Orthodox priests, the Orthodox to Catholics, neither caring

171

which was which, for the first and possibly last time. The Emperor was there, before the battle trumpets sounded and summoned him to the walls. Perhaps such a sight could inspire a man; certainly he was right in saying it was too late. A few hours later the troops burst in; many of the congregation were killed, the rest enslaved, and the next day the most venerable church of all became a mosque.

Argyll yawned and looked at his watch, then started with alarm. Six-thirty already. He'd been there for nearly four hours; the time had passed almost without him noticing. As he came back to the real world, he realized his back hurt and his shoulder muscles were protesting at the insensitive treatment they'd received. He began putting the books back on the shelves, then picked up the phone to see where Flavia was.

He was in a taxi minutes later.

Argyll found himself oddly hesitant when he found her. Even though Father Charles was a lunatic, he had sworn to keep his secret. On the other hand, he saw no reason why this should extend to the icon as well. And perhaps his case would seem stronger if he left out the information that he had it from the horse's mouth, so to speak. Flavia was unlikely to be impressed by being told his evidence came from a Byzantine Emperor who'd been dead for over four centuries. It cuts into your credibility. Come to think of it, and here Argyll did begin to think of it almost for the first time, it was a bit unlikely.

So he improvised a little. 'I've been through the documents, and done a great deal of work on the side. In fact, I've done so much so fast my head's spinning. And I think I've figured it out. The picture is – or at least your man believes it is – something called the Hodigitria. Does that mean anything to you?'

Flavia shook her head cautiously. 'I assume it's an icon.'

'Yes. Mary. With child. That's right. The distinctive aspect is that the child be on the left arm. There's thousands of them, it seems. One of the most common formats.'

'So? What's so special about this one?'

'By tradition they all derive from a single original. Painted from the life by St Luke. So called because of where it was kept in Constantinople. It was *the* icon of the Byzantine empire. The protector, and the supreme emblem of the empire. As long as Constantinople had it, the city could never fall and Christianity would hold sway in the eastern Mediterranean. And had a right to hold sway there.'

'Didn't work too well, did it?' Flavia commented drily.

Argyll almost felt offended at the aspersion. 'Officially, it was destroyed during the final assault by the Turks. The important bit,' he said sternly, determined to make the proper excuses, 'is that as far as I can see it wasn't. It was taken out of the city to safety. So its miraculous powers were never tested. I'm sure it wouldn't have made any difference, but there we are. It was brought to Rome by a Greek travelling under the pseudonym of Brother Angelus, and deposited in the monastery of San Giovanni, where it has stayed. Until a couple of days ago. That is what your man Charanis wants.'

'Is it the only contender?'

'Oh, no. There are more paintings attributed to St Luke than there are to Vermeer. Three in Rome alone. From what I've read, the pedigrees of these others aren't so good. Besides, that doesn't matter. This is the only one which can claim to be *the* Hodigitria.'

'And Burckhardt knew this?'

'So it seems. He was in the archives and even though I think he missed the whole story, he got enough to make some sense of it.'

'Is this thing real, Jonathan?'

He shrugged. 'Was it painted by St Luke? No; it seems to have been mentioned first in the eighth century. A Holy Fake, if you like. Whether it is the same painting, I don't know; there's a good chance. That's the target, anyway. Have you found it? Come to think of it, has this Charanis man of yours?'

She shook her head. 'He's still here, and still looking. Which gives us a chance of catching him. With Mary Verney's cooperation.'

'She's going to help?'

Flavia grinned nervously. 'I hope so. She doesn't know it yet, though.'

'What's her motive in all this?'

Flavia shook her head. 'Damned if I know. It's not money, that's obvious. This man seems to have a hold on her somehow. And it must be a tight grip for her to take so many risks. Do you feel like making yourself useful this evening?'

'I've been useful all afternoon.'

'In that case a few extra hours won't be noticed.'

'What do you want?'

'Go and keep an eye on Dan Menzies for me. I'll be round in an hour or so.'

15

Mary Verney was released by the police after about eight hours in the police station, and left the building with almost a light heart. She had withstood the pressure and kept her nerve. Initially she had been tempted to cooperate with Flavia; Mikis Charanis was a dangerous lunatic, and she was in too weak a position on her own.

But then Flavia overstepped. Once she knew they had no solid evidence against her, her hand was strengthened. And once she knew where the icon was, she had a motive. She could finish the job, with good luck. And surely she deserved some.

The problem, as far as she could see it, was perfectly simple. Charanis had her granddaughter and wanted the icon. She wanted her granddaughter, but didn't have the icon to give in return. Menzies did have it – or might, she wasn't so stupid as not to consider the possibility of Flavia being either wrong or devious – and so she would have to collect it from Menzies. Simple and easy. Just as well she had taken the trouble of finding out where he lived when she found out he was working in the church. And just as well he had never met her.

What was the alternative? Luring Charanis into a police trap? Fine; except his father would use every weapon in his considerable arsenal to get him released and would probably succeed. And even if he did go to jail, he still had his associates, and once it became clear that Mary Verney was responsible for his being in jail, then she and her granddaughter would pay a heavy price. She wanted no harm to come to her granddaughter, and did not want to spend the rest of her life looking over her shoulder.

She was not someone who was used to sitting back and accepting her fate; in her mind she saw her whole life as a struggle, to protect her and hers from the outside world. That was why she'd started stealing in the first place. She was used to doing things her way, at her pace, and for her own advantage. Being pushed and corralled by thugs on the one hand and the police on the other gave her such a feeling of being squeezed that she almost felt ill. Not that she had no sympathy with Flavia; one of the curiosities about her, so obvious that even she was aware of it, was that she generally regarded herself as a law-abiding citizen. And, apart from stealing for a living, so she was. She tutted over rising crime figures she read about in the newspapers, advocated stiff penalties for criminals and, generally, blamed the parents. Which she did in her own case as well. But, usually, she always managed to put what she did into a different category. Apart from the one occasion when she had been blackmailed, she hurt no one, and destroyed nothing. A redistribution of goods. She had few moral scruples about how she had spent her life; most of the people she'd stolen from could well afford their losses. But she had no illusions either, and had an odd sense of justice. Charanis offended that and there was nothing to be done about it.

She was pouring herself a drink when the phone rang. The porter downstairs. A visitor. Her heart skipped a beat. She listened for a while, then recovered slowly.

'What a surprise,' she said coldly when he'd finished. 'Perhaps you'd better come up, Mr Charanis.'

Mary hadn't seen him for years; not since she had personally delivered a picture, and ended staying on in his house for another month in what was one of the most delightful, if poignantly short, periods of her life. The most charming, and the most exciting, man she had ever known. And then he goes and does this to her; she was certain he must be behind this. She had only encountered his kind, personal side in the past; never before been in the way stopping him getting something he wanted.

But even now, with her in her fifties and him very much

older, her heart beat a little faster at the prospect of seeing him once more. And she was frightened as well; not just because of what he was doing to her, but also for fear that his ageing would confirm her own, and show her memories to be illusions.

Certainly he had changed; although as he stood there, bowed over now and old, the lopsided grin on his face and mischievous look in his eyes instantly made her begin to respond before she savagely repressed the impulse.

'A long time,' she said coolly.

'Far too long,' he replied in his thickly accented English. 'It's good to see you again, Mary.' There was a long pause as they looked at each other before he added: 'How are you?'

'It's strange that you of all people should ask,' she replied. 'Considering what you have done to me.'

He nodded. 'I feared as much. You are under something of a misapprehension. I have done nothing.'

'You have kidnapped my granddaughter, and left me with a high probability of going to jail. To my mind, that is not nothing.'

'Your granddaughter, is it? Have we become so old already?'

She poured herself another drink, and noted with pride that her hands were absolutely steady. Good, she thought. At least I can still control something.

'Tell me what has happened.'

There was something in his calm approach which stopped her making a sneering response and do as he asked. About his son, and the icon and her granddaughter. About the police and the murder of Burckhardt. The old man looked more and more sombre as she continued, his head bowed almost until he looked as though he was asleep. He wasn't, she knew; he had always done that when he was thoughtful.

Eventually she finished, and he sat there silently.

'Well? What is it? Are you going to say you have nothing to do with this? Or simply that you don't believe me?'

He looked up at her. 'I'm afraid I believe every word. But no. I have nothing to do with this. Nothing at all. Surely you realize I would never do anything like this to you, of all people?'

'I would have thought not. But I tried to talk to you and was fobbed off.'

'I was on retreat. I always give strict instructions that no one is to disturb me.'

'I find it difficult to believe that you cannot control your own son.'

'He is not my son.'

'Who is he, then?'

Charanis shrugged. 'He was born after you and I were together. It was an accident, but in a way my own fault. Your fault. I turned a blind eye, but was not a very good father. I maintained all the properties until a few years ago, and then my patience snapped.'

'Why?'

'He was dealing in drugs. For no reason; God knows he didn't need money and even if he did such a thing was unconscionable. I was father enough, or stupid enough, to use my influence to have the case dropped, but I refused from then on to have anything to do with him. I am old-fashioned, perhaps; but there are some things I will not overlook. Mikis kept on pushing until he discovered what it was. He has money enough, and neither of us miss the other's company. Since then he has become more and more evil. That is not too strong a word, believe me. He has used his money – *my* money, the money I made and gave to him in a fit of stupidity – to foment hatred because he sees himself as a future force in politics. And he is willing to do anything and sink to any depth to get some measure of power. I thought for a while it was just a period he would grow bored with as he's grown bored of everything else in his life, until I began to hear of what exactly he was doing. He is doing real harm, Mary. He may have killed people. He seems to think that will show how strong he is. There is only himself; he has no sense of right or wrong at all. And I am responsible. If anyone could have made him different, I could.'

'You didn't, even if you could have, which is doubtful. And he's on the loose now. Why, exactly, is he doing this to me?'

178

'About a year ago I had a letter from this man Burckhardt. He's a man I know well and trust. I've bought many things from him in the past. He is honest and reliable. He knew that I collected icons and asked if I wanted another one. I said no; I have five hundred and won't be able to catalogue even those by the time I die. But he said this would be the jewel of the collection. He came to see me and talk to me about it.'

'And?'

'He said he had found the Hodigitria. You know what what is?'

Mary shook her head.

'The holiest icon of Byzantium, and he could prove it. And he did. He showed me enough evidence to conclude that there was an reasonable chance that it was the real picture, brought by a fleeing monk after the fall of Constantinople. I told him to get it, no matter what the price.'

'Fine. But how the hell does this fit in with what's been going on here?'

'I initially turned him down, remember. And he touted the picture around other people. And also talked to Mikis. He didn't know I no longer spoke to him and hoped he would persuade me to listen. When Mikis heard what it was, he decided he could make use of it himself. Turn it into a banner, a standard for his particular brew of contemptible politics. At least, I'm certain that is what happened.'

'Burckhardt was operating for you, was he? I suppose I should have guessed.'

'You should have. I gave him a draft for up to a million dollars to get the picture and told him to come back to me for more if necessary. The last I heard from him was that he had struck a deal for a quarter of that sum. Then friends tell me the Italian police are making enquiries, and that Burckhardt had been shot. So I come to find out what is going on.'

'How did you find out about me?'

'There are ways,' he said with a wry smile. 'In this case, a friend in the embassy called Fostiropoulos.'

'How did Mikis find out about me? Why didn't he just hire some bruiser? It's not a difficult job.'

Charanis looked up at the ceiling for a few moments, and

thought. 'I suspect that is his sense of revenge. It burns strongly in him.'

'What on earth for? What have I ever done to him? The last time I saw him he was only six. He could hardly remember me.'

'He seems to remember you very well. You see, he blames you for the collapse of my marriage to his mother. He has rearranged the facts so that all was a veritable garden of Eden until you appeared. Not the case, of course. Yanna's behaviour was intolerable long before that. But we all must find reasons for things. He knew you stayed with me, and it was no secret in my family then that you supplied me with pictures. When the national museum queried the origins of one of them, he could easily have reached the right conclusion with a little work. I suspect he saw a way both of getting the icon and of visiting on your family some of the same misery you brought on his. Now tell me. Do you have the picture? If so, give it to me now, and I will sort out everything for you.'

'Thank you,' she said, meaning it. 'But I don't have it. I wish to God I did. I may have it soon.'

'Mikis mustn't get it. It would not only be dangerous, it would be blasphemous. I will not allow it.'

'I see things differently. If I had it, I would hand it over to him now, and hang the consequences. I want Louise safe, and frankly, I wouldn't care if the entire Balkans went up in flames as a result.'

Charanis shook his head.

'Will he harm Louise, do you think?' she asked, daring at last to hear the answer she most dreaded.

'That's your granddaughter's name? Not until he gets the icon. After that, I don't know. It is possible. Cruelty is the one thing he is thorough about.'

Her heart was pounding now. It was her worst nightmare. A straightforward bit of force she could deal with: a contract was a contract even if terms were violent. But she was dealing with a man who was unbalanced. She saw her options shrinking, then disappearing. If she refused to give him the icon,

Louise would die. If she gave it to him, she might still be killed. She had to tell him what she planned to do.

He thought a while, then sighed with bitter old age. 'Then I suppose there is no choice. I think I always knew it would come to this, sooner or later.'

Flavia called a conference of spare or underemployed troops late that evening. There was a lot to do, and she realized as well that nothing could be allowed to go wrong. And there was so little time. If they lost Mary Verney; if Charanis escaped them, the number of people who would protest would be enormous. It would not look good. She realized she was already thinking like the head of the department; she didn't want to give anyone in the ministry a reason for deciding she was too inexperienced, and shoe-horning in some outsider to take over.

She had thought about it long and hard, and come up with nothing better than the proposal she had already set in motion. A pity Bottando was not around; his advice at this stage would have been useful. He had disappeared to tramp the corridors of power, and there was no one else she could ask.

'Now,' she said to her assembled troops, 'this is going to be quite difficult. The essence of the problem is to make sure that Mary Verney never gets out of our sight. She wants that icon badly, and I have told her it was in the apartment of Dan Menzies. I assume she will try to take it. Whatever you do, do not stop her. And I will repeat that as often as it takes. Let her take it. And please, *please* don't let her see you.

'When she has it, let me know, and again stick to her like glue. If you don't, if you lose her, then we will blow the whole thing. I want to see her with the icon, I want to see her hand it to Charanis, and I want to see him take it.'

'Will she give it to him directly?'

'I doubt it. If she goes into any building and comes out, wait till she emerges. One person follow her, the other should go in and find out what she's been doing. She'll probably put it in a safe place for him to collect. She will assume she's being followed, so be ready. I want to use her to lure Charanis into the open, then I want him arrested. Simple enough. But he is a dangerous man. The carabinieri will have an eight-man team of their flat-foot thugs on call in their little blue trucks waiting for the call once we know where he is. They want him more than we do, and will make the arrest. Our job is to find him. Got that?'

They nodded. 'Good. Now, Mary Verney is in her hotel room. You, Giulia, will watch the lobby, and Paolo will back you up on the street outside. All of you take mobile phones and let us pray to God the things work. I'll want you two' – she gestured at the only other two people she'd been able to rustle up – 'to stay at either end of the via Barberini. If she gets out, one of you must see her. Please.'

They all nodded with varying degrees of enthusiasm. Giulia was still young enough to be eager; the rest merely saw a long boring night ahead of them.

Then Flavia walked to the via di Montoro and Menzies's apartment, where she found the American hard at work and Argyll slumbering on the floor. It was more comfortable than the sofa.

The icon, the Hodigitria, rested on an easel angled so that it caught the light. It was a small work, as Argyll had described, so dark that she had to peer at it to make out the slightly imperious face as it gazed distantly out of the old, worm-eaten block of wood it was painted on. Even though she knew it was a fake, she was strangely impressed, and could imagine the effect of the real thing in a darkened church, in its gold and jewelled frame and surrounded by banks of candles lit by devotees.

Something about the size, she thought. Small and under-stated, which is always more impressive than the vast and overblown.

But represented by a copy in a state of undress, so to speak, without frame or altar or smell of incense, it scarcely looked worth the trouble it was causing. And wouldn't have done, even if parts weren't missing, and even if the wet paint on the rest hadn't brilliantly reflected the evening sun.

'Oh, God,' she said. 'It'll never be ready.'

Menzies was not pleased by the remark, and scowled at her. 'If I may point out, I've only been working on it for four hours. I'm doing bloody well, thank you. And it will be ready in time. So you do your business and leave me to mine. Look.'

He took it off the easel and turned it round delicately. 'Old oak, an eighth of an inch thick. Filthy, and covered in dust. I had to cut it myself from a piece of the stalls in San Giovanni; which meant going there and finding something suitable. Only fifteenth century, but it'll have to do. Then the cut edges had to be dirtied up and darkened, and that took a long time. Then I had to paint the thing from memory. The painting used some form of tar as a base, and it was bubbling up and showing through the paint; getting that effect –'

'All right, all right,' she said. 'I'm just worrying. Will it be done?'

'How long do I have?'

'Until about eight tomorrow morning, I guess.'

He grimaced, calculated, then said: 'It'll be done. Could well be my finest work. Certainly my fastest.'

'Pity no one will ever know.'

'The greatest artists were anonymous ones. No one knew who painted the original, either. Anyway, if you'll keep quiet . . .'

He worked again in silence for a while, as Flavia paced around the room, peering at the panel every few minutes, until Menzies's patience snapped.

'Look, go away. You're not helping my concentration at all. Go and get a coffee; read a newspaper, or something. And take your friend with you. His snoring disturbs me.'

'What a nerve,' Argyll said a few minutes later. 'I helped him at the monastery, wielding his saw and collecting dust from behind the organ pipes; I've mixed paints and pounded powders and stuck my head up the chimney to get wood soot and brewed it up in ethanol for the backing. I've hardly had a moment's rest since I got there.'

He drank a coffee down in one gulp and ordered another. 'Great fun, though, I must say. Being a forger must be very rewarding. How did you persuade him to be so cooperative? Are you sure it will work?'

Flavia shrugged. Faking a painting in under twelve hours was not difficult; especially as Charanis had only a hazy idea of what it looked like, had never seen it out of its frame and because it was dirty almost beyond recognition. But it was too much to hope that he could ever fool an expert, or indeed fool anyone for very long, though she hoped that wouldn't be necessary. A few minutes would be enough. Subtleties, like getting exactly the right style, or trying to achieve the serenity of the original, were unnecessary for Charanis. But he wasn't the person who had to be fooled. Mary Verney would be more difficult.

And it was a pity they couldn't have used a professional, rather than Menzies. Someone like Bruno Mascholino, for example, would have been delighted to help, in exchange for a month or two off his sentence, and would have done a much better job. But he didn't know what to paint; only Menzies had studied the thing with any amount of care, when he was thinking about his restoration job. So, despite the disadvantages, he was the only person who could help. And even persuading him had been hard work.

'I told him I would issue a statement totally exonerating him from any involvement in this business; criticize the press for being vindictive and use all Bottando's influence with the Beni Artistici to get him the Farnesina contract.'

'Not a bad bargain. Is he the right person for the job?'

'He can make that ceiling look like Walt Disney for all I care at the moment. I don't even know if he's the right person for *this* job. But he is the only one. What do you think?'

Argyll scratched his chin and pondered for a moment. 'It might work,' he said cautiously. 'As he says, his great advantage is the dirt. And the fact that no one involved has ever seen it out of its frame, and that Mary Verney will assume it's just been restored by a total philistine. I'm coming to think he's not quite such a slash and burn man as they say. He's got a delicate touch. In fact, I've quite grown to like him. He's an awkward sod, but not nearly as repellent as he seems. We had quite a nice long chat, in between the pounding and the sawing.'

'Good,' Flavia said sarcastically. 'I'm glad you managed to

squeeze in a bit of the old male bonding. But will he finish in time? That's the only thing that concerns me at the moment.'

Argyll thought, then nodded. 'I think so. It's become a challenge. There might be a few rough edges, but he'll finish. I hope.'

16

Mikis rang the next morning, and Mary followed instructions dutifully, and with some trepidation. The usual phone call from Louise had not come through and she was sick with worry. But she wasn't going to let him know that. Instead, she calmly put the receiver down, walked out of her room and went to the nearest public phone.

'What about my grandchild?'

'All in good time.'

'Now is a very good time.'

'She is perfectly safe, of course, and has been moved closer to her home. You will get a call immediately after this if everything is well. Now, do you have that icon?'

She took a deep breath, 'Yes,' she said. 'That is, I will have it in an hour.'

'Where is it?'

'That's none of your business. Trade secrets.'

'Don't play games with me, Mrs Verney. I want to know where it is.'

'And I am telling you that it is none of your business. I will pick it up in an hour and give it to you later today. That's all you need to know. I'm not having you killing someone else. What did you do that for? It was stupid and unnecessary. All it did was stir the police up.'

There was a snort from the other end. 'I thought he had the picture and was lying when he told me he didn't. I wanted to teach him a lesson.'

'And I suppose you'll finish off with me?'

Charanis chuckled. 'Oh, dear me, no. We are partners, don't you remember? I'd never do that to a partner. Besides,

186

who knows when you might come in useful again. A woman of your talents. And such an unlikely person as well. Who would ever suspect you?'

'The Rome police, for one.'

'Ah, yes. So they do. What happened?'

'They pulled me in. Quite right too. This has been such a disaster I might as well have begged them to arrest me. Fortunately, all they have is strong suspicion. But I want this over and done with before they get anything more. So let's get on with it. If you want the icon, you have to keep to the deal. Let Louise go.'

'I have to see it first.'

'That's not necessary.'

'Oh, yes, it is. You will show me the picture. From a sufficient distance, if you wish.'

She thought fast. 'Very well. In an hour and a half you should be by the Ponte Umberto on the Lungotevere Marzio side. By the bus stop. I will come there and show you the picture. Then you will release Louise. When I have confirmation from her mother that she is free and unharmed, I will tell you where to get it.'

There was a long pause from the other end.

'One hour, then,' he said.

Mary Verney put down the phone, her heart beating hard. Now came the difficult bit.

'There we are. What do you think? Of course, it's a bit rough.'

Dan Menzies stood back nervously, and allowed Flavia to pick up the icon and turn it over in her hands.

'The face isn't right,' he went on nervously, like a chef fishing for compliments on his work.

Flavia studied the face carefully.

'And some of the scratches and scraped bits aren't perfect,' he added. Flavia switched her attention to these as well.

'But I'm quite pleased with the back. Quite pleased. Although with a bit more time . . .'

Flavia put it down, stood back and nodded. 'I think you've done a great job,' she said eventually. 'Better than I could have hoped for.'

'Do you? Do you really?' Menzies said gratefully. 'Of course, it *is* pretty good. Not many people could have done that, not in the time. Someone like d'Onofrio, you know. He'd still be picking the wood.'

'We chose well,' Flavia said reassuringly. 'I'm delighted. There is one thing, though. It still smells of paint, a bit. Is there anything you can do about that? I hope it won't matter, but you never know. We have some latitude as Mary Verney will think you've been restoring it, but I reckon she will spot it if there is too much.'

'How long have we got?'

She looked at her watch. 'Fifteen minutes maximum.'

Menzies thought for a second. 'Microwave,' he said.

'Pardon?'

'Stick it in.'

'Do you want it switched on?'

'God, no. I don't want to cook it. I just want a fairly airtight container.'

He fussed around fetching ingredients, and put them into a small metal bowl with a candle underneath.

'What's that?'

'Incense. Covers a multitude of smells and gives anything the true odour of sanctity. Plus one or two other ingredients that will smoke and give off a smell.'

'Such as?'

Menzies grinned. 'Dirty socks. Wool ones. Old friend taught me that. Ten or fifteen minutes should be enough to neutralize the smell of paint. Again, not a permanent job, but it should get us through the day. The knack is to make sure they smoulder, and don't burst into flame. Otherwise I'll have to start again.'

Certainly, the smell that came out of the microwave when he opened it up a quarter of an hour later had no traces of paint in it. And it was equally evident that the microwave would never be quite the same again, but no matter. Expenses would cover it, if all went well. And if all didn't go well, she'd have more to worry about.

'Good,' she said. 'Now I'll have to go. Could you keep an

188

eye on it until someone comes along for it? It'll be a woman in her fifties, who'll tell you she's in the police.'

'By all means,' said the suddenly friendly and cooperative restorer. 'No problem.'

And Flavia left. Paolo rang her up a few minutes later; Mrs Verney, he said, had left as well. Here we go, she thought.

Fathers Jean and Xavier sat facing each other in the hospital room, neither really knowing what to say. Father Xavier seemed tranquil and content, Father Jean was more perturbed. It was a lot to absorb, to be told that your superior general had acted in a way which was so – well, immoral. To go against the perfectly clear and unambiguous vote of the council, however narrow the majority, was shocking. Unheard of, in fact. It was even more disturbing that Xavier had chosen to tell him, of all people. The person who was most likely to act on the news. It was exactly what he'd wanted, of course; a handle to stop the man's reforming tendencies.

And he couldn't do it. There was no secret of the confessional involved, of course; but in the past few days he'd thought hard, reconsidered his own behaviour and judged it savagely. Had he known this a few days ago, it would have been very different. Now he felt that he should apologize, not the other way around. Rather than give his unquestioned obedience, as was Xavier's due, he had done his best to undermine his authority. He had caused this situation, and was responsible, every bit as much as the superior.

'I will of course resign as head of the order,' Father Xavier said after a while. 'And I am sure you will be elected in my stead. Perhaps that would be the best.'

'This may come as a surprise, but I would beg you to reconsider,' Father Jean replied quietly. 'This whole business was unfortunate, but I do not think you should resign. I was as much at fault as you, for not giving you the support that was your due. I am prepared to say so in council.'

Father Xavier looked up, half wondering what his old foe was up to now. 'That is kind, Jean. But no use, I'm afraid. I will have to relinquish the post. My error was too great, and

189

is bound to become public knowledge eventually. I do not wish to bring dishonour on the house. And, of course, my injuries will not mend so quickly.'

'The doctors say you will make a full recovery.'

'Eventually, no doubt. I hope so. But it will take time, and in that period I will be quite incapable of discharging my duties. It would be very much better if I stepped down. You must take over.'

Father Jean shook his head. 'Not long ago I would have grabbed the opportunity with both hands,' he said with a faint smile. 'But now I must conclude that I am not an appropriate person to lead us. I am too old and hidebound. If we choose someone else, and choose well, this episode can become a great turning point for us, rather than a period of sadness.'

'We?' Father Xavier said. 'We? I feel that you do not mean the council when you use that word.'

'No. If we can decide on someone, and both recommend him, then the council will agree. You know that as well as I do.'

'If we can agree. Who would you recommend?'

Father Jean shook his head, and drew the chair closer to the bed.

'How about Father Bertrand?' he asked. 'A man of no known political views and a good administrator.'

'And someone dedicated to his hospital in Bulgaria. You'd never get him to agree to come back. A good man, of course, but not for us. I thought maybe Father Luc.'

Father Jean laughed. 'Oh no. A saintly man, I admit. But he makes me seem radical. We'd be up all night flagellating ourselves with birch rods again if he took over. No, sir. Spare us from Father Luc.'

'Marc?'

'Too old.'

'He's younger than I am.'

'Still too old.'

'François?'

'Terrible administrator. We'd be bankrupt in a year. More bankrupt.'

They paused for thought.

'Difficult, isn't it?' said Father Xavier.

'What we need is someone new, not wedded to any faction, who could bring in fresh ideas. All these people we've been suggesting, they're no good at all. We all know exactly what they'd do. We need someone from the outside, in effect. Someone as different as Father Paul.'

Father Jean made the suggestion carelessly, but once it was made, the name reverberated around his brain. It was a shocking idea, he knew.

'He's in his thirties, has no experience of administration, no constituency in the order, he won't want the job and he's an African.'

'Exactly,' Father Jean said. Now the idea had occurred to him it suddenly gripped his imagination almost irresistibly. 'He's neither a reformer nor a traditionalist. The reformers will like him because he's enthusiastic about missions. The traditionalists will like him because he's very orthodox liturgically. When he's not in Africa, anyway. Heaven knows what he gets up to there. And he's a good man, Father. He really is.'

'I know. Father Charles spotted him, did he not? Brought him in? I was doubtful, I must say, but I've grown to like him.'

'The only hesitation I have is about what people will think,' Father Jean said. 'An African? The youngest superior we've had for three centuries?'

'Perhaps it's time not to think of such things. Besides, I hate to be practical, Jean, my friend, but it'll make us the most talked-about order in the church. Think of what that will do for recruitment.'

'Is he up to it, do you think? I must say, I believe he is. More than anyone I can think of. He has dedication and integrity. And common sense.'

Xavier folded his hands on his stomach with satisfaction. 'He will do very nicely,' he said with finality. 'Especially if we give him our support.'

'Will you?' Father Jean asked, conscious that a momentous decision was on the verge of being taken. 'Give him your support?'

Father Xavier paused for a fraction of a second, then nodded. 'With my whole heart.'

'And so will I, then.'

Father Xavier chuckled for the first time in days. 'In that case, we have a new leader. We need to draft some memoranda for the committee. For my sake, I would like it done as quickly as possible. This afternoon, even. A letter from myself stepping down, and a joint note from both of us recommending Father Paul. I will make a few phone calls when you leave, but you will have to run the meeting. The problem is Father Paul himself.'

Jean shook his head. 'I think it would be best not to tell him in advance. He would only refuse to stand. If it's sprung on him in the meeting and we have a quick vote . . . well, he won't have any choice.'

Xavier lay back in his bed. 'My goodness, Jean, my goodness. This'll make the Jesuits sit up and take notice.'

Father Jean stood up to go, feeling as though an immense burden had been taken from his shoulders. With a small tear in his eye, he clasped his former leader's hand, and shook it firmly. 'I'm so glad,' he said. 'Do you know, I believe we have been guided?'

17

Menzies sat on his sofa contemplating his handiwork. He was an egotistical man in all areas of life except where his work was concerned; in that he was extremely self-critical, to himself if not to the outside world. But even he, as he sat and looked, then got up and picked up the icon, turning it over, brushing it with his finger, then looking at it critically once more, was satisfied. Was it perfect? he thought as he wrapped it carefully in a cloth. No. Could he tell there was something wrong? He wondered as he covered this in newspaper and tied it with string. Certainly, although it would have taken him some time to figure it out. Would anyone else? He paused reflectively. He didn't think so; really he didn't. It was a decent piece of work. In the circumstances, a brilliant one.

He was still judiciously congratulating himself when Mrs Verney, posing as a police messenger, came to pick it up. Would she notice anything wrong? he wondered anxiously.

'You'd better check it,' he said with concern as she took the carefully wrapped parcel. 'I don't want it damaged and you coming back and saying it was like that when you picked it up.'

'I'm sure that won't be necessary.'

'I insist,' he said. 'And I want a receipt.'

She sighed heavily. 'Very well.' And began to unwrap it. 'Fine.'

'Look at it carefully,' Menzies said.

She looked it over. 'Seems OK to me. Have you done any work on it?'

'Some,' he said. 'I was just starting.'

'I'm sure you'll be able to finish later.'

'You're satisfied?'

'Oh, yes. Now I must go. I'm late.'

'My receipt . . . ?'

With barely concealed impatience, she put the parcel down and hurriedly wrote out a note. Received from Sig. D. Menzies, one icon of the Virgin belonging to the monastery of San Giovanni. Menzies took it and regarded it with amused satisfaction. A certificate of competence, he thought. Something to show his friends.

'Now, I must go.'

'Splendid,' Menzies said. 'Take care of it. It's caused enough trouble already, that has.'

'Don't I know it.'

And Mary Verney, with the icon under her arm, walked out of the apartment block and turned left up the street.

A man sitting at the little café over the street saw her come out, and picked up his phone.

'You can add impersonating a police officer to your list of crimes and misdemeanours,' he said quietly. 'She's got it, and heading into the Campo dei Fiori. I'm right behind her.'

Mary Verney took a taxi from the rank outside San Andrea; it was busy, as the market was still in full flood, but the rush hour was over, and she didn't have the alarming problem of having to stand in the open with a stolen icon under her arm for too long. She got off to a good start by giving the driver 100,000 lire.

'Now, listen carefully,' she said. 'This will be an unusual drive. I want you to do exactly what I say; if you do, I'll give you another 100,000 at the end. Is that understood?'

The driver, a young man with a malevolent smile and a bad squint in one eye grinned horribly at her. 'As long as you're not going to shoot someone.'

'You'd object?'

'Charge you more.'

'I see I picked well. Now, at three o'clock exactly, I want you to be driving south down the Lungotevere Marzio, towards the crossing with the ponte Umberto. Fifty metres up, there is a bus stop. Near it, there should be a man standing. You with me so far?'

The driver nodded.

'You will get into the lane closest to the pavement, and slow down. When I say stop, you stop; when I say go, you go again as fast as possible. Then I'll tell you what to do next. Got it?'

'One question,' said the man, who Mary Verney suddenly realized had a thick Sicilian accent.

'Yes?'

'Where is Lungotevere . . . what did you call it?'

'Oh, Christ,' she muttered under her breath. 'Do you have a map?'

Five minutes later, they were under way, Mary Verney clutching the map in one hand and the icon in the other. She thanked God they didn't have that far to go. Otherwise they'd have got stuck in the traffic and never made it. The driver took the route up the via della Scrofa, then swung round at the Porte Ripetta, and headed south again. Mary's heart began to thump with nervousness. She took the icon out of the bag she'd been carrying it in, and laid it on her lap.

'Into the nearside lane now,' she said, noting that the traffic was heavier than she'd hoped. 'Slow down.'

Then she saw him, standing beyond the bus stop, hands out of his pockets.

'Stop.'

The taxi stopped, and she held up the icon to the window. Mikis stared at the icon, and she stared at Mikis. It lasted for about ten seconds, then he nodded, and took a step forward. He put a hand in his pocket.

'Now! Go! Fast!' she shouted. 'Get us out of here.'

The car lurched forward as the driver, now thoroughly enjoying himself, slammed his foot on the accelerator and let out the clutch. There was traffic everywhere; twenty metres further on the lights were at red and the road was blocked with two large trucks.

'Keep going,' she shouted to the driver. 'Whatever you do, don't stop.'

He needed little encouragement and swerved with a thump

on to the pavement, put his hand on the horn and his foot on the pedal. The taxi shot along, gaining speed until the pedestrian crossing at the bridge; then he cut left across the traffic, swerved to avoid a tourist and barrelled over the crossing so fast that, had anything been coming towards them, they could not possibly have missed it. He went faster and faster in the direction of the Piazza Navona, then cut right down the old cobbled streets that surround it.

'You're going to kill someone,' she shouted as he swerved to avoid an old tourist eating an ice cream.

No reply. He kept on driving, almost like a professional racer. Then he slowed abruptly, and turned sharply into a cavern underneath an old apartment block.

The engine died as he cut it off, and the pair of them sat in silence for a few seconds. Mary was trembling from terror.

'Where are we?'

'My brother-in-law's garage.'

He got out of the car and pulled the big old doors closed, cutting out all the summer light with a frightening suddenness. The weedy light bulb he switched on was no substitute. Mary breathed deeply several times to calm herself down, then fumbled in her bag for a cigarette, and lit it with shaky hands.

'Thank you,' she said when the driver came back. 'You did a marvellous job.'

The driver grinned. 'Normal driving for Palermo,' he said.

'Here.' She handed him a bundle of notes. 'The additional 100,000 I promised. And another 200,000. You never saw me before. Don't recognize me.'

He pocketed the money, and gestured to the door. 'Thank you. And if you ever want another lift . . .'

'Yes?'

'Don't call me.'

Mary nodded, dropped her half-finished cigarette and ground it into the dust with her feet, then picked up the icon in its wrapping.

'How far is it from here to the via dei Coronari?'

The taxi driver, pouring himself a drink from a bottle he'd

found in a rickety desk, pointed. She walked out, back into the brightness of a Roman summer.

Five hundred metres away, in an entirely different street, pointing in the wrong direction and encased on all sides by cars and trucks, Paolo wept with frustration and humiliation. It was the sudden acceleration and the appallingly risky driving of Mary's taxi that had caught him unawares. When pushed to the test, he wasn't that willing to die. He beat his fists against the dashboard of the car, then picked up his phone and spoke reluctantly into it.

'Lost her,' he said.

'Oh, Christ,' Flavia said, her heart sinking. 'Paolo, you can't have. Tell me you're joking.'

'Sorry. What do I do now?'

'Ever thought of suicide?'

'What the hell are you playing at?' Mary Verney, now she'd had a drink and had calmed down, was furious by the time she found the public phone in the bar and called Mikis again. 'We had a deal. You had nothing to gain by pulling a gun.'

'I was not pulling a gun,' Charanis said at the other end.

'Oh, come on.'

'I was not pulling a gun,' he repeated. 'As you say, what would I have to gain by shooting you? Nothing. So stop being hysterical. I want to get this over and get away.'

'Did you see the picture?'

'Yes.'

'Are you satisfied?'

'Enough. Until I can examine it properly. In about quarter of an hour you should receive a phone call. I will ring back in half an hour and you will tell me where the picture is. And it had better be there.'

There was no pretence at the urbane suavity he normally affected; he was serious now. Mary Verney looked at her watch; somehow she felt the next fifteen minutes would be vital. It would either work, or blow up in her face. Dear God, she wished there had been another way. If anything went wrong . . .

She looked at her watch again, thirteen minutes. She lit a

197

cigarette, another one but at her age what did it matter, and ran through the list of things that could go wrong.

The phone went. She grabbed it, fumbling slightly in her impatience.

'She's at liberty.' Oddly formal in its phrasing.

There was a click and the line went dead.

She dialled her daughter-in-law's number, fumbling badly and dialling the wrong number the first time she tried, and the second. The third time it connected.

'Hello, Granny.' The bubbly, infectiously childish voice at the other end brought tears to her eyes; the moment she heard it she knew she'd won. She'd done everything she set out to do. She managed to mumble back a few words, but Louise would have to wait.

'Is your mummy there?'

She stopped her daughter-in-law from talking; she'd always talked too much, and once she got going it was difficult to stop her.

'She's all right?'

'She's fine. I don't know what happened . . .'

'I'll tell you later. Take Louise, get in the car and go.'

'Go where?'

'Anywhere. No. The police. Go to the nearest police station. Sit there as long as possible and say you want to report a missing dog, or something. I'll send someone to get you when it's all over.'

'When what's all over?'

'Just do it, dear. It should only be another hour, or so.'

Her heart sank as she put the phone down and looked at the small package by her side. She would now have to deliver it and hope nothing went wrong. She took a deep breath, and walked off to begin the final stage.

When Flavia picked up her phone and heard Paolo's frustrated, apologetic explanation of how he had lost Mary Verney in the traffic, she all but hurled the instrument across the room in rage and frustration. Of course there were risks something would go wrong. Something always does. But already, and such an absurd blunder? Paolo had years of experience; he knew the streets of Rome better than anyone. He was an alarmingly fast and incautious driver. Of all the people who should have been able to hang on to a foreigner who barely knew the city, he would have come top of her list.

And now it was all over. They would have to sit back, and hope that they could pick one or both of them up as they left the country. How very disappointing. How embarrassing. How humiliating. How stupid.

She paced up and down, not because this ever helped her think much, a process always done better horizontally, but because it provided some vague illusion of doing something. There would be a handover. Obviously a cautious one, or it would have already taken place. Mary Verney had driven past Charanis, then accelerated away so fast Paolo had lost her. She didn't trust him; that was obvious. He saw she had the picture, and presumably had to do something before she would hand it over.

So where would the handover take place? She walked next door to find Giulia, who had come back to the office and was waiting to be given something to do.

'Your notes,' she said. 'Reports. Of when you were following Mrs Verney.'

The girl opened her desk drawer and pulled out a sheaf of paper.

'Where did she go? I know she went shopping, went to museums, and so on. Where else did she go?'

Giulia shrugged. 'Dealers. We went round almost every dealer on the via dei Coronari. Then she took me for a long walk. She said she always likes to walk four or five kilometres a day.'

'Where did you go?'

'Down the Corso, across the Campo dei Fiori and across the ponte Sisto. We stopped for a coffee opposite Santa Maria in Trastevere. Then we walked up to see the Bramante chapel in San Pietro, then we ended up watching the sun go down from the Gianicolo. Then we took a taxi back to her hotel. I was exhausted. It didn't seem to bother her at all.'

'She didn't do anything unusual? Didn't seem particularly

alert at any moment? Wasn't checking anything out? What did she say?'

'We talked all the time. She's a very nice person. But she didn't say anything which struck me particularly.'

'Try a bit harder. She's going to hand this picture over to Charanis soon. She must have a handover spot. Somewhere quiet, where there won't be any witnesses, somewhere where she can put it down and leave very fast. She doesn't trust him, and I don't blame her. She's frightened of him. Where can she leave it which is quiet and with good transport?'

'In Rome?' the girl said. 'Nowhere. Besides, if she wants to put a safe distance between herself and this man, why not give it to an intermediary?'

'Like who?'

'Like one of the dealers.'

Flavia looked solidly at her. Maybe she had a future in the police after all. 'Who did she visit?'

Giulia handed over her list. Flavia went through them. 'She introduced me as her niece at all of them.'

'She knew them?'

'Oh, yes. They all greeted her very fondly. Some with a bit of caution, but they all put on a show for her.'

'Including this one?' She pointed at one name, halfway down the list.

'Including that one, yes.'

Flavia all but kissed the girl with delight. 'Yes,' she said triumphantly. 'Yes, yes. That's the one. It must be.'

'Why?'

'Because you say she knew him and when I met him the same afternoon he denied ever having heard of her. Giuseppe Bartolo, old friend, I've got the both of you. At long last. Come on. Let's go. There's not much time.'

Flavia did her best to summon reinforcements, but knew as she and Giulia ran through the streets, across the Piazza Navona and down the via dei Coronari that the chances of anyone getting there quickly was slim. The rush hour was beginning, and none of her comrades were in walking, or running, distance. She was on her own, with Giulia. Nor did she have any idea of what she was going to do when she arrived. Hang around outside and wait? Then what, even assuming they were right? She hated guns herself and was a terrible shot. She assumed Giulia had received the standard training, but also remembered that trainees weren't allowed to carry weapons. What, exactly, was she meant to do if Charanis turned up before her support, and refused to stand there and be arrested?

Running and dodging the crowds and concentrating on arriving as swiftly as possible gave her little time to dwell on this problem. She had one chance to catch this man with the icon and link the entire case together, and she wasn't going to miss it again. She only hoped that her guess about Mary Verney was right. What if, at this moment, she was standing on top of the Gianicolo handing the thing over?

If she was, she was. Too late to do anything about it. Besides, there was the gallery. She slowed down, waited for Giulia to catch up, and stood uncertainly, getting her breath back.

'What do we do now?'

'Wait. And hope.'

Flavia looked around. 'Might as well sit down and look inconspicuous, I guess.'

She led the way over to a café, and commandeered a table which gave a good view of the gallery and its approaches.

'What about a back entrance?' Giulia asked.

'There isn't one. I know this place.'

She ordered a bottle of water and drank, opened her bag and peered anxiously at her gun. Then she scrabbled around in the depths to find the bullets she kept in a little purse. As a matter of principle she always refused to go around with a loaded gun in her pocket. Rules now said she had to have one. They never said anything about it being ready to go off at any moment.

Giulia looked nervously at the unpractised way she loaded it.

'Quite right,' Flavia said grimly. 'The only time I ever tried to fire one of these things in the past, I nearly killed Jonathan.'

The trainee smiled wanly.

'How do we know he's not already been and gone?'

A good question. Flavia looked up as she considered an answer, then frowned. 'Because he's coming down the street now, that's why.'

She nodded in the direction of the Piazza Navona, and Giulia peered round to see in the flesh the man she'd only seen before in a grainy photograph. He was tall, quite handsome, apart from an incipient paunchiness, and very, very businesslike. The sort of person who was not going to frighten easily and might well not come quietly.

'I think,' Flavia said, 'the best thing to do would be to leap on him from behind as he comes out of the shop. He'll be holding the icon, so will have one arm occupied, and two of us should be able to get him on the ground. Once he's collected the picture he should relax a little as well.'

Giulia nodded stiffly.

'Nervous?'

Another tight-lipped little nod.

'Join the club. Come on,' she said as Mikis vanished into the shop. 'Stations. You take that side of the door, I'll take the other.'

She dropped a note on the table to pay for the water and the two women walked across the street, desperately trying to look like a pair of shoppers concerned with nothing more than buying a small memento for a beloved aunt's birthday.

Flavia was sweating with nervousness, and she noticed that Giulia was trembling with simple fright. She hoped the girl wouldn't make a mess of things. If both of them did what they should, they stood a decent chance. But if Giulia froze, then she would leave Flavia in deep trouble.

They took up positions on either side of the shop door, Flavia consulting her watch and trying to look like a girlfriend on the verge of being stood up, Giulia concentrating her attention on a red open-topped car with two men in their twenties in it, playing their stereo at an unsociable volume, glancing around to make sure everyone else was looking at them, deliberately doing their best to incite hostility by their noisiness. Don't go over and ask them to turn it down, Flavia thought. Please. All around, the street was full of people, coming and going, walking arm-in-arm, enjoying the sunlight

202

and warmth. Peaceful and normal people leading a peaceful and normal life. And not a sign of Paolo, nor of anyone else. Where was everyone?

And then it was too late to hope for reinforcements. The door of the gallery opened, and Charanis, with a parcel under his arm, walked out. He paused in the little entrance way before stepping out into the street. Flavia made sure she could grab her gun, the youths in the car turned up the volume still further, and drummed a beat on the side of the door, bobbing their head in time to the music. Giulia looked desperately at her, waiting for a sign, a look of grim determination on her face.

Flavia nodded, and leaped forward to grab Charanis's free arm, and was relieved to see that Giulia did the same. 'You're under arrest,' she said.

She felt Charanis's muscles tense up and noticed that the sudden movement and shout had drawn the interested attention of the men in the car, as well as one or two passers-by. One of them got out of the car to see what was happening. Charanis dropped the picture, and began to crouch down to fight for his freedom.

But the man in the car walked forward just as he was beginning to use all his strength to wrench himself free. 'Help us,' Flavia said. He looked her straight in the eyes, then gave a strange little smile.

There was very little noise and it was almost completely muffled by the cacophony of drumming coming from the car; but Charanis suddenly doubled over so violently that he broke free from Giulia's grasp, and collapsed on to the floor. The young man calmly picked up the package with the icon, walked over to the car, and got in. It screamed off down the street. No more than seven seconds. There were no screams and no rush of pedestrians to get out of danger. It had been so quick, so neat and tidy, no one had even noticed. Until the thick stream of blood ran away from Charanis's collapsed body and gathered in a large pool in the gutter.

Flavia recovered her senses first; Giulia was standing looking down at her dress and the red stain that had spread down it. 'Call an ambulance,' she said once it was clear that she hadn't been injured. 'Quickly.'

And she bent on her knee to feel for Charanis's pulse. It was a waste of time. A crowd was gathering, talking nervously and excitedly, and she should have taken control and made sure they kept their distance. But she didn't. She just sat beside the body and stared into space. She had no idea what had happened or why.

She didn't notice the one person who could have explained it to her. At the back of the crowd, a small old man with grey hair and a grim look on his face had watched it all stonily and impassively. From the moment he had left Mary, he had worked hard. He had made sure she was followed every step of the way to keep her safe. And when she had told him where the handover was to be, he had given his orders. He felt it was his duty to be there. In all his long life he had often been ruthless and often cruel, but he had never been a coward and had never walked away from his responsibilities. He fixed his mistakes, and he had now fixed his biggest mistake. After a few moments, he turned round and walked down the street to where his limousine was waiting to take him to the airport.

18

Argyll's section of the city was less violent, but hardly more tranquil. He didn't know about the incipient elevation of Father Paul; nor, as yet, did Father Paul, who went into the meeting that had been hurriedly called hoping that he might be able to make out his case, yet again, for being allowed to go home. No; Argyll's disturbance came from the bundle of documents that he was inching his way through, painfully, word by word and with frequent references to the volume of teach yourself ancient Greek that he had borrowed from the library. If what Father Charles had told him was true, rather than senile fantasy, then a lot of the bits of paper were missing. That hardly bothered him; there was enough to suggest that the general outline was accurate enough, even though proof of the identity of Brother Angelus seemed hard to come by. Practically speaking it didn't matter, although it was tiresome.

The trouble came from the long reflective pauses that his labours forced him to make. It was a boring job that he was doing, and he was tired. The pauses, as he stared vacantly out of the window, got longer, and the thoughts that filled his mind as more conscious activity took over became more haphazard and random. And, ultimately, more provoking.

For example, he found himself considering the one little detail which, as far as he could tell, everyone else had forgotten about entirely. Which was, if none of the obvious candidates had bashed Father Charles on the head, who had? If the refuse collectors had seen no one but Burckhardt and Mary Verney leave by the church's main door, how had it got out of the building?

He had a meditative stab at the irregular subjunctive for a

while, then considered another matter. He had bought the shopping at the market that day. Now why did that occur to him, apart from the fact that he had to do the same again today? And something else. Burckhardt had a bag with him. Too small, by the sound of it, to fit the picture in. Must have been the money, and he must have left disappointed. If Father Xavier had come to the church shortly before, he must have unlocked the door. He was then attacked. Burckhardt arrived and left without the picture. Therefore the picture disappeared before the door was locked and could not . . . Did that stand to reason? It did, he thought. It did.

He stood up. A man can only stand so much Greek in one day, and in Argyll's case the limit was about two lines of the stuff. He'd have another go at Father Charles. He could read it to him, if he was in his right mind. If not, then who knew what he might tell him today? Might conceivably tell him where Atlantis is. Or the lost Treasure of the Templars. Besides, there was no one else around. Everyone had scurried into the library with earnest looks on their faces and had not yet emerged.

Father Charles was not only aware, he seemed in better form than before, even pleased to have a visitor. He took the proffered manuscript with a light smile.

'Do they not teach Greek in English schools?' he asked with surprise.

'A bit rusty,' Argyll explained.

'Oh. What have you learned so far?'

It was like an exam and, as the old man clearly had no remembrance of what he had said the previous day, Argyll responded in a traditional manner. He cheated, and laid out a brief summary of the conversation.

'It sounds unlikely, but I wondered whether this monk, this Brother Angelus, was some high dignitary of the eastern empire. And that he brought the icon with him.'

Father Charles's eyes twinkled. 'Very good, sir. Very good. I'm impressed. He was, as you say, a high dignitary, whose identity is unknown.'

'Is it?'

The old man nodded. 'It is. A very closely guarded secret at the time, and a very closely guarded secret now.'

'It was the Emperor.'

Father Charles raised an eyebrow. 'What makes you think that? There is no evidence.'

'Yes, there is. But you are sitting on it. You took it out of the folder.'

'Goodness, that was very clever of you.' He looked puzzled. 'I really can't imagine how you figured that out.'

Argyll decided not to tell him.

'Still, you are right. It was the Emperor.'

'So why hide the information?'

'To preserve his memory from people like you. And those other people who came nosing around. It would spoil the story, don't you think? The image of the courageous last Emperor, falling on the walls in the midst of the battle; it is one of the great moments of our history, I always think. How sad if it had to be replaced by a tale of his sneaking on a ship, leaving his men and hiding out in a monastery for the last miserable years of his life.'

'But he was planning a counter-attack. Wasn't he?'

'Yes. I believe so, but like most of his projects it came to nothing. His main supporter, Pope Callixtus, died and his successor was more interested in nepotism and works of art than in the safety of Christendom. Constantine – that's the Emperor, by the way – died a year or so later. Suddenly.'

'How suddenly?'

'He was struck down by violent stomach pains one evening, after dinner. He died in great agony two days later. Personally, I think it had all the signs of poisoning. That would not have been surprising. There were a large number of people who had a vested interest in the papacy not wasting money on crusades. More for them. Besides, everyone was already negotiating deals with the Turks. Another war would not have been in the interests of the papacy, nor of Venice or Genoa. Constantine was a dreamer and an embarrassment. And he died, allowing the story of his heroism to live on.'

'And you're making sure that happens.'

Father Charles nodded. 'I am not such a vandal that I have destroyed anything. But all the essential bits of paper are well hidden. It would take months of searching to piece the story together again, even if you knew what you were looking for. Do you know what the icon is?'

'Yes. The Hodigitria.'

Again Father Charles indicated his approval. It was strange, Argyll thought. Like talking to two entirely different people.

'A leap of the imagination on your part, and very impressive, I must say. Yes. That is what it is. Painted by St Luke himself, and left by the Emperor in the monastery under the guardianship of his servant Gratian and his family. He gave instructions that it should never leave the walls of the monastery unless it returned in state to a Christian Constantinople. And cursed be he who disregards that charge. The Emperor himself swore to destroy anyone who laid impious hands on it, and got his servant to swear the same.'

And then, with a leap of the imagination which was real this time, rather than fake, Argyll knew exactly what had happened. It was so clear and obvious, that he was slightly surprised he had not figured it out before.

'You were in that church that morning, weren't you? When Father Xavier was attacked?'

He nodded. 'It is my habit, when I am well, to pass an hour in contemplation early in the morning, before the others get up. That morning I was indeed well enough.'

'So you saw what happened?'

He smiled, then shook his head. 'Not a thing.'

'You're lying.'

'Yes,' he agreed equably. 'I am.'

'Did you take the icon?'

'Of course not. She doesn't need me to look after her.'

Argyll looked at him steadily, and Father Charles gestured around the almost bare room. 'You may search if you wish.'

'No,' Argyll said. 'I don't think I will.'

'She is safe, you see. She is under divine protection as laid down by the Emperor and nobody can harm her. So there is

no reason for the police to concern themselves any longer.'
He looked at Argyll, in no doubt that he would understand.
Argyll nodded.

'Yes,' he said. 'Thank you.'

Argyll walked thoughtfully back to the archive room so he
could tidy up and put away the documents he'd no longer be
needing. Caravaggio would just have to wait until next week.
At the foot of the stairs that led up to Father Charles's room,
standing in the open doorway and staring across the courtyard, he saw a gloomy-looking Father Paul. He looked terribly
tired, as though he'd aged thirty years in the past few days.

Argyll coughed slightly; Father Paul turned, then stood
politely out of the way.

'Cheer up,' Argyll said, when he had seen a bit more of
that despondent expression. 'Things can't be that bad.'

'They can, Mr Argyll,' he replied slowly. 'They really can.'

'Not allowing you to go back home, eh? Sorry to hear that.'

'No, they're not. Ever.'

'Surely in another year . . . ?'

'We had a council meeting. Father Xavier sent a message
he was stepping down.'

'Reasonable. It will take a long time for him to be on his
feet again.'

'Yes. And they elected a successor.'

'Ah. Who's the lucky man, then? Can't say I envy him.'

'It is myself.'

'Oh.' Argyll peered with genuine concern at the man's face
and realized the pained look wasn't merely a conventional
disguise for satisfied ambition. 'Oh, dear. That must have been
a bit of a shock.'

Father Paul looked at him sadly.

'Can't you say no? Say you're too young?'

'I did.'

'Too inexperienced?'

'I tried that as well.'

'Married with three children and a drinking problem?'

Father Paul smiled. Only faintly, but it was a start. 'I didn't think of that. But I doubt it would have served me. You see, we are under vows of obedience. We cannot refuse.'

'How long is this job for?'

'It is a life sentence. Or until infirmity renders you unable to discharge your duties.'

'You look terribly healthy to me.'

He nodded.

'You really don't want the job?'

'I can think of nothing I want less, Mr Argyll.' Argyll saw that he was close to tears. 'I want to go home. There is so much to be done there. This is not my place at all. Every day in Rome is a torment.'

'Who was it said the only people who should be given power are those who don't want it?' He thought. 'Can't remember. But I think you will be a wonderful superior. It may not have been very kind of them, but for the sake of the order I doubt they could possibly have done better. It was an inspired choice.'

Another twitch. 'I fear you are wrong.'

'Listen,' Argyll said kindly. 'You know Flavia?'

Father Paul nodded.

'She's been offered the job of running the Art Theft Department. She's terrified at the idea, and has been in a bad mood for days, especially as she thinks I don't want her to take it because she will be working even harder than she does now. It's a lot of responsibility, plenty of trouble when mistakes happen and she will always be compared to her predecessor. But she will be very good at it, however frightened she is.'

'You think she should take it?'

'I do. She'll be miserable otherwise. And she knows, really, she can do it well. And so do you. You both need practice, that's all. Bottando knows what he is doing. And so do the people who put you up for this job.'

Father Paul smiled wanly. 'That's kind of you. But they need a politician and an accountant, not someone like me.'

'You can hire those. What do you need an accountant for, anyway?'

'Father Xavier, it seems, had lost a great deal of money on rather foolish ventures.'

'Ah. I see. So you're in the hole. How much?'

'A substantial amount.'

'Why don't you sell something else? Like that Caravaggio. It shouldn't be there, anyway. Even Menzies thinks it looks silly.'

'Considering what happened last time . . .'

'Very different. This time you should have a proper intermediary, acting with a reputable institution. One with a lot of free wall space. You'd get a fair amount for it.'

'How much?'

'That depends. It's really only attributed to the great man. But, if it can be pinned down, you're talking about several million dollars. If not, then you're still likely to get a couple of hundred thousand. It's not one of his best, and would require work to establish its credentials.'

He had grabbed Father Paul's interest, there was no doubt about that. But then the priest's shoulders sagged again. 'We need the money now, Mr Argyll. Within a week. It must take longer than that to sell a picture.'

Argyll nodded. 'I don't know that I can help you there. I could make discreet enquiries for you, if you like.'

'You?'

'Oh, yes. I used to be a dealer.'

Father Paul thought carefully. 'No harm in that, I suppose. Although I'm afraid the council is in a recalcitrant mood. I doubt they'll agree to anything concerning pictures after last time.'

'Better get the icon back then.'

Father Paul laughed. 'That, I fear, would be something of a miracle.'

'"Oh, ye of little faith,"' Argyll said. 'I always wanted to say that to a priest. Miracles do happen, you know.'

'They are rarely there when you want them.'

'I have the same trouble with taxis. But they do turn up.'

'I don't know whether we deserve one.'

'Do you have to earn them?'

'Are you teaching me theology, Mr Argyll?' the priest said with another ghost of a smile.

'Oh, no. Just reminding you that you shouldn't give up

211

hope. You've barely started. What would you do if the icon came back? Sell that too?'

He shook his head fervently. 'No. She would be returned to her proper place. And the doors would be opened again.'

'Is that an official decision?'

He thought, then smiled. 'Yes. Why not? My first command.'

'Good. Could you spare me half an hour or so this evening? About nine?'

When Argyll got home half an hour later, he found Flavia slumped in the armchair with a stiff drink in her hand. She looked exhausted, and moody.

'How did it go?'

'Worse than you can possibly imagine.'

'You didn't get him? Oh, Flavia, I am sorry.'

'We got him.'

'What's the problem?'

'He's dead. Somebody shot him. It was terrible. In cold blood, right in front of my eyes.'

'Who?'

She shook her head, and took another gulp of whisky. 'Damned if I know. All I know is that it was professional. Very calm, unhurried and effective. Just walked up and walked away. The damnable thing about it was that they even paused to take the icon as well. Makes me look like a total idiot. I can't do this job. I'm going to tell Bottando tomorrow. They'll have to bring in an outsider. I'm not up to it.'

'Nonsense,' he said.

'No, it's not.'

'Yes, it is. This isn't your fault. Heaven only knows why he was shot. Nothing to do with you.'

'Mary Verney got away as well.'

'So? If you'd been persecuted in the way she'd been, you'd leave the country as well. It's not as if she stole anything. Except for what you more or less told her to take. You have to think Bottando-ish here. How would he deal with this?'

She sipped her drink and thought. 'He'd go into full damage limitation mode. He'd ascribe the attack on Father Xavier

212

to Charanis and say the shooting was drugs related. Some nonsense like that. And he would also point out that it would be a help if we had the icon back.'

'And so it would be,' Argyll said, pleased that she seemed to be coming out of the depths. 'I do believe I can help you there. In fact, before Bottando goes public with the idea of Charanis being the one who attacked Father Xavier, you might want to know what really happened.'

'You know?'

'I figured it out this afternoon. Nothing like an archive for aiding the mental processes.'

'So? Tell me.'

'No.'

'Jonathan . . .'

'On one condition. Two conditions, in fact.'

She sighed. 'And they are?'

'One, you stop this self-pitying nonsense about not taking up Bottando's offer. You are far the best person to run that department and you know it.'

'You said a sensible person would go for the money.'

'A sensible person would. You are not a sensible person. I know you. I'd rather see you occasionally when you're content than all the time when you're ill-tempered and miserable. Which you will be if you spend your time doing a job you think is worthless. You'd be a rotten bureaucrat. Even filling out expenses forms makes you bad-tempered. So stay where you are.'

She looked at him fondly, then leant over and kissed the top of his head. 'You are sweet.'

'It's one of my better qualities. So, such as it is, that's my advice.'

'I don't know whether you're right.'

'I'm always right.'

'The second condition?'

'That when I complain about living out my life in lonely solitude you adopt a suitably understanding attitude and move heaven and earth to take some time off. Starting now.'

'Now?'

'Yes. I want to go away for the weekend.'

'I can't . . .' She stopped and considered.

'Make up your mind.'

'All right. We go away for the weekend.'

'Splendid.'

'Now tell me where the icon is. When did you figure this out?'

'This afternoon. Through a combination of skill, intelligence and shopping. And a tip-off from a source.'

'Who?'

Argyll grinned. 'Constantinos XI Paleologos Dragases, Emperor of Byzantium, Noblest soul, God's vicegerent on earth, heir to Augustus and Constantine.'

Flavia cocked her head and looked disapproving. 'Not now, Jonathan. I know you're trying to cheer me up . . .'

'I mean it. I've been having long and fascinating conversations with a Greek Emperor who's been dead half a millennium. Do you want the full story?'

He had, of course, promised Father Charles not to say, but he reckoned that a small exception was justifiable. She needed cheering up, and they were going to get married, after all. What was hers was his, and so on. So he told her about Father Charles's periodic wobbles.

'Now, what he was doing was merely taking everything he knew about the history of the monastery and funnelling it through his dementia. As far as I could check, everything he told me was true. I couldn't check it all, of course, as he wouldn't let me see most of the documents. What I could fitted perfectly.'

'Why has no one else mentioned this? I mean, if he goes around thinking he's an Emperor, wouldn't one of the brothers have told you?'

'I don't think he does. I think he was jolted into it by shock. The shock of seeing Father Xavier attacked. He's an old-time priest; believes in the old routine of getting up at dawn and praying. The middle of the night, sometimes. I'm certain he was in the church that morning, when Father Xavier came in. He denied it, and then told me he was lying.'

'He attacked him?'

'No. He was just in the church when Father Xavier arrived,

unlocked the door, and took the icon out of its frame.'

'Who did attack him?'

'Constantine charged his servant Gratian to look after it and make sure it never left until Constantinople was Christian again. So we ask the servant. Simple. And obvious when you remember market day.'

Flavia snorted. 'I think you've become as crazy as he is. And what's market day got to do with it?'

'The local market operates on a Wednesday and a Friday. Father Xavier was attacked on a Wednesday.'

'So?'

Argyll grinned and threw her jacket over. 'Figure it out yourself on the way. It's a nice evening for a walk.'

In that, at least, Argyll was right. It was one of those soft, warm Roman evenings when everything is all but perfect, at just the right moment between the heat of the day and the cold of the night. When the air had a golden glow which was beautiful, however much it might have been due to exhaust fumes, and when even the low sound of the traffic and the tooting of horns was restful and reassuring. The restaurants were full and overspilling on to the streets, the tourists were happy and the restaurateurs happier still. From the open windows of the apartments down the narrow streets came the sounds of television and eating and conversation. Adolescents on little scooters puttered past, trying to look as though they were driving Harley Davidsons. And for the rest, they leant against walls, or walked up and down, arm-in-arm, talking quietly then bursting into loud greetings as friends appeared.

Despite everything, and despite the fact that they were not merely passing the evening in restful idleness, Flavia and Argyll walked arm-in-arm as well, their pace slowing and becoming more tranquil as the city wrought its irresistible magic on them yet again. It was the sort of evening that made the cares of the day seem unimportant, no matter how terrible they really were. It was, in a word, what made an overcrowded, noisy and smelly city into one of the most magical places on earth, and ensured that both of them would fight desperately never to leave it.

They walked past the little throng of vigil keepers still camped out on the steps of the church, noting that, if anything, the crowd had grown slightly. Some Argyll recognized; others were couples just sitting, drawn by the crowd that was already there, and some were long-distance students who decided that the old rule of safety in numbers made this a good place to unroll their sleeping bags and settle down for the night. Somebody – Argyll suspected the café owner across the street – had confiscated some of the round black oil lamps, very much like cartoon bombs, still used for illuminating roadworks, and placed them on every second step, giving the whole scene a mysterious, almost medieval air, as the flickering flames cast soft shadows over the figures sitting between them.

'Impressive, don't you think?' Father Paul said after they found him and Argyll led the way back into the street. 'There's more of them every day. They come with prayers, and food.'

'Food?'

'Old custom, I'm told. More southern than Roman, but it seems to survive here. If you ask a saint for something, you bring a present in return. Food, or money, sometimes even clothes.'

'What do you do with it?' Flavia asked as they'd looked enough and turned to walk down the street.

'Give it to the poor, what else? Some of us are shocked, but I have no intention of discouraging it. Where are we going?'

'Nowhere. We've arrived. It's in here, I think,' Argyll replied. They were a few hundred yards down the road. It was a ugly run-down block, old and disintegrating. The main door should have had an intercom, but it had long since stopped working. Instead, the door was roughly propped open with a brick. Argyll checked the names on the buttons. 'Third floor.'

The lift didn't seem to be working either, so they walked up, then along the narrow corridor of the floor, until he peered at a bell, then pressed it. To make sure, he knocked firmly on the door as well.

The television inside stopped abruptly, and was replaced by the sound of a child crying. Then the door opened.

'Hello,' Argyll said gently. 'We've come for your Lady. She's perfectly safe now.'

Signora Graziani nodded, then opened the door. 'I'm so glad,' she said. 'Do come in.'

Flavia gave Argyll a strange look, then followed him in. Father Paul, quite impassive, brought up the rear. The little living room was cramped and overstuffed with television, washing and grandchildren; the furniture was old and battered, the walls covered with crucifixes and religious pictures.

Flavia was a little perplexed by all this but, as it seemed that Argyll knew exactly what was going on, was content to stay in the background and keep quiet for fear of saying the wrong thing.

'You are sure it's safe?' Signora Graziani said with a burst of anxiety.

'Quite sure,' he replied. 'The picture will go back to its proper place and stay there now. Father Paul is determined to keep her and give her the honour she is due. Aren't you, Father Paul?'

Father Paul nodded.

'I'm so glad,' she repeated. 'When I heard what was to happen I said, "This is not right. This is a bad man, to do such a thing."'

'You were cleaning, and overheard? Is that it?'

'Of course. Wednesdays I get there early, because I have to work in the market at eight. I had just prayed and was getting my bucket, when I heard Father Charles – such a good, kind person, poor soul. He was almost in tears, pleading with the superior not to sell the picture. He said the order had to guard her. Foolish, of course; everybody knows it is the other way around and that she guards them. But Father Xavier said it was too late and said, very cruelly, that Father Charles was a superstitious and sentimental old man.'

She looked momentarily terrified, lest Argyll impute evil

thoughts. 'I prayed to My Lady to defend herself, and offered what help was needed, as my family has always done. And she told me I had to stop this man. She told me; I had no choice, you see.'

'I hit him, with my broom. I didn't mean to hurt him, really. But my hand was guided, and he fell and hit his head on the stone steps. That wasn't me, you see. I scarcely hurt him at all. It was her. When she chastises, she can be very severe. She was out of her normal place on the altar and looked so forlorn and lost. And I knew, it was almost as if someone told me, that I had to hide her away until she was safe.'

'So you took her home?' Flavia asked. Signora Graziani looked shocked.

'Oh, no. She must never leave the building. I wrapped her in a plastic bag and put her in my little room across the courtyard. Where I keep all my cleaning equipment. In a large empty packet of soap powder.'

'And you left Father Xavier . . . ?'

'I did, and I'm sorry for it. I didn't realize he was so hurt. But I left for a while, to tell the people at the market I couldn't work today, then came back. I was just going to make sure he was all right . . .'

'Thank you,' Argyll said. 'You have done your duty, as you were ordered.'

'I have,' she said with satisfaction. 'I do believe I have. We have served her faithfully for as long as I know. What else could I have done?'

'Nothing,' Father Paul said. 'You did exactly the right thing. You kept your word better than we did.

'I will put it back myself,' he continued. 'And we will have a mass tomorrow to celebrate. I hope very much you will come, signora.'

She brushed away a tear from her eye, and bobbed her head in gratitude.

'Thank you so much, Father.'

'Bloody hell,' Flavia said angrily once they had left the apartment and the door had shut. 'You mean to tell me this whole thing was caused by a stupid old woman with delusions . . . ?'

'That's one way of looking at it. Personally, I believe her.'

'Believe what?'

'That a member of her family has been charged with looking after that picture for ever and a day. Or at least since the servant Gratian left the monastery when his master died. It's what? Twenty generations? A blink of the eye for this city. An old neighbourhood. Quite possible.'

'Jonathan . . .'

'There's a family in the city called the Tolomei, you know. Claims it goes back to the first Ptolemy, illegitimate half-brother of Alexander the Great. Nearly seventy generations, that. It's possible for a family to have stayed more or less in the same neighbourhood for a few hundred years. Perfectly possible. Assuming they survived the sack of Rome in the 1520s, not much else has happened in Rome since. If it was charged with enough importance, there is no reason why the family practice shouldn't continue as the name of Gratian slowly got italianized into Graziani. It's just very rare to have some sort of independent confirmation. Not rational and police-like enough for you?'

'No.'

'Thought not. But effective enough to find the icon, nonetheless.'

'Assuming it's there.'

'It'll be there. How are you going to deal with its reappearance?'

Father Paul shrugged. 'I can't say where it was, because that would involve explaining how it got there, which would be a pity. So maybe the best thing would be just to put it back.'

'And I will have to make out a report,' Flavia said.

'Oh,' Father Paul said with disappointment. 'Do you have to?'

'Of course I have to. We can't just have the thing turn up.'

'Why not?' Argyll asked.

'What do you think, why not?'

'Well, if you make out a report, then you also have to say that Signora Graziani stole it, that Xavier had planned to sell it illegally, that the order had got itself up to the eyes in debt.

219

Lots of scandal, just as Father Paul here is taking over, poor fellow. Then whoever shot Charanis might come back for the real thing. Whereas if we quietly put it back, and were as surprised as anyone that it was there tomorrow morning, then you could forget about the whole thing. Apart, of course, from putting it around that it was probably a copy to replace the lost original or a piece of tiresome absent-mindedness on the part of the monastery. Then everybody would be happy and you could have the weekend off and we could go away for a few days.'

They walked in silence for a few minutes while Flavia turned this over in her mind. 'I'm not happy.'

'If I were asking you to surrender a great success that would bring credit on the department, then I would never dream of suggesting it. But it's really just a scruffy painting that went missing for a few days. No big deal, really. Then you could make out that the Charanis business was nothing to do with your department at all.'

'Well . . .'

'Why don't you ask Bottando when he comes back tomorrow morning? Get him to decide.'

She thought again. 'Oh, very well. It's got to go somewhere, I suppose.'

19

'It was there?' Bottando asked.

'In a packet of washing powder. Non-biological. Quite undamaged. What do we do now?'

'I think your Jonathan has the right idea,' Bottando said, swinging in his chair as he listened to Flavia finish her account of the previous evening. 'Minimize our involvement. There is a time, you will discover, to advertise our activities, and a time to keep your head down. Let's keep it all as undramatic as possible, shall we?'

'Undramatic?' Flavia said incredulously. 'I've just had Father Paul on the phone. That icon's reappearance has triggered a major religious revival. It was bad enough before, but when it turned up overnight, the entire neighbourhood went crazy. Father Paul ordered the doors opened and a mass celebrated and they had two hundred people in there. Standing room only. More people than they've had since the cholera epidemic in the nineteenth century.'

'Not a police matter,' Bottando said mildly. 'I have always been of the opinion that people get the miracles they deserve. As these things go, this is a perfectly agreeable one. Besides, it will make them look after it more carefully. Is Jonathan right about what this thing is?'

She nodded. 'Possibly. I haven't seen any of the evidence and you know how he gets carried away sometimes. But it is perfectly possible.'

'In that case it will be very much better if it is kept out of circulation. Better that it should work miracles in Rome than around the Black Sea. So leave it be. Are the carabinieri content? They're not going to cause a squall?'

'The man responsible is dead, so they're happy to close the book.'

'That's good. I'm glad. Now, more important matters; have you decided what you are going to do?'

Flavia took a deep breath, and nodded.

'And?'

'I'll stay here and run this place.'

Bottando beamed. 'I'm so glad. I would have hated to hand over to anyone else. You'll do wonderfully. By far the best person.'

'I'm not sure.'

'Oh, yes. You just have to learn a few tricks of the policing business. Like lying, cheating, that sort of thing. I'll be around, after all. You can consult me whenever you want. After all, I will still be nominally in charge.'

And he smiled fondly at her. 'Thank you,' he said.

Flavia grinned back. 'Thank you. Would it be setting the wrong tone if I started by taking the weekend off?'

'You can do whatever you want.'

'Advice?'

'I think it would set the tone perfectly. Go away and refresh yourself. As long as you have a really good time.'

And she left, shaking his hand, then giving him a kiss on the cheek as well. She could have sworn there was a slight moisture in his eye as she left.

Because Flavia had been in a hurry to get to the office to see Bottando, she'd left the apartment early. Because of that, she'd missed the post. Because of that, she missed the last detail as well.

Argyll, in contrast, caught it all, mainly because of his idle habits and insistence on greeting each new day in a slow and methodical fashion. Up, coffee, shower, coffee, newspaper, coffee, toast. After the second coffee he went out to get the paper and collected the mail on the way back in. Two bills, one circular and a thick white envelope in an unfamiliar hand. Being a believer in getting the bad news out of the way first, he opened this last. Inside was a key and a short note with the heading Rome Airport.

Dear Jonathan,

You will forgive me, I hope, for writing to you in such a hurried fashion, but I have a small favour to ask and am anxious to leave Rome as swiftly as possible. I am going on holiday to Greece for a while; I'm sure you understand. The icon is now in the hands of its rightful owner, to whom Father Xavier originally agreed to sell it. In order that this matter be brought to an end once and for all, and so that there should be no further recriminations or enquiries, he is anxious that the order should be paid, in full, the agreed price. This was $240,000, and was due to be delivered to Father Xavier before he was attacked. Peter Burckhardt deposited it in a left-luggage compartment at Ostiense station, and it is now in the Central Terminus. How I came across the key need not detain you here, but I would be grateful if you would discharge the duty of delivering the bag of money to the order as quickly as possible. I am writing to you to preserve the purchaser's anonymity.

I've no doubt that your opinion of me is now even lower than it was when I arrived last week. For this I am truly sorry. Now is not the time to explain my involvement in this business, although I hope one day to do so. I do want you to understand that I had very good reasons which had nothing to do with any personal gain. I am glad to say that the result seems to have been as good as I could have hoped, and I am now able to return to retirement – this time, I hope, forever.

Please give my very best wishes to Flavia, and apologize to her on my behalf for causing so much trouble. I would have been more cooperative had it been in my power.

With fond regards,
Mary Verney.

PS: The bag containing the money is due to be removed from the left luggage compartment at the terminus at eleven a.m. on Wednesday. Could you make sure you collect it by then? Otherwise someone might open it and steal it. You know how dishonest some people are.

Argyll read it through twice, thought it over, and ended by grinning broadly. He had a strong suspicion that the woman had planned to take the money herself, but her hurried exit from Rome made it impossible to collect. So she had turned necessity into graciousness. Quite neat. He looked at his watch, and started up. It was twenty-five to eleven. He might just make it with a bit of luck and if he didn't wait to tell Flavia.

He walked out of the apartment to give final proof to Father Paul that miracles do indeed happen.

SILENT KNIGHTS

Other current events titles from Brassey's

The Fate of America: An Inquiry into National Character, by Michael Gellert

A Chain of Events: The Government Cover-Up of the Black Hawk Incident and the Friendly-Fire Death of Lt. Laura Piper, by Joan L. Piper

The Gulf Between Us: A Story of Love and Survival in Desert Storm, by Cynthia B. Acree with Col. Cliff Acree, USMC